For Catherine for her continued support.

With a special thanks to Gerald Braude for his editorial expertise, without which this novel never would have made it this far.

PART I

CHAPTER 1

The sharp glare of the enflamed sunset only intensified the sight of his father's blood. Leon kneeled, then became still. He stared into his father's black face, mesmerized by the return stare. Had Leon not been born, Big Leon wouldn't be lying in the mud, and the blood stained grass would not be flattened against the wet ground. Had Leon not learned to read, his father would never have run from the shack, pushing Leon ahead of him, roughing his hair, knocking him over a time or two. Had Leon not loved the landowner's daughter, his father would not have been shot through the heart and head, eyes gazing into the near-night sky as if terrorized by fear. Big Leon pleaded blankly for his son, Leon, to understand some long-kept secret that wasn't much of a secret at all—that they were not truly related by blood. With the noise of pursuers all around them and getting closer, Leon still didn't move.

*   *   *

Leon didn't remember being born, but had heard often enough of the blood and gush of it. Martha referred to the sound. Edna referred to the smell. "A dark smell," she called it. "And a white chile. Even though the father be black black coal."

Leon had heard the story of how Big Leon tried to knock his little body out of his mother's arms. "Just as he seen ya, after farmin', he tried it," Martha told him. "But Bess, she hole tight, turnin' in circles until the all of us come down on Big Leon, stoppin' him. When we let 'im up off the floor he leave the shack for two days. 'Course he daren't leave the farm, so he work all night and all day until after two of them he can't see black or white, and he come back to the house. But Bess knowed not to trust, maybe the sense of it just be deeper in her than him. After that he hardly make mention of it. Always tryin' to get her trust back, I suppose."

Leon sat on a fruit crate while Martha talked. He listened and watched as she washed herself in the shallow sink basin in the back of the shack. Her big brown breasts hung down as she bent over. She took care to soap and wash her face and head, then her arms, shoulders, and trunk. Last, she slid her slippery hands all around and over the front of her breasts, the black nipples hardening into stacked buttons. She talked all the while she washed. She told Leon stories no one else would tell him. "I tell you these things 'cause I have a love for you that yo' mama's and pappy's grief don't know how to give. I see things goin' on where they spite each other even in their man-woman relations."

At age four, Leon didn't understand some of the stories she told. But he remembered them. As he aged, familiar phrases dropped from Martha's lips dragged images of her handsome, swaying breasts along with them, like the words needed the image for authenticity.

Leon understood he wasn't all black and wasn't all white, but that's all he understood. Somewhere between two colors he stood fenced out of the only two worlds he knew. The other Negro children called him Mix-up. Whenever he complained, Bess held him close and whispered, "They scared 'cause you better than them."

Martha said, "There's nothin' one can do about hows they look, but you got all them choices for hows you acts."

Bess cooked for the Carpenter family. Breakfast, lunch, and dinner. Sometimes she'd leave well before light and not return until well after dinner and dark. Leon wondered whether she ever got to be outside at all and felt sorry for her. Big Leon, on the other hand, practically lived outside. Martha told Leon that about a year before he was born, Big Leon was made foreman of the Negro farmhands. Mr. Carpenter acted as his own overseer. "That no position easy to get if you as black as Big Leon," she told him. "Even after the war and emancipation."

Leon sat with his skinny legs out straight and his back against the outside wall. Dim light penetrated the stained window, speckling Martha's face, arms, and torso with light and dark, like pebbles at the bottom of a slow moving stream. The air brushed in chilly from the open door. Martha's bare skin stood goose-pricked and tight. Martha had ordered the other children to gather wild mushrooms from just inside the woods.

Leon wiped a tear from his cheek. The verbal beating he had gotten from the other children now kept him inside. Martha wouldn't let him go into the woods, "Lest you get a physical beating too," she said. He rubbed his head where he had been knocked with a stick. He kept his mouth shut.

Soaping up, she turned to look at Leon. "Yo' daddy deserve that position better than any man, but sometimes he don't believe it. He think it's tradin' that happened. He still act like a good boss-man to the others though. He don't beat nobody even if he get beat. You ain't likely to see it yo' self, but yo' pappy got the kindest heart of any man I know, black or white."

Leon looked into Martha's broad face, admiring her dark eyes and flat nose. He loved her big bones and strong arms. She could hold him tight when she hugged him. Or she could shove him against a wall when she got angry. She spoke tenderly of Big Leon, more than she did for her own sister. As if it were her whole name, Martha called her sister Poor Bess.

Martha's job was to keep children safe and to clean the six hastily whitewashed shacks hiding behind several layers of trees beyond the main house. Only in winter, when the snow lay thick, cold, and white, could anyone glimpse the leaning buildings behind the dark trunks and branches of the bare elms, white ash, and black cherry. Even then it took the black line of wood-smoke that rose through the trees to announce their location.

The children knew to say yes ma'am to Martha. As the oldest Negro woman, her child rearing duties meant that she taught the children to be respectable slaves.

After dinner, Martha cleaned up and retired to her corner of the shack where she would hum or sing softly while Big Leon, Poor Bess, and Leon would live like a family. That privilege, according to Martha, was something many slaves never got to do, as they were sold almost as soon as they were born, eliminating any family allegiances that might arise.

Most nights, summer and winter alike, Big Leon took long walks returning exhausted.

Late in the evening, Bess talked with Leon and played tickle games. Once a week she washed him and took him to bed with her.

"You my little one?" she'd ask, sniffing his hair.

"Yes, Mama." Martha had taught Leon what his answers were supposed to be. The teasing went on for years.

*   *   *

"You a beautiful boy." Her fingers danced over his seven-year-old face.

"That tickles."

"Oh, does this tickle?" She ran her fingers lightly down his chest and stomach and Leon tightened up, squeezed his shoulders close to his head and bent at the waist, all the while trying to keep Bess's fingers from touching him.

She laughed and moved her hands around to his sides.

"No," Leon said under his breath so that Bess couldn't hear. She didn't hold him as Martha knew how to do. Yet those moments of play were the only times Bess seemed happy, so Leon wanted the play to last as long as it could. As long as he could bear.

When the door opened and Big Leon entered all play stopped. Outside air churned up the inside air. Candle lanterns flickered and twisted the light inside the shack. Shadows rose and dropped. Sometimes Big Leon laughed and asked the same question he always asked when he caught the two of them together, "Playin' with yo' beauty?"

Bess did not answer.

Although the meaning of the question changed for Leon from year to year, it finally settled into what he considered a curse.

After asking that one question, his jaw set and his hands twitching, Big Leon sat and looked out the back door. He lifted his hand for a moment and everyone fell silent, except Martha whose humming softened, but remained.

In her straw bed, Bess positioned Leon to face away from her. She ran her fingers up and down his side, his stomach, and along his neck. Leon knew to stay quiet. He tensed, bearing the sensations of his skin until near tears. His dislike for the stimulation turned to hate that night. He got sick to his stomach, too, from all the tickling and the tension it brought on. For years, Leon vomited in the evening after play, erasing everything before it, miraculously relaxing him and enabling him to enter a deep sleep.

Had Big Leon come home and asked Bess, "You my woman?" Leon would be allowed to go to his own straw covered floor space. Bess would answer, "You know whose woman I am." Those words, too, changed in meaning for Leon as he got older. The words also saved him, many times, from his mother's attention, from sickness, but seldom from sleep.

CHAPTER 2

Burdened as an only child, Leon lived in a camp where many children meant family. When old enough to understand the concept, he learned of Bess's repeated miscarriages. He witnessed several of them himself. Each time it happened, Big Leon stayed in the fields for a day or more. Leon discovered him sleeping against a tree one night and told Martha about it later that day.

"Early up and late down," Martha said. "He's feelin' failed."

"It ain't him, though, that lost it," Leon said.

"No, but it him that brought it on. And he knowed it."

Leon watched Martha as she washed herself. It was their time to talk, as Martha cleaned up after a hard week.

"You playin' with them white boys again?"

"How you know?"

"See it in you. You walkin' funny. Now do yo' chores."

"Yes ma'am."

Before Leon could head outside to fetch water, Martha said, "Work with Big Leon?"

"Did."

Two boys ran into the shack, Edna chasing them. "Here now. Here."

Martha looked up, her breasts, Leon noticed, swaying heavily around with her body as she turned to see what came through the door. "Edna?"

Edna's two boys, Tunny and Bud, stood there smiling. Bud stared at Martha.

"What's it boy, you ain't never seen no teats afore?" Martha snatched up a rag and dried herself.

Leon jumped up to hide her nakedness from Bud's stare. "Ain't nothin' to see."

Bud started laughing and Tunny joined in.

"Those evil laughs," Martha said. "What goin' on?"

"Somethin' not good," Edna said.

"Mix-up, he in trouble," Tunny announced.

"You gonna get a beatin'" Bud said.

"Maybe hanged," Tunny said stretching out the 'h.'

"Ain't nobody gettin' hanged here," Martha said. Mr. Carpenter never done that as long as I lived. He might beat his Negroes, but he never kilt none."

"He ain't never had his own boy kilt," Tunny said.

"Shush now, I be tellin' her," Edna pushed at the smiling boys.

"Lord, my, what happen?" Martha pulled on her shirt and moved to stand near her straw bed in the corner. Edna followed after shooing the boys outside. The boys waited, still in view, just beyond the door.

Leon took on a fear like never before. He stood transfixed, thinking and listening at the same time.

"Little Freddy be playin' in the barn. A plank let loose up high an' he fall smack on his haid. I heared that the brains leak out his ears and eyes. I heared he was crumpled like a old rag, limp and lifeless."

"Mix-up done it," Tunny yelled from outside.

"Leon been here with me lately," Martha said, snapping Tunny's sentence at the end.

"Hank and Earl sayin' it's all 'cause Mix-up here—"

"Leon his name," Martha said, jutting her chin out at Edna.

"You wanna hear this?" Edna pursed her lips.

Martha lowered her head.

Edna quieted her voice and said directly to Martha, "I said evil when I smelt evil."

Leon pretended he didn't hear what she said. He felt Martha's humiliation in the presence of Edna's arrogance and wished to save her. He didn't move.

"Them other Carpenter boys say Leon suppose to fix the planks and miss one on purpose."

"That weren't true," Leon shouted. "I never been told to fix them planks!"

"What you told, boy?" Martha said.

"You don't believe me?"

"What you told?"

Leon closed his eyes for a moment. "Freddy come out—"

"That the oldest?" Martha asked.

"Yes, ma'am. He come out and said stack the hay ready for feedin', then help in the fields. I done the stackin', then went to Pa like they tell me."

"I believe him," Martha said.

Edna laughed at her. "Don't matter what you believe. Only matter what the white boys say."

"We'll see."

Edna stepped to the door as if she was in a huff. "Maybe we see how special yo' family be now. See how special Bess is, too."

"We suppose' to stick together," Martha said.

"We was," Edna said. "We did too, til the evil come on us."

"The evil," Tunny echoed.

Martha ran at the door. "Shoo!"

When Tunny was gone, she turned to Edna. "Bess ain't the only woman done—"

Edna interrupted. "No, but he the only child look like that." Her long finger pointed at Leon.

"He ain't got nothin' to do with how he looks."

Edna huffed again and double-stepped down the path, her two boys falling in line.

Standing in the doorway, Martha yelled to them, "Ain't no evil here. And ain't none comin'." She walked back to her corner. "Come here and sit with me a spell. They be comin' soon if they not already here."

No sooner did she take Leon into her arms, Fred Carpenter Senior came through the doorway. His head appeared first, like an olive colored mask. The man's wavey hair shook as his jerky, unsure movements settled to a calm. Fred's slight frame removed nothing from his regained sense of authority.

"Ain't nobody done nothin' wrong," Martha shouted.

"No need to speak up. I hear just fine," Fred said.

Leon saw in the man a kindness rather than an anger, and didn't know what to make of it.

"Yes sir," Martha said. "Can I speaks for the boy, sir?"

Fred's answer was interrupted as Bess pushed into the room around him. She ran for Leon and held him. His body stiffened out of habit, even though her hug was firm rather than light and ticklish. He felt as if he might throw up again.

"I didn't—" Leon stopped and swallowed.

"Shush, now," Bess told him. With her head turned from Leon's gaze, Bess looked into Fred's shoulder. "He's my boy," she said in a shivering voice.

A softness came over Mr. Carpenter's face long before Bess turned to confront the man, even as Mr. Carpenter watched her from behind.

"Bessy. Dear Bessy, I can't just leave it. I have to do something. If I drop it altogether, my own kind won't understand."

Bess pulled Leon in front of her. She lifted his face toward Mr. Carpenter's.

Leon knew he wasn't to look Mr. Carpenter in the eye. But Bess held his face up. He tried to shift his eyes to the left, then to the right, but everywhere his eyes moved, there was the landowner's face. So he closed his eyes.

"Look at him!" Bess yelled. "Take a look."

"Don't need to. I seen him before. Mona pointed him out a long time ago."

"Mona don't know you like I knows you." Bess's hand shook against Leon's chest.

Fred then did something very uncharacteristic of everything Leon knew about white men. He closed the shack door and said, "Nobody knows what goes on here."

Bess let Leon's face go and turned him, then handed him to Martha.

Leon sat obediently.

Fred spoke in the quietest tones. "I whoop my boys pretty hard. Done it out of sadness. Little Earl, not knowing why I was doin' it told the truth of it. They was playin' hard like I told them not to and pushed Freddy off a high brace. That's what happened." He paused and reached out to Bess who let him touch her neck with his hand.

Leon squirmed to get up, but Martha put light pressure on his legs, and he sat still.

Evening sunlight angled through an open window. The softness of the shadows reduced the scene to a fantasy. A fantasy Leon couldn't quite grasp.

Leon let his mind stretch as far over the experience as he could. He tried to understand all the words and motions and their meanings. No matter how hard he tried though, he felt left out. The words didn't say everything straight enough. And the actions confused him. He never saw a white man touch a black before. Not with such gentleness and compassion. Not without a strap between the two of them.

"If it were Mona, she'd have him gone," Fred said.

"He ain't the only boy here," Bess said.

"There's no need," Fred said.

Bess was a thin and shapely woman from behind. Her face, Leon knew well, showed no worry, no pain, but showed no life either. Bess's face was smooth as a young girl's, which seemed unnatural. Leon watched as his mother lifted thin arms and held onto Mr. Carpenter's forearms. "Ain't Mona's decision."

"No, it ain't."

"She beat him plenty when he little."

"I know," he said.

Martha turned her head away as if she didn't want to witness the two of them.

"Then let him be," Bess said.

"Caint." Mr. Carpenter pulled away and turned to face the door. "I got to mark him. If I don't nobody'll be happy. But, I promise you this, I'll do it quick and easy as I can."

"That yo' decision?" Bess said.

He looked at her once again. "I decided that. And I decided he's going to replace my boy. He's going to do all Freddy's chores and his own. I'll tell Big Leon."

"I didn't do nothin'," Leon whispered.

Fred looked over Bess's shoulder at Leon. "This is good for you, boy. The best that could happen. There's much worse. Most would've sold you long ago."

"Still not right," Leon whispered.

"Shush," Bess said. "Don't sass him."

Betrayed, Leon lowered his head in silence.

Mr. Carpenter nodded to Bess, then to Martha. "Let's go, boy."

Big Leon opened the door. He gave Bess a stern look, and she backed away from Fred. "What you doin' with the boy?"

Leon had made a step toward Mr. Carpenter and stopped when his father entered.

"Don't you look at me," Fred hollered.

Big Leon stared into the man's face. "The boy?" he said. Big Leon's arms shined with sweat. His thoroughly soiled shirt held tight to his toughened skin.

"I told the women folk. Now, don't push me or I'll be forced to do more." Fred walked to Leon and grabbed his arm as if it were a fly bothering him.

Big Leon moved out of the doorway.

"You watch how you're walking." Fred said in the angriest voice Leon had heard since the landowner's arrival.

Big Leon looked down and let Fred pass.

Leon led with Fred's thin fingers laid across his shoulder, shoving him forward. Leon heard his father say, "Dammit woman, you always takin' my strength from me. What I done for it?" The voices stopped after that one statement, but now Leon let it ring over and over inside his head as Fred, using one firm hand, guided Leon down the path and around the barn.

Behind the barn, Mr. Carpenter pulled his belt off and with the metal steer-shaped buckle slapped Leon across the face.

Leon fell to his knees and touched his bleeding cheek.

"Take off your shirt."

Leon obeyed.

Mr. Carpenter hit him hard across each shoulder. Then he picked Leon up and made a quick scrape down his chest with a steer horn, opening the skin to the hot air.

"You a pale black, boy."

Leon didn't know whether to respond or not and stood quietly waiting for another blow.

"Your daddy love you?"

"He don't say," Leon answered.

"You work with him?"

"Yes, Sir."

"He teach you the work?"

"Yes, Sir."

"And he don't say you his boy? Back there, he called you the boy, like you not his. You know why?"

"No, Sir."

Fred scraped the buckle across Leon's chest again. "Sounds like you got the nigger brains, but not the nigger skin." He shoved Leon. Shoved him hard. "Don't know why I'm bein' easy on you, except that your life must be hard enough. You can go home now. Be ready to work at sunup, boy. And wash up first. You stink and I don't want that smell stickin' to my boy who's left."

Leon walked into the shack, and Bess was already gone.

"Boy, you look a mess," Martha said right off. "I clean you up."

The sun was all but a sparkle from setting.

Martha lit two candle lanterns and wet and soaped a rag. "This goin to hurt, but not like yo' beatin'."

"Weren't no beatin'." Leon said. "More like a scrapin' and a smackin'."

"You lucky as much as you unlucky."

"Why don't Mr. Carpenter be upset at Freddy diein'?"

"He upset. He fightin' with his own self. I seen it. Like the devil fightin' with the Lord. Men folk always like that. They always fightin' with demons. He have plenty a demons, that man do. He down right guilty. But thinkin' about this evenin' he sharin' his guilt with this family."

Martha prepared a dampened rag and ran it across Leon's scrapes, first his cheek, then his chest.

Leon tightened at the sting. "He say I stink and to clean up."

"You don't stink. He just don't like the smell of work. Or maybe the smell of truth."

"I don't mind smellin' different."

"You fine." Martha said.

After a moment, while putting his shirt on, Leon asked, "Does Pa love me?"

Martha stopped fussing. She looked out the window for a moment. The light from a half moon flattened her face and put a shine in her eyes. Her teeth, too, shined when she spoke. Her lips quivered. "Yo' Pa love you, boy. Yo' Pa love everythin'. He love everybody. All except his-self. And that hard to get out of."

Leon breathed. He had been holding his breath. His cheeks tightened near tears even though he didn't know why. "I love Pa. I be proud he boss of some of the work. I be proud he look Sir in the eye. I love him 'cause he my Pa. Just 'cause." The tears streamed down his face.

Martha took him to her breast. "Now, boy. You stay proud. You keep lovin' yo' Pa. No matter what you learn, Big Leon yo' Pappy. You remember."

"I don't want extra chores. I don't want to work with those white boys all the time. They try not to do nothin'."

"I know. I know." Martha rocked Leon while they stood there.

That night Big Leon didn't come in until very late. Later than usual.

Bess had returned to the shack and Leon lay on the floor with her, his muscles so tense they hurt. He lay naked after being washed. Bess ran her fingers absentmindedly up and down Leon's body from knees to neck and touching everything between.

The cool night air blew into the shack, shocking Leon at first. Then he rose from beside Bess and walked to his own corner. His body relaxed instantly. He slipped on his shirt. In slow silence, Leon reached and touched his father's hand briefly before going over to lie on his own straw bed.

Big Leon pulled a tattered blanket up and around Leon's shoulders. Then with his big hand, he patted Leon on the back and brushed his face where it had been cut. He slid a vegetable crate to the back door and stared into the black woods.

CHAPTER 3

In the fall of his twelfth year, the air deep with winter urgings and blowing at him through the barn door, Leon busily mucked stalls and transferred feed barrels. By his side were Hank and Earl, who were alternately cruel and kind to Leon, one moment ordering him around, the next asking how Leon thought they should fix the barn door. Leon settled into his position as half slave and half older-brother. His weak stomach had him throwing up once a week, mostly late in the evenings and well after dinner, after being tickled or played with by Poor Bess.

After spending the morning to early afternoon with the Carpenter boys, Leon worked in the fields with Big Leon. One day Leon reached for Big Leon's hand, but the hand was pulled away and Leon didn't try again for years.

By this time Leon had learned why the other Negro children called him Mix-up. He learned that he could be an instrument of cruelty in his own family. And he learned that Hank and Earl's sister, Hillary, grew older, just as he did, but that she blossomed differently.

Mona had kept Hillary away from the help for years. By the time Hillary turned twelve, though, Leon had not only been introduced to her, but also saw her often while cleaning the garbage from behind the house or whenever she strolled out to the barn to call for Hank and Earl.

Although stout like her mother, Hillary's face didn't carry the same weight of anger and cruelty that Mona's face displayed. Not that Leon saw Mona's face often. He tried to stay away when she was around. She'd holler and threaten to beat him.

Hillary was talkative and curious at the same time. Sometimes she'd ask Leon a question, then suggest three answers even before he could think what to say. He learned to think faster and it became a game for him to come up with an answer before she could.

Hillary slipped through the barn door. All the boys stopped working at the same time.

"What you doin' here?" Hank hollered.

Hillary pointed at Leon. "His mama sent me to fetch him for garbage cleanin'."

"Why don't she fetch him herself?"

"Why *doesn't* she? Don't you hear any of your learning?"

"No need for it. Anyhow, you didn't answer." Hank put down a feed bag.

"She's busy."

"Well, you go tell her he's busy too," Hank said.

"Pa said it was okay. He's talking with Bess about something."

Hank smiled and looked at Earl. They both started to laugh. "Nigger soup," Hank said.

Leon turned away.

"So, where's Ma," Hank asked Hillary.

"Sittin', like always."

"She's burstin' with crazy," Earl murmured.

"Stop it," Hank said.

"You're jokin', why can't I?"

"Don't matter what I do. Just stop it about Ma." Hank glanced at Hillary. "Take 'im. But bring 'im back straight away."

Leon didn't need to be ordered. He followed behind Hillary as if she were leading him with a rope. "Why it need cleanin' now?" Leon said once they were outside.

"'Coons got in the garbage last night and made a mess. Pa wants it cleaned up before the house stinks. You know what to do with it?"

"Throw it down the holler."

"What do you do when you're done work?"

"Go back to the barn."

"I mean after that."

"Help Pa."

"I mean after that, too."

"Wash up for dinner. Go to bed."

"You don't do any reading? That's what I do. I'm reading parts of the Bible on my own. I have been for a long time now. Mrs. Milner said I'm smart. Smarter than those two back there in the barn. I'm going to go away when I'm old enough and keep learning until I'm smarter than anyone." She looked into Leon's face.

Leon turned his eyes away.

"You look smart."

"I not."

"What do you read and I'll tell you how smart you are. Earl is only about first grade smart and trying to sit in the fourth grade." She laughed at herself.

"I don't read. Negroes don't read."

Hillary stopped in the path and touched Leon's arm to stop him as well. "I already told you I'm smart. I know you're not all Negro. I know you're part of my pa. That's why my ma is crazy. She hates him and loves him. That's like a hook in a fish's mouth. You love the taste but can't get away."

"You wrong, Miss Hillary. I all Negro and Big Leon the only pa I ever knowed."

A breeze blew up and the scent of forest bottom consumed Leon. His skin pricked up in the chill.

"You be that then," Hillary said. "You be what you want. But you're still smart, and I bet I can teach you to read real quick."

They walked close to the back of the house before anything more was said. "You didn't answer," Hillary said.

"Didn't hear no question."

"I'm going to teach you to read. After dark. I want you to come 'round to the back here."

"Can't."

"You won't get caught. And if you do, I'll be there too and tell them it was all my doing."

"I don't think so," Leon told her before she left him in the back.

Hillary smiled back at him. "Oh, yes you will."

Leon began cleaning the mess of garbage, putting everything into burlap bags kept near the kitchen door. When he was through, he took the bags three at a time into the side woods where the land dipped toward Lower Run. On the first trip, Leon dumped the bags and shook them empty. Then he sat down.

The damp air of the woods wasn't so cold. The wind slowed too. Afternoon clouds slipped over the treetops as they ruffled and shook leaves, in small bunches, down onto the ground. The place already looked more brown, yellow, and red, than it looked green. The place already felt ready for winter.

Leon relaxed his back against a tree, the same tree he'd relaxed against many times before. His only rest came when he took it. He learned in a few years how much time he could take without looking lazy, without looking as though he wasn't doing his job. Leon learned how to work hard then rest, rather than work slow like some of the other Negro boys. Rather than being noticeably lazy like Hank and Earl. Even the white farmhands spent more time discussing how to do things rather than just doing them, stretching their days longer, and leaving no time for themselves, or so Leon imagined.

During short rest periods, Leon noticed the beauty of the world around him. Martha had taught him what to look for by pointing out the shapes of clouds, the colors of trees, and the sunset, what she always called "The Lord's sweet song into night." Leon hummed as he relaxed, learning that, too, from Martha. When he hummed, though, he heard words playing in his head. He suspected, but didn't know for sure, that Martha heard only her own humming, even though she sang once in a while.

His words told him things about himself, like "I'm a loner in the wood/ bein' forgotten by my own./ I'm a loner in the wood/ feelin' like I got no home." The words also informed him about what he enjoyed or hated. "The trees come a laughin' with me/ like I be their friend." or "Tunny too ugly to like anyone pretty as me." He also whispered what he observed. "The girl done crazy 'bout the nigger in the barn/ think she can teach him and that it won't do no harm."

That day, after each of three trips to the hollow to dump garbage, Leon sat and sang, satisfied with his life as it was.

After finishing his barn work, then working with Big Leon in the fields, Leon returned home and got ready for sleep as usual. Bess arrived home early and insisted on washing him even though he protested.

Martha retired early, humming loudly, and in an agitated manner. Something out of sorts must be going on. He would remember that humming. He would remember later that evening too. But years would go by before he remembered what happened between the two.

Late, and after Big Leon returned, Hillary tapped at the back door, then boldly stepped into the shack.

"What in the Lord's name girl?" Martha said.

"Come to talk to Leon."

"What you want wit him?" Bess asked. "He sick tonight."

"I teach him to read."

"Not my boy," said Bess. "I tole you, he throwed up."

Leon wanted to escape that night. Looking from Hillary to Bess, he stood between them unable to say his peace. He felt embarrassed to have Hillary standing on the dirt and bark floor, embarrassed that she might see his flattened form in his straw bed or the stains on the walls.

"He goin' nowhere," Bess said.

That's when something sudden, strong, and unusual occurred. Big Leon stood, shirtless, skin-shining, and firm. It was as if he had risen from the ground, large and black. "Let him go," he said.

"You got no say," Bess shouted.

Big Leon turned to face Bess. "I got say now woman."

Leon heard Martha say, "Um, um," before she turned away from the action.

"You go on son. You learn to get outta here."

Leon had never heard Big Leon call him son, and suddenly felt proud to be a consideration in the man's life at all.

"In the South they hang you if you teach a nigger to read," Bess said to Hillary.

"We ain't in the South. Anyway," Hillary said, "I'm doing this here for me, too."

"Enough. He goin'." Big Leon nodded and Hillary and Leon left before another word could be said.

CHAPTER 4

When Mona Carpenter died, Fred made everyone on the farm, blacks and whites alike, go to the funeral.

Hillary told Leon it was her father's way of doing the least he could. Honor her one last time for putting up with him.

Leon didn't want to go. Mr. Carpenter had stayed out of his life and he wanted it to remain that way. Yet he had a precognitive sense, like leaves turning up before rain, that changes would occur after Mona's funeral. And those changes all seemed to stem from the family tensions of that day, starting with Big Leon's refusal to let Martha be excused from the funeral. "We all gotta go," he told her.

"I don't owe that woman or that man for nothin' 'cept messin' with a good family."

"We goin'," Big Leon said, finalizing the conversation.

Bess mumbled something under her breath as she was known to do more and more often.

"Quit mumblin' woman."

Bess mumbled again and Big Leon ignored her.

Leon stayed out of the conversation. He dressed in a clean shirt and trousers. Big Leon gave him a hat to wear, "For the day," which made Leon feel like a man. At fifteen, he was a man as far as workload was concerned. With the hat on, his step turned more deliberate and controlled.

Once dressed, Leon stood outside the shack.

Tunny and Bud walked by. "Mix-up," one of them said.

Leon hadn't heard that for a long while. Tunny and Bud seldom spoke to him except when necessary. The whole family maintained an invisible existence soon after Freddy's death.

Leon didn't mind being called Mix-up as much as he hated being called Nigger Soup by the Carpenter boys. He thought about all the names he had and which ones he liked best and which ones he liked least. He liked it when Big Leon called him Son, even though it seldom happened. He liked how Martha called him boy most of the time. Martha spoke in changing sounds unlike anyone else Leon knew. Most often boy was a loving and familiar word, but Martha could change the sound so it came out like a curse. Her humming had the same range. Leon liked the way Hillary called him Leon. His name so seldom uttered in his own house that Hillary came to mind whenever his name was used. There was the exception though. Bess called him Leon, but she always prefaced it with my. My Leon. He hated that sound.

Martha came out and interrupted his name game.

"We leavin'?" he asked.

"Not yet."

"Why not?"

"Big Leon claimin' his rights to Poor Bess before he have to look into Sir's face. I reckon he want to be the first man of the day." Martha spit the words out.

Leon turned his head away.

"Don't like the truth? Well it disgusts me. Right now ain't the time. They almost started in front a me. Afore I even ready to go. You don't like me sayin' it, but theys the ones disrespectful." She walked down the path. Her shoulders and back rounded, folding in.

"Where you goin'? We gotta wait here."

"I'm goin' this far, no farther. Don't want to hear no ruttin'."

Leon followed her. He shook his head as he walked.

"Mona be lucky she done with it," Martha said.

"Hillary told me she's been crazy for years."

"That what it'll do to you if you let it. Poor Bess ain't too straight already."

"It must have been hard for Mona," Leon said with careful thought to use the proper English he had learned from Hillary and his reading and writing lessons. He envisioned the words even as he spoke them.

Martha's face softened. "Hard for you, but you here."

"I'm not here. I'm separate. I don't belong anywhere."

"Those some big thoughts boy. Careful you head don't break open. 'Cause you here, all right. You here."

In a moment he said, "They abuse each other. It's all the hate in the world, isn't it?"

"Not all the hate in the world, juss the hate on this little piece of property. One time I love my sister Bess. I love Big Leon even more. Now Poor Bess goin' the way of Mona and it not from losin' all them babies. Big Leon stay with her from spite and pride. He hate his-self for it, but can't get loose. She hate him and Sir and now you too, I'm a-feared." Martha stopped and peered directly into Leon's eyes driving the words home.

He was filled with discomfort, as if he had eaten too much supper then found the meat was bad. His stomach turned. He searched the trees and the sky for a sense of belonging. He hummed. A warm breeze reminded him it was almost summer. This eased his stomach somewhat, until he heard Bess cry out and a moment later heard Big Leon.

In five minutes they both came out the door.

Leon ran his fingers along the rim of the hat. He stood tall. Bess turned from his gaze when he glanced into her face. Big Leon snatched the hat from Leon's head. Martha jumped back.

"Change my mind. You not wearin' no hat," Big Leon said.

Leon's shoulders raised. He was about to protest, but then Big Leon slapped him along his ear. "Take it inside." He handed Leon the hat.

Leon cupped the top of it in one hand and took the rim between the fingers of the other. He gritted his teeth. "I'll do it, all right." As he turned to go back into the house, Big Leon slapped him again. This time Leon pulled his head down and his shoulders up in a protective motion.

"Don't sass me, boy."

"I puttin' the hat inside."

Stepping into the shack, Leon noticed the thick line of faded leather around the rim of the hat. A crust of dried sweat, white-stained and salty, also rode the rim. Leon threw the hat onto the unmade bed where Big Leon and Bess had been. The smell was harsh and musty in the room. Leon picked up the hat again and spit into it. He threw it back down and joined the others outside.

Big Leon led, Bess and Martha behind him, then Leon. Martha wouldn't look at Bess.

The family cemetery stood atop a small hill overlooking the north field. Leon had been there before, trimming the weeds next to Freddy's gravestone. He had fixed the fence surrounding it several times.

The path the help took to the cemetery meandered along the woods. Stone fences rose inside the tree line, sometimes separating property, sometimes as a place to put rocks collected from the fields.

Leon had walked the path many times, but never in such a long row of people. And most everyone had his head down. Big Leon held his high, but Leon sensed false pride in it.

Leon looked around, taking in the scent of the blossoming trees and sprouting oat fields. He let the air shift around him, cool in the shade of woods, then warm as the procession turned the corner around a field and stepped, one-by-one, into the sunny hillside. Being spring, the creek ran deep and loud. From the side hill near the cemetery, patches of running water showed through where the swampy areas lay in the valley not far off. The creek flooded every year making new tributaries through the lowland area.

Leon became the flowing water, hearing it louder and louder in his ears. He became the spring scent on the wind, the odor thickening inside his lungs. Stepping blank-faced and steady behind a long row of blacks, he became the woods and the field, the shadow and light of himself building in contrasts his eyes were unaccustomed to.

Soon a hawk-call broke his meditation. He stood on the ridge overlooking the valley, spring-brown creekwater throwing itself Southeast, completely unaware of the dead body poised over the dark cavern of a grave high on the hill.

Leon stopped in the back of the crowd. He watched the grass, its green tips rising toward the sun.

A preacher read from the Bible. Near the edge of the crowd, Hank and Earl poked at each other. Hillary came around to reprimand them. Light glistened from her eyes as she turned in the morning sun.

Leon was surprised to see her so emotional about her mother's death. She seldom had a kind word to say about Mona. She told Leon once that she thought her mother had given up.

Her dress was clean and fit tightly to her skin, a Sunday dress she had outgrown awhile ago.

Mr. Carpenter kept silent, staring down at the pine box all the while the preacher talked.

Hillary made her way toward Leon. "Hi," she said, standing next to him.

Martha glared at Leon.

"You should be with your pa," he whispered.

"He needs to be alone."

"I reckon."

Martha shook her head at the two of them. A cautionary reprimand.

Hillary leaned into Leon and spoke into his ear. She smelled clean and good. "Meet me at the creek flat," she said. "After."

They had met at what they called the creek flat on many occasions. That's where Leon had learned to read in the late evening, near sunset, in the summers. Usually they met at the creek flat for half an hour or so. It was his favorite place to read, the sound of water in the background, an occasional birdcall.

The creek ran high and the flat—a stony and gravelly area near a bend in the flow—was smaller than during the summer months. Only one creek flat developed close enough to their homes, much of the rest of the creek banks were either deep drop-offs or swampy, depending on where the creek cut through the land. The mud and swamp areas were shallow with broken branches of the creek meandering, making a wide sweep into the valley. Little islands of green, frog-filled areas rose and sank each year as spring flooding of the valley altered the creek's flow toward the Susquahanna River.

Leon clenched his jaw without answering. To meet at the creek flat during the day would be a treat. He knew work would carry on later in the day, but by the time everyone slowly made their way back to their shacks, he and Hillary could meet, read, and he could run back home, hardly missed.

Martha glanced back, disapproval shadowing her face. Leon knew that Hillary shouldn't be so bold as to talk with him in front of everyone. He figured that everyone knew or thought they knew about him and Hillary. Leon had heard things said. He had heard different folks questioning his new speech, the 'proper language' they called it. He even tried to speak one way when people were listening and totally different when Hillary and he were alone together.

Leon recognized very well what language was proper and what wasn't, and it occurred to him that the difference usually meant saying the whole sound of a word instead of clipping it off at the end. That and sometimes the order in which the words came from your mouth made all the difference. He had learned, from Hillary's continual scolding, to dislike the way most people spoke, including Hank and Earl who had no regard for learning.

Excited about the possibility of reading something new at the creek flat, and in bright daylight, Leon could hardly wait for the funeral to end.

His wish came true, as there wasn't much to say about Mona. As suspected, everyone walked away even slower than they had arrived. Idle time was not unheard of, but it was cherished.

At the nearest edge of the woods, Leon took off running downhill toward the creek. He heard Martha grunt some words out, but they weren't recognizable. The sound itself was piercing and sharp-edged even though the words were unclear. Still, he knew what she was trying to say. No one else made a sound, and Leon didn't look back to see whether anyone had moved to stop him.

He stopped at a slope that fell off and into a deep, swift creek-flow. A maple tree had fallen over and bent to the movement and power of the water. He looked into the deep green and saw the torn carcass of a deer hanging loosely, caught in a tangle of bark-stripped branches. It had been there since the prior winter. No acrid smell of rot lifted from the remains. Most of the meat and bone were gone. Only strips of skin and parts of limbs hung onto the tree, a final but futile attempt at life.

Leon made his way up creek to where the land flattened out and the creek made its turn, cutting into the opposite bank and leaving bare the creek flat.

The rumble of water rushed into his ears, a steady background blocking out the whistling of wind through the trees. The creek galloped toward the river, and the river slipped past towns and cities.

Leon had an urge to jump into the creek and float with it until he hit the river, then float with that until a friendly town sprouted up. He'd stop there and work hard, so he could buy books and read.

He watched as drops leaped up, somersaulted, and landed back in the stream only farther down, closer to the river. He picked up a stone and pitched it into the water. He picked up another and threw it at a tree on the opposite bank, hitting it squarely.

"Hey," Hillary shouted over the roar of the creek.

Leon went to her. "You got something to read?"

"Not this time. I thought we'd talk a little."

"You upset about your mama?"

"A little."

"She was crazy."

"That's Pa's fault. Pa and your ma."

"My Ma's crazy too. Worse than ever. She scaring me." He shut up, wanting not to think of Bess.

"She scares you," Hillary corrected.

"She scares me," Leon said.

Hillary turned away. "Can we sit in the grass?"

Leon followed her up the bank and over to where the sun reached a clearing and a soft patch of fresh grass lifted up.

Hillary leaned into Leon. He stiffened.

"What's wrong."

"We're not supposed to touch."

"I need comforting. Besides, you're my half brother. It's okay."

"I'm nothin' but a farmhand. And a Negro one, to boot. I got too much of my mama in me to be called a half-brother to anyone."

"Your nose ain't even flat."

"Don't matter."

"It doesn't matter."

"We still shouldn't be touching this much."

"This isn't touching," she said while leaning into him farther. "I know what touching is."

"How do you know?" Leon focused on his words.

"Jacob."

"Who's that?"

"He's a man I see sometimes from across the valley."

"A man?"

"He's twenty."

"You best be careful."

"Better. You had *better* be careful," she said.

"You'd better be."

"Don't act like that. I do things you wouldn't know."

"I don't want to know."

"Like real touching."

"I don't want to know," Leon repeated.

"Like this." Hillary brushed her hand over Leon's leg.

Something in his mind exploded. He pushed her away. "What you doin'?"

"Don't shove me like that. I was showing you what you don't know."

"I tell you, I don't want to know." Memories rushed into Leon's thoughts. Things he didn't want to remember like guilt, pain, and hatred. As always his stomach ached. He didn't know from where his feelings originated.

"I want to know," she said.

"No ma'am."

"Don't talk like that."

"Don't be angry. I'm just scared." Those were his only words.

She sat up and unbuttoned her dress, then pulled it open. Her breasts were white as a new snow. They were thick too, as thick as her body allowed.

Leon tried to look away but couldn't.

"If you don't, I'll say you did."

"No," Leon said.

"I'm grieving and need comforting."

"Not by me," he said. "Please Miss Hillary. Go see your Jacob. Go on."

"I'll tell Pa you did it."

"No. Why you doin' this to me. We supposed to be friends."

"We are friends, that's why. No one has to know." She pulled at the rope around his waist and then pulled her dress over her head.

Leon's body weakened. He tried not to do it, but his body and Hillary's didn't listen.

It was quick and she started to cry afterwards. "I'm sorry Leon. I'm so sorry. I'm crazy like my ma and pa. I'm crazy and pulled you into it."

"Don't be crazy," he said. "Please, don't be crazy. We'll never do that again. Go see your Jacob." He held her as she hit her fist against her thigh. He pulled her tight to his chest and rocked her. His eyes were open wide. He remembered Edna's words. He was evil. And his evilness affected everyone around him. Hillary was next in line.

"You got to go," he said. "You got to be quiet."

She stood naked before him, bending to get her clothes. The smell of them rose with her and came putrid to Leon's nose. A tart and sweet smell together that didn't fit into the world quite right. Her heavy breasts hung down as she bent over and his bare penis rose again.

Hillary noticed and said, "That's pretty." Then she burst into tears. "What did I make you do?"

Thankful that she took the blame, Leon also feared who she might confide in. Her vulnerability could turn on them both.

"You're my brother," she said.

"I'm all nigger. Really, I feel it inside."

She shook her head.

"No ma'am, Miss Hillary, no, I'm not your bother. Don't think it. Please, say you know different."

She put on her clothes and hugged him. "I won't tell. I know I sinned, but it'd be a bigger sin if I told."

"They'd lynch me," Leon said as though they both didn't already know it.

"It's a burden I'll carry now."

Leon pulled his pants on. He calmed. "I got to go home."

"Me too," she said.

"I'm sorry," he said.

"It's my sinning mind. It's the sinning I was born into. My pa did it and now I did. I think Hank did it too, with a shack girl." Hillary touched Leon's shoulder and reassured him one last time that she'd keep quiet.

When she was out of view, Leon ran along the creek, back into the woods, and all the way home.

CHAPTER 5

S weat dripped from Leon as he approached the shack. He slowed to catch his breath, then entered. No one was there except Martha. She accused and judged him. He knew the look.

"I'd a thought that white blood a made you smart, but you got nigger brains inside your white head."

"You right. You right."

"Don't use that poor-boy talk no more. Not to me. It like you talkin' down and I ain't less than."

"I'm sorry, Martha."

She took her time moving across the room. "I don't have no idea what you sorry for, boy, but I know guilt when I sees it."

"I done nothing."

She pierced his words with an outstretched finger.

"I didn't do anything," Leon corrected.

"You lie."

"Martha."

"Don't keep lyin' to me. Just don't say nothin'. Just go help your pappy. And pray to the Lord."

Leon left the shack and searched for Big Leon. He ran into Tunny, who told him that Big Leon headed out to check the north field for varmints.

Leon ran until he saw Big Leon standing mid-field with his head held high as he scanned the property. Big Leon's blackness belied his relation to Leon.

Leon watched his father for a moment and wondered whether Big Leon wanted to be alone. They both knew where Bess would be: soothing Sir's sadness. What of Hillary now that she was through with Leon? What of Martha, who must know the unsaid details of Leon's trip to the creek flat?

A cool breeze shifted the tops of the trees and a hawk cried, then flew down to snatch a field rat or rabbit. It was too far off for Leon to notice which.

Big Leon raised his arm. He held a revolver. Leon had never seen one before and had no idea why or how Big Leon would get his hands on one. One shot rang out and Leon saw a ground hog drop. Big Leon lowered his head, then kneeled onto the ground as if praying.

Leon took some steps toward his father, then stopped.

Big Leon turned. "Where you been?"

Leon walked closer so he didn't have to yell an answer. As if yelling the location would carry with it what he had done there. "The creek flat."

"Readin'?" Big Leon seldom mentioned what he had been instrumental in allowing.

"Not this time."

Big Leon stood and went over to Leon, grabbing his face by the jaw.

Leon tried to pull away.

Big Leon jerked the boy's head and shoved him onto the ground.

Leon looked into the sky above his father's head. He rose to one elbow. He said nothing.

Big Leon pointed the revolver barrel at Leon's head. "I should kill you. Put you outta you misery." He lowered the gun. "You stink in a bad way," he said. "You in danger?"

"No." Leon said. "She wouldn't."

"Don't blame you. Them white folks can make a preacher sin. They supposed to be smarter'n us."

"I tried not to do it."

"Can you read?"

Leon hesitated. What did that have to do with it? "Yes, sir."

"Listen."

Leon sat up and focused on his father's face.

"You listenin'?" He pointed the revolver at Leon again.

Leon crabbed backward, crawling away from the black iris of the barrel. Would his father really pull that trigger? Perhaps a blessing if so.

"You have to think white. You have to read white. You have to speak white." Big Leon spit and it landed near Leon's hand. "I don't truss 'em." He grabbed Leon by the neck and lifted him onto his feet. "I know too much. You been used to kill me. Everybody use you to kill somebody else or somebody inside they self." He shook his head and walked off. "It ain't you fault, but you might get kilt for it."

Leon stood and watched as Big Leon left the field and entered the woods.

Leon's knees shook and his teeth chattered. He didn't know how to think white. Even if he were evil, he couldn't think as evil as how whites appeared to think. Leon peered into the woods after his father. He thought about the deer he'd seen. If he were to jump into the creek, he wouldn't float to the river. He'd get hung up on a felled tree and drown. He breathed short, fearful drowning breaths.

He too hummed. Tried to forget what Hillary and he had done. All around him the field smelled of the new growth of spring. The woods let out the winter smell still, rotting leaves and a depth of cold not quite free of frost. Soon, Leon thought, the creek would peak then slow. He knew the sound. One night he'd hear the creek get quiet, the noise no longer strong enough to lift up through the woods to the six white-washed shacks.

Humming helped him to feel better, to think. The words he put with the humming reviewed his day, which started out in death, moved to orgasm, climbed into fear, and ended -- as Leon saw it -- with being evil in the eyes of those who loved him. Both Big Leon and Martha labeled him. Hillary did too in her own sinful and crazy way.

Leon thought about what his father had said. He wasn't white, though. And he didn't feel Negro. Besides a great uncertainty about himself and a greater uncertainty about where his life was headed, Leon sensed only guilt and fear.

No one spoke to him that night. He ate out back, alone, and cold from the night air.

When he went back inside, Bess lay in her corner, spider threads glistening in the deep dark near her head. Big Leon stood near a splintered window staring into the darkness. Martha hummed in her bed, in her corner of the room.

"My Leon," Bess said.

Leon tensed. He was no longer anyone's Leon, least of all Bess's. Yet, he had been taught to respect his mother.

"Let me have your sweetness," she said, shifting back close to the wall, leaving a space on the straw for him to lie down near her.

Leon looked at his father who let too many things go on. "No," Leon whispered. "I'm going for a walk. I'm in a thinking way and I'm going."

Leon noticed Big Leon smile to himself. A sign of approval?

Bess screeched, surprising them all. Then she covered her head and mumbled a long sentence that kept going even as Leon left the shack.

The cold bit hard, but he stepped lively into the darkness. The moon had remained low on the horizon and could not be seen from the woods. He knew his way to the creek. The closer he got the louder the sound and the colder the night air. At the creek flat, Leon kneeled down and hugged his knees to conserve a little body heat.

He tried to feel white, but nothing came except images of Hank and Earl and Mr. Carpenter. He couldn't even conjure his own face. Then there were white women, but only a few. Mona, in his memory, always stared ahead, seldom looked around. It was as if she had been dead for years, like Bess was becoming dead. Mona moved slowly. Hillary had talked about how Mona mumbled, not ever saying any real words, agreeing and disagreeing with herself at the same time. The tones involved were what had made Hillary think so. And now Bess mumbled.

Thinking of Hillary also brought up other images. Her hanging breasts, thick arms, and wide, when she bent to pick up her dress, butt. Leon laughed out loud. She smelled like sweat and sweet water. Her big arms were made for work, but since she did little of that, they were flabby and soft.

He pictured lying atop that big softness and felt the itch to do it again.

Still, in his imagination, he didn't look or feel white.

He spit onto the rocks. Moonlight edged onto the flat from behind him, scattering the pebbles and stones into shadow and light. The creek sparkled.

He pictured Big Leon, Tunny, Bud, and all the other shack people together. Picturing him with them made it plain as day that he wasn't black either.

"I nothin'," he said. "Evil have its own look."

Hearing his voice, Leon heard again what Big Leon had told him that day. 'You have to think white, read white, and speak white.'

Big Leon never said feel white. He never said be white.

Leon didn't feel white, but he knew how to speak white. In fact, he spoke better than most whites. Leon didn't feel black either, but he could speak black.

He spit onto the rocks again. He looked into the trees on the opposite bank. The moonlight brightened the branches and highlighted the new life, the spring buds searching for a place in the world. Was he evil? He sensed pain and sadness inside him, but also song and delight. Perhaps Mix-up was an appropriate name for his feelings as well as his heritage, as well as his appearance.

A great horned owl hooted and Leon saw it high in a tree waiting for the stirring of a mouse.

He spit once more, then stood. Cold air brushed all the newly exposed areas of his skin. He rubbed his arms. In a slow careful run Leon headed to the only family he knew.

He sneaked into the shack, undressed and lay on the cold straw floor, pulling a blanket over him. There had been a fire in the fireplace earlier, but only embers glowed now. He stared across the room into the red and black mystery of the dying fire. He listened to the shallow breathing from the other bodies who shared the shack with him. He attempted to sense a connection, a kinship, an instinct, between him and each of them. Only thoughts of Martha brought that family feeling. For Big Leon he felt respect. He felt pride. For Bess, even the thought of her made him tense up and pull back. He closed his eyes and thought of Martha again. She had been his mother and sister, his only playmate when the other children teased him.

They all lay quietly, spread around the shack to create as much privacy as possible. But there was no real privacy, only a false sense of it. Surely, everyone in the shack new what went on in there, but each in his or her own way ignored or forgot or hid behind those truths as lies, and hid behind the lies as truths.

That day Martha worked hard to break that notion down, Leon thought, then Big Leon took a step in that direction too. Even Leon had changed the course of events when he left that evening. What strange chain reaction did all that signify? What would break down next? He thought he knew the answer. He closed his eyes harder against the thought. His mind racing, Leon lay still until he fell off to sleep.

*   *   *

Leon woke groggy and slow. Bess had already gone off to the big house. Big Leon stood naked, raising his pants from the floor. Martha sat with her head turned from Big Leon.

Noticing Leon's movements, she said, "Don't think Leon should do no white chores today. Got a bad feelin'."

"Not ours to say," Big Leon said.

"If you need him more? You could say that. You boss of it."

Big Leon looked over at Leon then pulled on his shirt. "Feed him. I'll see."

"What are you feeling?" Leon asked.

"Feelin' those boys a his gonna be rammin'. They gonna feel righteous."

Big Leon left without another word.

"I don't care," Leon said.

"This is a bad time, boy, a bad time. People be confused what's right. They feelin' guilt now it's too late. They want to hide their guilt behind wrong doin's. You don't get in the way of that, you hear?"

"I hear you, but I don't know what I can do about it. Like Pa said, 'Ain't our say.'"

"Don't mock your pa's speakin' ways."

Leon pulled on his clothes. "I didn't mean to. I was just saying what he said."

Martha got up to feed him. "He tole me what he tole you in the field."

She put a chunk of bread in his hands.

"What was that?"

"You know. You doin' it. You talkin' white. You remember how to do that. It save your life out there." She pointed out the window. "I'm thinkin' you be workin' with your pa today."

"I'm not afraid." Leon bit off some bread and walked outside. He skipped heading for the barn and went straight to the house, collecting the kitchen garbage from the back. The kitchen help heard him and someone he didn't recognize peeked out at him, then jerked back inside.

After he had everything bagged, Leon carried two bags at a time into the woods. As was his habit, he emptied the bags and sat for a moment.

He watched three squirrels appear from nowhere and chase one another along a felled tree, up another, and across a branch to a third tree. Their tails fluffed and twitched. They chattered and ran, bumping into one another, rollicking and chattering some more. He laughed at their play and wished for the return of his own innocence. When he decided to retrieve two more bags from the main house, the squirrels scurried away. Leon looked into the ravine. The run flowed steadily, still high from thaw. He breathed deeply, letting out a long relaxing breath, then repeated the act allowing his shoulders to loosen and drop.

Two more bags, another, shorter stay in the woods, and Leon headed for the barn. Hank and Earl weren't there. Leon knew the chores that needed to be done and set to work filling feed bins and water buckets, setting hay and cleaning stalls for when the horses came back that evening. He worked until early afternoon, deciding to ready a place for new hay even though that was months off. He didn't mind organizing bales and cleaning the bays. He enjoyed the calmness of the broom swing. In all, the first part of the day went smoothly. Leon did what he knew to do.

He stopped in to see Martha, but she was working in one of the other shacks. He scooped some water and broke some bread to eat while heading out to Big Leon.

Spring plowing also meant rock collecting. It seemed no matter how many years the fields had been planted, about the only thing the ground grew consistently was rocks. Every spring a new crop had to be gathered and added to the stone fence barely inside the woods.

"They's less of 'em every year," Big Leon said, but it always seemed there were the same number to Leon.

"The land just chucks 'em up," Leon said.

Five men and seven children stood abreast and walked each field up and down, pulling and passing they called it. The rocks accumulated in number as they were handed, thrown, or kicked from the center to the edges of the field.

Leon, coming on late, was told to gather and stack, which meant he'd work alone. He'd take the stones from the edge of the field into the woods and add them to the fence. Since the planting fields were rotated, a fence would grow in size slowly over the years. Once high enough, new fences would be started, or old ones curved to section off a new area.

Leon gathered and stacked. The wide band of black men and boys walking up through the field were too far away to talk to.

This activity continued from field to field until the last field was stripped of rock, then a flurry of work hovered around the stacks until the fence stacking job was complete. Even then, Leon worked around many people, but remained alone.

That evening, Leon walked down to the creek flat before nightfall and found Hillary waiting. Excitement and fear stood side by side when he recognized her form in the half-light.

"I brought a new book."

Leon couldn't wait to read whatever it was she had. "What is it?"

She held it toward him. "One of my mama's. Pa said I could have whatever I liked."

Leon took the book. "Henry W. Longfellow," he read. "I've never read poetry except the Bible."

Hillary beamed. "It's pretty new."

"But she didn't read lately, did she?" Leon asked.

"I think when alone she might have been different." She went to touch Leon on the chest. He stiffened. "What is it?" she said.

"I don't like to be touched."

"You mean by me."

"No. I just have to be ready. It's all right. I just get tickled at first."

"It seemed like you were all right before."

"Miss Hillary, please, you have your Jacob." Leon held the book to his chest, partly for protection and partly to possess it.

"I been thinking about what we did. Sometimes it's right and sometimes it's wrong," Hillary told him.

"It's not right."

"You don't like me 'cause I'm not skinny and pretty."

"No. No. I didn't say that." He stumbled back a step.

"I'll tell you, though, skinny girls don't have a bosom like mine."

Leon closed his eyes as Hillary opened her dress. In his mind he could see her, though. Her breasts reminded him of Martha's when he was younger and used to watch her wash. They reminded him of a human warmth that was almost gone from his life now.

Hillary took his hand and leaned into it.

Leon shook his head back and forth protesting what he knew he would do. "My body ain't listenin' no more," he said.

"It's listening to the call of nature, that's all." Hillary led Leon to a soft bed of pine needles hid by low branches.

Leon's actions and emotions shot in opposing directions. Fear rose inside him even as he let his trousers fall to the ground. He understood sex as a weapon and a pleasure. After the pleasure of release, fear dominated.

Hillary cried afterwards, claiming, once again, that her body had sinned like her father's had before her.

Leon could not feel any worse. Nothing good could come from their act but the act itself. What's more, she could break down, or worse yet have a two-headed child, as his imagination told him. He remembered her soft body and strong breath, the pungent and sweet scent of their bodies after lovemaking. He often thought of them together when they were not together.

Hillary let Leon take books home to read. No one would find them missing, she told him.

Leon read by the dying embers and by morning's first light. He read to remember and he read to forget.

CHAPTER 6

Y ou stinkin' like sin," Martha said.

"It's the fish fryin'." Leon uncovered a book from his sleeping corner.

"Don't hide in that there thing."

"I'm not."

"But you will. I knows you better'n you knows you."

"I'll wash then."

"Can't wash sin away, not even with lye."

"Leave me alone. There's more sinnin' going on around here than in hell itself," Leon said.

"Not in my place."

"Your place is a corner. In your corner there's hummin' that's supposed to keep everything out. But outside your hummin' door, there's evil beyond thought."

Martha slapped a hand to her thigh as though she were reprimanding a dog. "You stop. It's the white man put this in our house. We juss play-actors in a white man's animal-sick play. Now you stuck twice in it."

"I know what you mean. But I only got stuck in it once. When I was too young to fight. When I was too young to know better. Because of it, my pa hardly comes home and my ma is going crazy."

"You stop right there. You respect—"

"You don't respect her."

Martha's brow tightened.

"The truth," Leon said. "She sinned me out of her body to kill Pa. Pa freed me to kill her. And, maybe to save me, though I ain't his to save."

Martha stood silent and firm, as though the truth had never been spoken so clearly or so openly.

"Nothing is said here. Everything is covered over like putting straw over horse shit. In books people talk," Leon said.

"We ain't books. And you ain't talkin' to that girl."

"You've always been more mama to me than my mama been," he said through tears. I want you to see."

"I see, but I don't know that you see."

Leon slumped down and sat on the floor, letting the book drop to his side. "I'm scared."

Martha grabbed his arms and lifted him to his feet. She held him in front of her.

"I can't stop and she won't let me stop," Leon admitted.

"It's a tangle in a web. It all sticky and sweet, frightful and glorious."

"What do I do?"

"It can only lead to no good, boy. You tell that girl, you done. It not right. She knowed it ain't right too. She can see. She juss as tangled as you. She juss as sorry and juss as glad. Somebody got to be strong."

"I'm not strong enough."

"You as strong as you pa, but you don't know it."

"My pa's a white man who can't whip a nigger boy."

Martha pushed him away. "Your pa the man who here. He the man who teach you farmin'. He the man who set you free."

Leon ran out of the shack, the smell of trout burning in the pan behind him.

Big Leon came down the path.

Leon pushed by him.

"You stayin' for dinner," Big Leon said.

Leon ignored him.

"Boy!"

Leon ran to the creek, not the flat, but where it straightened, where maple and pine stood in small groves near the edge. Leon flowed with the creek, swift and deep. He yelled at the woods. He cried with the insects, sirens of the quick life, the sudden death.

Stepping too close to the bank, he slipped and soaked his foot. The water felt cool on that hot night. The woods breathed humidity and the scent of loam. A crow cawed and flew off. Leon wondered why black birds could rule much of the area, when black men could not.

He sat and rubbed his hands over his foot until it became dry. A clatch of gnats moved slowly on a breeze coming his way. He got up, swatted at a mosquito and walked farther down-creek toward the river.

He hummed as he walked, listening to the sound resonating through the back of his jaw and into his skull. He wondered what difference there might be between a black man's skeleton and a white man's skeleton. When he died, would anyone be able to guess what color he had been? Being both black and white, were there extra pieces inside him? Or missing? What was the difference if everybody were blind?

Leon heard a noise and stopped humming. He saw movement in the fading light. A potato sack shirt, lighted by a deep violet sunset, slipped behind a tree. He waited, but nothing more moved. Thinking clearly what to do, he walked backwards. In a few steps, Tunny peeked around a tree. At that moment, Leon understood how stupid he had been night after night. The humping. The nakedness. It had all been known.

Tunny stopped as though he thought Leon couldn't actually see him.

"How many times you follow me?"

"We know what you 'bout," Tunny said.

"Git, then." Leon ran toward Tunny, who shoved Bud out from behind a tree and ran after him.

Leon watched. Neither of them looked back to see whether he'd stopped or kept following. A darkness deeper than night set over him. He picked up a rock and threw it as hard as he could toward Tunny and Bud. It crackled through leaves then thunked into a tree trunk or branch and fell to the ground. He picked up another and threw it harder. His breath came hard. His teeth clenched. He scanned the area for anyone else who might have followed him. Shaking his head, Leon walked back to the shack. He felt hungry. He hurt for the comfort of food. Even cold fish would be better than nothing.

Big Leon was not home when Leon arrived. When he came inside, Bess mumbled in the corner, called, "Sweet Leon." When he ignored her, she rolled into the space nearest the wall, the thin blanket falling and her bare shoulders and buttocks showing. Martha presented Leon with a plate of fish and a biscuit as quickly as she could. She blocked his view of his mother by standing between them, the plate held out.

The room smothered him with the odor of sweat and compression of night heat. His hunger was deep and covered many areas of his life, many emotions. He hated Tunny and Bud. Their knowledge disgusted him. What they do with what they know didn't matter any longer though. How could they alienate him more than he already felt?

Leon left the heat of the shack and ate, sitting on a rock out back. Using a biscuit, he cleaned the last of the grease from his plate. He set the plate down at his feet and leaned back against the shack. Stars and fireflies blinked in and out of life overhead.

His head against the shack wall, Leon heard Bess and Martha arguing. None of their words came through clearly, but the tones of their voices belied their exchange. He let the sounds comfort him, like humming a ruckus song. Their discourse took place in a rapid-fire question and answer format. He imagined how they might hold back conversation that he and Big Leon were not invited to hear. When alone, those two could lash out with no need to pause unless one of the men came walking through the door. How amusing it was to hear so much talk coming out of them now. At times they both talked simultaneously. He giggled. All the talk of respect that Martha delivered suddenly felt—and sounded—like a complete lie.

Remembering Tunny and Bud once again, Leon wondered where Big Leon went on his walks. Did he follow Leon as well? Nothing seemed real or honest. Even the fireflies were false stars.

Leon stayed outside, swatting an occasional mosquito, until the anger inside the house slowed, until the humming began.

He usually met with Hillary three times a week, sometimes more. He questioned his own intentions and wondered what would happen, truly, if he refused to meet her, like Martha suggested. Should he test this new idea?

The thought of Hillary caused his heart to beat faster. His body reacted against the memory of her touch, yet his mind leaned toward it. She had a peculiar smell about her body and a strong scent from her mouth. When tender her manner was superior. Was he her nigger, like Bess was her father's nigger?

Enough pain slithered through their little shack even before he was born, was he to carry that pain through, add new ingredients, and make it venomous? His mind boiled and his body ached. The way Hillary rubbed against him made his skin crawl, yet the way she moaned made him hard.

Leon dashed the thoughts from his mind. He grabbed his plate and stood quickly, exerting his body to release its hold over his thoughts.

He never had to make a decision on his own, but it was getting to that time and he could feel a decision standing over him like a large man in a black cloak. He couldn't let Tunny and Bud see him with Hillary again. He couldn't imagine his father watching. And Martha knew. Bess? His stomach churned and his throat opened. He squeaked and groaned. He gagged at the combined thoughts of Hillary and Bess and their awful connection through him, through Sir, through Big Leon, who knew too much about his own family to stay inside the same shack for more than a few hours at a time. Hell could not be a hotter, more sinful place.

Leon wiped sweat from his brow. He used a shoulder to wipe his mouth dry. His hand and shirt were rough and scratchy, work heavy and sweat soaked. He remembered as a child being hugged by Martha and caressed by his mother. He had wished to be touched by his father, but that never or seldom happened except by accident. His mother's touch soured. Martha retreated. Now his skin tightened at anyone's touch except his own. He'd move out of the way to avoid being brushed against. As Hillary searched his body, he squirmed and shifted claiming that it tickled or scratched or hurt.

He kicked the dirt, sending dust into the air. He swatted at a mosquito using his empty plate. He breathed deeply, looked to the sky, said a silent prayer for himself, for Hillary, and for the rest of his family. He had decided. No matter the outcome, he could go on no longer. Not as things were.

Big Leon returned home. He sat near the wash basin, then lifted his eyes to stare out the window, his head held high, his eyes fixed on a cloud, the sky, the treetops. Neither Leon nor Big Leon spoke. Leon set his plate with others on the ledge. In his own corner of the room, Leon sat on his bed of straw. He reached down and back with his hand, touched his book, the one he'd kept, Wordsworth.

Martha lay flat, barely visible in the dark, yet she was the witness in the family. Bess lay curled facing the wall. A thin cover lay over her back now. Martha must have covered her. Still her bare shoulders shined with sweat. Her neck looked soft. That single thought shot guilt through Leon. How could he think such a thought? What tenderness he felt for his mother was tarnished and although it was tenderness he wished for, he could no longer accept it. That he knew. Martha seemed to know it as well. Big Leon appeared to deny it.

An urge to stand and shout came over him, but he did not move.

Big Leon must have felt the boy's energy. He turned and looked at Leon. "Go to bed," he said. "Rest."

"Yes, Pa." He wanted to hear his own voice as he addressed his father. He heard the familiar sound, but it stood riddled with untruth. So many untruths lived in that one small shack. In that room. At that moment. Leon nodded and Big Leon returned to his eyes-fixed position.

A heavy breeze blew in. Leon wiped his mouth dry. He undressed and lay down. He felt like pissing, but wouldn't get up to go outside. He fell asleep with the slight pain of an unreleased bladder. Horrible dreams plagued his sleep. He could do nothing inside them without an audience, without being watched. The woods were riddled with people watching him. His home was no better. Faces peered in the windows, from every corner, in through the door. Leon tried to run, but faces appeared in the sky, in the trees, and in the rocks along the river.

He awoke before sunup, shaking, exhausted. He pulled on his trousers, held them at the front and ran out to pee in the bushes that grew along the side of the shack. Nothing felt quite right that morning. It began in physical pain and with an uneasiness that followed Leon all morning. Grits and bread for breakfast. That was a treat. No one spoke, though, only grunted and hummed.

Leon hurried to Sir's barn to settle the stalls, ready them for evening. The teams would already be out. He planned, too, to clear the kitchen garbage, relax and make up songs, then head for his father's side to work out the remains of the day.

The plan was right. It reeked of familiarity clear up until his rendezvous with Hillary. Already, early in the day, he knew it would be different from all their other meetings.

Leon glided through the day, an uneasy feeling thick in his chest and throat. Hank and Earl weren't much help, but they weren't much hindrance either. Leon took orders from them without comment, without acknowledging them except to respond.

On his way to the back of the house, he saw Hillary for a moment and she winked at him. From that time, it took an hour to adjust his mind. He thought of her thick legs and soft breasts, the wetness between her legs and her moans of pleasure. From there, he imagined her smell, then her threats and rudeness when he didn't respond the way she wanted. This all flowed, like the creek where they met, into thoughts of Hillary and her other man, Jacob.

Stamping his foot and hitting one fist into the other palm didn't fully illustrate Leon's anger or pain at the thoughts he brought up. Nor did it belie the confusion of those emotions. He loved and hated her. He feared what she might do. He loathed himself for the power he let her have over him, for it was not merely the power of ownership, but of much more. As much as he didn't understand that power, he also knew it well and from more places than he should. Leon accepted his own feelings. He spit, trying to reduce the acrid taste in his mouth. He pissed onto the garbage trying to empty the poison that was building up inside him. And he hummed and sang with teeth clenched and fists tight to draw his mind back into harmony.

Before heading for the fields, Leon pushed his back straight, his head high, and let his nostrils – those white-man's nostrils – flare out and suck in the world as he knew it. The rest of the day, Leon worked hard, often to exhaustion. At one point, Big Leon asked whether Leon was all right. A moment of fatherly concern Leon would remember. Yet, he was never able to respond.

That evening, near dusk, Leon carried his anger to the creek flat.

"What's wrong with you?" Hillary said.

He wondered how she could possibly know his thoughts were torn? Did he walk differently? Was his face twisted, tightened, or expressive in some other way?

"Nothin'," he said, but knew she wouldn't have it that simple.

"You mad at me for not stoppin' to speak today?" It sounded as though her guilt had come to the creek flat with her.

"That weren't no reason."

"Why are you talking like that?"

"I wanna."

"You know how I hate for you to talk that way."

He stared.

She walked closer to him, her eyelids lowered to a seductive half-closed position.

Why he said what he did, he would never know. "You juss want me to sound white so's you done have to think about who you sinnin' with. So's you can imagine it be Jacob stickin' you and not some nigger farmhand."

It was his delivery more than his words that hurt Hillary. He could feel her pain as the words were delivered, and if that weren't enough, he could imagine her pain being worse from the way her face twisted hideously into a snarl.

"How dare you?" She fell to her knees, ready to cry.

He leaned toward her...his hand reaching out. Then he held his position. "You can't love no nigger. And you can't, you show can't, love you half-brother." He pulled his hand fully back. "You an evil woman. We both evil. I evil the day I's born of this world."

Hillary looked up as if she couldn't believe what she was hearing, her face streaked with tears. The setting sun set behind Lean; she squinted.

"I know." Her whisper was so soft Leon wasn't sure he'd heard the words correctly.

"We stoppin' the sin now."

"You have no right to decide."

"I have the say," he shouted.

Hillary curled back from his voice.

Leon searched the woods for movement. How did this scene look? How did it sound? He tried to think from outside his small world. His stomach burned and his throat locked shut. Nothing made sense. He wanted to run away and hold her at the same time.

"Go," Hillary said. "I hate you." She crumpled sideways onto the ground. "You're just a lousy nigger. Like your mama you enchant us with the idea of forbidden fruit, but you're nothin' but flesh. You're flesh and blood and bone like us all."

Leon turned to leave. He bent over and coughed, sensing bile rise in his throat, surprised he didn't vomit.

"I'll make you sorry," she cried.

Her words shoved at him until he ran stumbling over roots and stepping into holes.

As the light burst across the horizon before the sun disappeared, Leon came to a stop. Bending forward, his hands on his knees, Leon spit. He gulped hot humid air, like trying to breathe under water. He waited, sending his will to his lungs, trying to get them to operate more slowly, more efficiently.

Suddenly, Big Leon stepped out of the bushes.

Leon's eyes stretched as wide as they could. "What?" was all he could muster.

"Need your help," Big Leon said.

Leon spit again. He glanced up through the twilight.

"A late calf comin'. I need a hand. It may be breached."

Leon wondered why him, but didn't ask. He followed Big Leon to the South barn where they kept the few head of cattle Fred Carpenter owned.

On the way Leon asked why one of the other men wouldn't do it.

"Cain't."

Leon didn't ask why.

At the barn, a cow lay in its stall bleating like a sheep. Big Leon and Leon were the only two there.

"Why not Tunny?"

"Toll 'em all to scat home." Big Leon kneeled next to the cow and stroked her neck.

"How you know it's breached?"

"Said maybe. She breached last year."

Leon kneeled near the cow's back and laid his hand on its bulbous belly. They waited for a while.

Big Leon stood and paced for a moment.

The barn stood quiet now, with only an occasional creaking sound from the wind. A breeze blew through the open doors scuffing up loose straw.

Leon noticed how well kept the barn was. He wondered briefly why Tunny and the others were sent home.

Big Leon leaned against a stall post. He stared out the barn door at a dark sky. An owl hooted. "I always hated you. You face mostly, that white ugly."

Leon kneeled, silent, listening to Big Leon's even tone.

"And you mama, she could-a died instead a birthin' you. Lord knows I died. Still do when I looks at you. And I know she hate you too, only she hate you and love you. They's always opposites. When they's sun they's night. When they's poor they's rich. And when they's divine, they show-'nuff be sin to go with it.

"What I sayin', boy, is with all my hate, they's love too. I cain't see you gettin' kilt for nothin'. And white girls, they jus' nothin'."

Leon's questions never got out.

The cow bawled and action occurred.

Like a dream, the world took over and Big Leon's words faded as though never said.

The next day the two men separated early in the morning and went on with their chores.

Hillary was missing and Leon heard snippets of conversation that suggested she had become unstable, "Like her momma," someone said. He heard she'd run off.

After dinner, he sat out back, waiting for Big Leon to return from his walk. But he didn't return and Leon went in to get some sleep. Martha and Bess had already fallen off.

He slept after the long day of fence post repair, wagon wheel greasing, and animal feedings. He slept exhausted by the birth of the new calf the night before. He slept in his own sweat beaded along his neck and shoulders, in his own dirt and grime from a long day's work after a night of no sleep. Leon slept soundlessly until Big Leon woke him with a start.

CHAPTER 7

F ace to face, Big Leon's black eyes bordered by white indicated
fear. "We gotta go."

Leon pushed onto a shaky elbow.

"I got somethin' for you." Big Leon held a burlap bag tied at the
top with a rope.

"Why?"

"White girl been talkin'."

Leon lowered his head and whimpered. Big Leon placed a huge
hand on the boy's shoulder. His whimpering stopped and his mind
cleared.

At that moment, nothing mattered to Leon but life. Nothing felt
so new and so fresh, nothing more deliberate than his immediate
actions. Awareness of the pending darkness outside frightened him.
Yet, there was no escaping it. Run. That's all he could think. Run into
the woods, through them like a finger pushes through axle grease.
Get slippery. Come out the other side into the reflective sheen of
escape.

For his size, Big Leon ran fast and sure-footed. At first, he
sprinted ahead of Leon as though he knew exactly where they could
find safety.

It was daybreak and the world leaned into awakening. Birds
chirped and squawked as the eastern sky blossomed. The running
footsteps of two Negroes broke the typically quiet summer morning
like an egg dashed to the rocks. A crackle and snap, the brushing by
of leaves, the hiss of heavy breathing followed them through the
woods and along the creek.

They headed south where the lowlands turned to swamp, thick with vegetation. Eventually the broadening of the creek joined the river.

Leon had never been that far except in his dreams, but he had heard about the terrain and seen it labeled on maps.

Big Leon halted and before he could say listen, before his hand raised into the air to quiet all sound around them including nature's noise, Leon heard the distant yelp of dogs. He turned to run, but big Leon grabbed his shoulder and pulled him back.

"Boy, you been done this to. I know you not bad. You change the future for yourself, hear?"

"I'm evil."

"You listen here. You had evil happen to you. You have evil around you. But you not evil in you-self until you accept evil."

"What I did—"

"Is called learnin'. You good at learnin'. Learnt everythin' I teach you, before I finish. Faster 'an any the others. You got white smarts inside, and you got to use 'em."

"They're getting closer," Leon said.

"We can outpace 'em for a while if we keep movin'." Big Leon stood as tall as his muscular frame would allow. He looked around. He listened. "You go ahead. I'll keep my eyes on you."

"Don't—"

"You listen up, son. You change the course of yo life. Don't be no dumb nigger."

"But, Pa—"

Big Leon pulled the boy close and squeezed him to his chest. He held tightly as if he didn't want to let go, as if all the hugs he hadn't given to Leon were shoved into that one embrace. Then he shoved Leon hard. "Go!"

Leon ran ahead. His father never said where to run to, but Leon figured, for now, toward the river.

To slow the progress of the dogs pursuit, Leon and his father entered and exited the creek in only the most gravelly and rocky areas, eliminating the chances of muddied water giving them away. Balancing over the rocks slowed them down, but it was worth it until the sound of barking dogs got too close. Then they'd leave the water and sprint through woods and underbrush. The closer they got to the river, the lower the stand of vegetation, the broader the flatness of muck. Nothing was said, but Leon knew they'd eventually be in the open.

Rest was limited to moments of heavy breathing, bent over, with hands on knees and back bowed by the weight of exhaustion.

Leon's feet were cut and bruised. His knees weak. His mouth frothed and felt thick with saliva.

Late in the afternoon, less than a mile from the river, Big Leon sat down.

"What are you doing?" Leon burst out between breaths.

"Restin'."

"The dogs. We're almost there."

" Cain't leave," Big Leon said.

Leon understood. It was his wrong the men were chasing down, not his father's. Yet he knew that Big Leon would be beaten and his responsibilities reduced. All for helping his son.

Leon kneeled next to his father. He bent over and hugged the big man across his broad shoulders. He smelled Big Leon's sweet breath and felt its heat on his cheek. "I love you, Pa."

"I'll slow 'em down. I'll give up. You have-ta crawl to the river. Be sure not to shake the bushes as you goes."

"What will they do?"

"Nothin' much," Big Leon said while he stood up. "Now go."

With that, Big Leon ran from the underbrush and into the muck as though the river lay fifty feet from them in the opposite direction. He ran with his hands waving in the air as though trying to frighten away a mountain lion. But he had something in his hand that Leon had not noticed before. The sun glinted off the metal.

Leon stood in silence. From somewhere he couldn't see, he heard a shot, then two. His father fell. Leon crawled out to him.

Before Leon reached his father, the setting sun broke below distant clouds, producing a flash of color over the area.

Big Leon's eyes were open when Leon reached his side. They stared up at him.

Leon waited for the sound of the dogs to break from the hollow confinement of the lowland trees and underbrush, and into the broad expanse of clearing.

Leon wiped mud from his hands.

He reached over and closed his father's eyes, then stroked his bloody face one last time. The sound of pursuers increased as they stepped into the clearing.

Leon heard a familiar voice call the dogs back. "Slow down," the voice told the men. "Easy does it from here."

Leon held onto the burlap sack Big Leon had handed him, and scuttled across the ground on all fours, careful not to make the bushes quake. His hand landed on the revolver that Big Leon had waved around. He brought the gun around and shot repeatedly through the tall weeds in the direction of the voices. He didn't wait another second. He crawled as fast as he could toward the river. There were two things that he would never know: Did his father run into the line of fire on purpose? Did Fred Carpenter slow down his pursuit to give Leon time to get away?

PART II

CHAPTER 8

After shoving a felled tree into the river, Leon spent the most frightening hours he had ever known, death-gripped to the floating tree. He could not swim, and before long the tree floated mid-river with no way for Leon to get to shore. He had dropped the gun into the sack, which he held perched atop the root system he gripped, shaking more from fear than the cool water.

A bare branch weighted the trunk and kept it from rolling completely over. The roots created hand grips near the thickest part helping Leon keep his shoulders and head out of the water. He could not see into the cloud-filled night. His nose, so close to the tree, smelled dirt, rotting wood, and the clean scent of river water. His arms ached, but when he tried to swing his legs up and onto the tree, it rolled in the water. Once his head entered the water. After that, he tried not to move at all. When the river currents turned the tree, Leon whispered a cry into the darkness. He feared for his life and mourned his father's death alternately. To this point, his life had been spared. As though angels were watching over him, he had escaped the harsh beatings some of the others got, he had been let loose of his cage of ignorance, and now had his life and freedom provided. But at what cost? The life of one father and the humility of the other? And now, was he to drown in the river?

Hours turned seamlessly and silently. Summer nights are the shortest of the year, yet to Leon, an eternity of darkness plodded by. He imagined that he traveled through Hell to pay for his sins and, as the Bible says, the sins of his fathers. If he were protected by angels he would be redeemed by the light at the end of his journey.

As he drifted, subtle sounds of the river became more acute. He heard the difference between lapping and flowing, indicating when the edges of the river slipped onto a stony beach rather than an embankment. When the river narrowed, current flow increased and the whooshing became louder. As the river widened again, a soft and distant quiet fell over him. At one point in the night, he heard insects chattering. He was close to shore, but wasn't positive how close. He could feel the woods bearing down on him. For a moment, he let his legs stretch down, toes pointed, hoping to feel bottom. The tree shifted. He pulled up and gripped tightly, his muscles clenched around the roots, his fingers locked into place.

The hell he lived broke open, a crack in the sky, a haze over the water. Leon's legs felt numb when he moved them. He shivered. His teeth chattered. He turned his head. The opposite shore lay closer than he had thought. His ears had betrayed him. Still, the distance was great. *The river would claim him before he could struggle his way over.*

Ahead of him the river narrowed and turned. Leon knew from tossing twigs into the creek that the log would work its way into the faster, deeper section of river. They were already floating into the current.

There could be felled trees there too, and an embankment, which would make it difficult for him to climb to shore. The trough made from the stronger current could pull him under. Yet, the tree he held to would most likely slam into the bank.

He had few choices. The water pitched him and the log. It rolled and turned, unstable in the rough current. The tree turned to meet the water's flow pattern. He held to the wrong side of the trunk. The opposite side would slam into the bank and he couldn't reach over the log far enough to secure a grip on any hanging branches. His heart pounded. He took a deep breath and plunged into the water, banging his head on the underside of the log. Seconds later he emerged on the opposite side. The current shoved against him like a childhood bully. He reached for his burlap sack and stretched as far out of the water as possible. He shifted his body near the bend between the tree roots and its trunk hoping to protect his head from getting smashed. He got ready for action.

The current quickened. Leon threw his burlap sack over his head toward shore. He lost his grip. The roots rolled. Underbrush hung over the embankment into the river. If he gripped the wrong bush, it would tear loose. He would plunge into the undercurrent and be gone.

He waited. Surveyed. Could he choose fast enough? He reached out, grasped, and held tight. Held on for life.

With one fist full of grass and dirt, and the other gripped to a thin pine branch, Leon let the log scrape past him. The roots poked his face and chest before the tree twisted from the bank and slid downstream. The grass in his one fist gave way, but the pine branch held tight.

Leon thanked the river for giving him up. He clamored, hand-over-hand, up the branch and crawled into the woods, away from the river noise. Away from its smell.

Under a grove of pines, Leon sat upright and rubbed his legs and feet until they tingled with new life. He shivered in the shade of the trees. After a moment, he lay back flat against the soft needles and listened to the whisper of wind. He let the sound of the river fall into the background, let it disappear into the recesses of his mind, a memory no longer worth his focus. He slept until his shivering body woke him.

Leon sat up and closed his arms around his shoulders. His skin had dried, but his clothes remained damp, drawing in the cold from the shade. The air felt balmy. He stood for the first time since shoving the tree into the river the night before. He stamped the ground trying out his legs, then bent down and stepped out from under the hanging branches. As he moved his body warmed.

As much as he wanted nothing to do with the river for a while, Leon headed straight for it. When he broke into the sun, the warmth helped to lighten his step. He walked upriver, searching for and finding his sack resting in the thick branches of a small mulberry bush, sun-struck with golden light.

He retrieved the sack and sat down a short distance from the riverbank. He untied the knot at the top and poured the contents onto his lap. There was bread and jerky and the book he kept under his cot. A knife glistened in the sun, as did the gun Big Leon had been carrying. And there was one other item. A hat. The hat he had spit into. The hat he had claimed. It was now his.

Leon placed the damp hat onto his head. He cradled the wrinkled pages of the book in his arms and cried. After a while he pulled the hat off. He straightened the brim and brushed loose shreds of burlap from its surface, then placed it on his head once again. He took a deep breath, stuffed all but a chunk of bread back into the drying sack, and stood. The sun had nearly finished its job of drying his clothes. He bit into the bread and walked east.

Wooded areas along the river came and went as the ground pitched slightly along it. The river was his road and his life for now. There were fish if he could find a way to catch them. There was water to drink. Even so, he kept his distance, the constant sound of its flowing always in the background. He kept his distance, too, from the wagon paths that followed the river.

That night, the sky cleared to partly cloudy. Leon knew how to make a fire having done so in the coldest mornings in the shack. He cleared a spot, collected dried grass from the river's edge and dried twigs from the ground. He rubbed a sharp stick between his hands, causing enough friction to light the dried grass. By the time the sky blackened and the moon rose, he had a small fire, but no food to cook.

He reached into his sack and pulled out one of the last two pieces of jerky. He sat cross-legged before the fire enjoying its peaceful crackling. The moon peeked from between clouds, a crescent shaped messenger of God.

Leon sighed. He felt alone. His mind wandered. He thought of Martha and smiled. He thought of Hillary and his groin shifted. He laughed out loud, the echo coming back to him from inside the woods, a quieter version of his own laugh. Leon felt lucky to be alive, and that gave him something to build upon.

After eating, his stomach still not satisfied, Leon piled some thicker pieces of wood onto his fire, curled next to its heat, and waited for sleep to come for the second time that day. He woke once in the chilly night, crying out to Big Leon, then slept until the morning sun woke him.

He ate the last of his bread and jerky, rocked slowly to a song he had heard once, and waited for his body to warm before he stepped into the new day.

At the edge of the woods, fog obscured both the tops of the trees and the ground. The middle sections were blurred. River fog slipped into the field but burned off quickly in the hot sun.

Leon headed to the river for a drink. He splashed his face with water and rubbed the cool liquid into the back of his neck before heading downstream. He stayed close to the river hoping to find calm areas where he could catch a fish to eat for supper. But after high noon passed, Leon felt too weak to plow through the underbrush along the river. He had yet to find a place where he could walk into the water, a place where fish might rest. The ker-plop of a trout or pike breaking the surface to swallow a bug was the only thing that gave him hope.

Late in the day, after pulling away from the riverbank overrun with underbrush, Leon stumbled by a stand of blackberry bushes that stretched thirty feet along the river's edge. He ran to the area chasing several deer into the woods. They stopped and Leon pulled the pistol out, already tasting meat. He pulled the trigger and it clicked. No bullets. He picked berries and shoved them into his mouth as quickly as he could. Most were fat with juice and stained his fingers, lips, and chin. He ate until he felt full. He circled the area where he thought the deer had gone, unsure of what he might do if he found them. By early evening, Leon, thinking only of his hunger and a juicy breakfast, decided he could spend the night near the blackberry bushes.

He gathered wood and started a fire once again. Before sitting next to the fire he picked a shirt-full of berries and laid them next to him, plunking several into his mouth from time to time, humming a blackberry song. "Juicy and sweet, somethin' to eat,/ makin' my belly full."

By nightfall, his stomach ached. He couldn't sleep. He marched to the riverbank where he had a miserable case of diarrhea. He moaned in pain, stumbled back to his fire and laid flat on the ground next to the flames. He arose twice more that night making two more trips to the river's edge. By morning he felt empty and exhausted. The skin around his anus had blistered. He hobbled uncomfortably to the river where he cleaned up, then waited to dry. The sting reminded him of the blackberries. He was hungrier now than he had been the day before.

He walked slower. The sun beat hotter. He took the blackberries with him, but ate them more sparingly until he fell to another bout of diarrhea, at which time he dumped the remainder of the berries onto the ground. He longed for a piece of meat.

Leon stumbled along, the sun draining remaining energy through his skin. At a beach made by a turn in the river, Leon waited for the sun to angle down so he could see clearly into the shallows. The fish were small, hand-sized. He reached in, but his reflexes had been compromised by his weakness. A hawk squealed overhead.

As nightfall approached, Leon went into the woods and carved a forked spear from a thin branch. He carved barbs into each point. With his spear, he headed back to the river flat. Leon missed his mark repeatedly, the trout easily slipping away until, apparently, tired of the game it swam deeper into the river.

Leon plopped down on a stone with his feet in the water. His eyelids closed and he rested until, nearly asleep, he started to fall over. He wished he had blackberries, regardless of their painful effect on him.

Pushing up into a crouched position, he grabbed his spear and lumbered into the woods. Although the woods were already dark under the canopy of trees, something drew him deeper. He heard laughing. Stumbling forward, Leon tried to count the number of voices, but kept getting confused. Then, in the middle of a count, he smelled food cooking. Rabbit or chicken.

He crept on all fours, his sack in his teeth. In a small clearing a fire burned bright, snapping and sending cinders into the warm night air. His hunger pushed him on. The ground felt damp on his hands and knees. When his knee snapped a twig and the conversation halted for a moment, Leon became motionless.

"Juss a deer," he heard someone say. Then the talking, the storytelling started up again. Soon laughter and the sound of people eating filled his ears.

Leon leaned against a tree. He planned to wait until they fell to sleep, then sneak in and dig the bones out of the fire. He'd break them open and suck out the marrow. He'd lick them so clean they'd shine in the sun. His mouth watered. His tongue slipped over his lips. He slept and dreamed of eating.

His dream shifted to him being dragged behind a hay wagon. His shirt had gotten torn. His face was being slapped by newly felled hay. When he woke, he was being dragged, but not by a hay wagon.

Leon kicked his feet. He felt the grip of an enormous hand let go of his shoulder. Then his hat and burlap sack fell next to his face.

"There it is," the big man said.

Leon put his hat and sack in his lap and shot up into a sitting position. His eyes burned. His mouth watered. He waited for something to happen. The big man lowered his body down on a log next to a smaller man with a pearly-white beard. Two more men sat on another log and one man leaned on an elbow perched against the second log. All five men were old. All five were black.

"Gonna steal from us? Kill us in our sleep?" The man leaning against the log said.

"I wuz gonna steal bones and lick 'em clean, is all," Leon said.

"Hungry," the man said to the rest of them.

"You runnin' son? You awful skinny," the man said.

"You a criminal? You kilt somebody?" Another one of them asked.

"I not runnin'. I never laid a hand on nobody," Leon said.

"You look familiar. You the son of that farmer we take those eggs from two days back? You trackin' us?"

The leaning man looked over at the man at the end of the log. "Hell, Jesse, who send a boy out to chase down five old niggers robbed a han-full a eggs?" They all laughed.

"You don't know what white folks do with they kids sometimes," Jesse said.

Leon listened to them. His stomach cried out.

The smaller man who sat next to the giant who had dragged Leon into their camp said, "The boy's hungry." He pointed at Leon. "You hungry?"

Leon nodded his head.

"I'm feedin' 'im," the man announced.

"Ain't juss your food," the leaning man said.

"This piece is." The man crouched down and stretched an arm toward Leon as if he were a wild animal. A half-eaten chicken leg pushed out from the man's greasy fingers.

Leon took the leg and popped it into his mouth, holding the bulbous bone in his fingertips. The meat slid off into his mouth. He chewed and swallowed, then licked and gnawed at the bone.

"What yo' name, boy?" The man who had given him the chicken asked.

"Leon."

"Leon what?"

"Juss Leon."

"No need to be scared. We ain't hurt no one." The leaning man lifted slowly to a standing position. "Ma-name's Cracker-Jack." He took a breath. "That there, who give you his chicken bone, that Buddy."

Buddy nodded.

"Next there, that Big Josh." Cracker-Jack pointed to the opposite end of the log. "You probably got that there Jesse."

Leon waited, looking at the last man. The other four looked at the last man, too. Then they started giggling.

The last man looked from one to the other of them. "Well, God-do-diddly-dam," he said. "My name's Bob."

Everyone burst into loud laughs except for Leon and Bob. Cracker-Jack slapped his thighs. "He named Bob after an old white man's horse. He not even named after no man."

"Ain't so do-damned funny to me," Bob said. "Looka him." Bob motioned toward Leon. "He got a nigger's name. What you suppose his ma and pa thinkin'?"

"Maybe they foreigners and don't know no better. He do look a little I-talian," Cracker-Jack said.

"He look dirty white to me," Buddy said. "He been in the sun all summer, I 'spect."

Big Josh handed another piece of chicken over to Buddy, who handed it to Leon. Leon ripped some breast meat from the bird and stuck it in his mouth.

Cracker-Jack, obviously in charge if anyone was, motioned for Jesse to hand over some bread.

Leon took it right away and stuffed it into his mouth beside the half-chewed chicken breast. He stared at the ground waiting for the hammer to fall.

CHAPTER 9

D espite the conversation of the five men, their through-the-night discussions, singing, and laughter, Leon seldom woke, and when he did, he only rolled over and fell back to sleep. In the morning, he awoke to the sweet smell of breakfast stew. His arm had fallen asleep. His hands, together like in prayer, rested under the side of his face. The stoked cooking fire burned against his back. He sat up, dazed and hungry. It took a few minutes of rubbing his arm to bring life back to it.

In daylight, without the shifting light and dark, the appearances of the five men were more accurately revealed. They were very old. Leon didn't know how old, but they all moved slowly, showing wrinkles like ripples on water, and had white hair.

Jesse stirred the pot hanging over the fire. "Where Buddy wit them mushrooms?" he asked no one in particular.

"He comin'." Cracker-Jack said.

Leon had thought to eat mushrooms when he was hungry, but never learned which were poisonous. He hoped Buddy knew.

Bob hobbled over and kneeled next to Leon. "What you real name?"

Leon looked into the deep chasms of Bob's face.

"Come-on. You runnin'? Kilt somebody?"

"It's Leon. My real name."

"Naw." Bob laughed. "I got one boy name of Leon. Ain't heard a no white man namin' his boy Leon."

"I'm not white."

Bob slapped Leon's face lightly with a leather palm. "You ain't black neither."

"I know."

"So, we got that cleared. Now, what you really doin' here?"

"I free to do what I want, ain't I?" Leon said.

"S'pose you are. You don't fend well, though. That tell me you a cared-for nigger if you one at all, or a set-free white boy don't know what he got his-self into. I be-diddly-do-thinkin' you mixin' a bit a truth wit yo' big lie."

Cracker-Jack shuffled over to them. He had a long look to his face, which made his flat nose appear extra wide. His skin looked as though it had swallowed all the night shadows, so black it was almost featureless. "We don't need to know no truth. Yo' truth belong to you," he said.

"Juss curious," Bob said.

Leon turned away without saying anything.

Bob moaned into a slouched stand. "Don't want this boy slittin' no throats while we sleepin'."

"He won't slit nothin'."

Bob followed Cracker-Jack back to the log. He yelled over the fire, "I know you white 'cause I see that book you hidin'. Unless you steal it from your master outta spite."

"Ain't no masters," Big Josh said. "And, Negroes can read too."

"Yeah. You right. Look at us," Bob said, "we're five fish-flaimin' freeee niggers who be too damn-dimmidy old to clean pots or sweep out stalls."

Buddy showed up with an armful of cleaned mushrooms that he threw into the pot Jesse attended.

They all laughed at Bob's joke.

Leon, though, sat up straight, curious at their laughter. He didn't understand. "What's funny about being free?"

"Free," Cracker-Jack yelled, and they all howled louder. "Boy, we ain't ask to be free. We set free. You know why? 'Cause we ol'. We can't labor no more. Maybe they ain't no slavery, but they ain't no jobs neither. Not for ol' Negroes like us."

"But my Cookie can work," Bob said. "She can still swaddle a chile and cook a good meal." He quieted. "I miss my Cookie."

"Boy, we all got wives who probably work 'til they dead. We no good fer nothin' 'cept roamin'. We roamers," Cracker-Jack said.

"Not Big Josh," Jesse said.

Cracker-Jack glanced over at Big Josh. "Nope. Big Josh ain't got no woman. Ain't no woman wanna be poked every night by his big stick."

Leon's throat hardened and his chest felt compressed. He imagined Hillary's bare breasts. He recalled Big Leon and Bess and how they related, how sex had tortured his whole family. Oh how he wanted it all gone. Forgotten. After all, he'd gone through the river of black hell and wanted it – his past – to disappear.

"Stew's ready," Jesse announced.

Despite his shyness to this point, Leon perked up and crawled around the fire to Jesse's side.

"You lucky we got a extra pot we can feed you in," Jesse said.

Buddy stroked his beard while Jesse dished out breakfast and handed plates around. "You know, young Jimmy White here could run for us."

Several of the men nodded.

"He does owe us a couple meals," Cracker-Jack said.

Big Josh, speaking for the first time said, "He small enough to shove through a window."

Leon didn't like the word shove, although the idea was accurate.

"We could use a younger helper," Buddy said.

"Lick-bam-dibbledy," Bob said, "you like to be our boy? Our Jimmy White?"

Leon swallowed. "Ain't nobody's boy. But I'll help you. You been kind."

"Ding-dong-dilly," Bob slapped his knee, 'we turning the tables. Got ourselves a white boy."

Leon laughed.

After breakfast, all except Leon joined in for cleanup. Cracker-Jack and Big Josh bundled the blankets, Buddy reduced the fire to cold with a pot of water, then smoothed out the pit until it nearly disappeared. Jesse cleaned up the cookware and handed it over to Bob, who packed it into a bundle no bigger than a size ten hat.

Leon stayed out of the way.

When the others stood ready to go, Leon put on his hat and grabbed his sack.

"Take that." Cracker-Jack pointed at the larger bundle.

Leon weighed the situation.

"You work for you food."

Leon bent down and picked up the bundle. He followed tentatively as they walked deeper into the woods.

Jesse, Buddy, and Bob chatted about their wives and children. Leon stayed behind the men and listened when the conversation became loud enough. He lost long portions of information, but gathered that at some point each became too old for hard labor, and was set free to roam, torn from their families.

The stories included beatings and killings, having children sold, sisters sold and fathers set free against their will. Between the three men, they had some twelve or more children, many of whom were either taken from them or sold soon after birth. Some landowners let their Negroes have families, though, and he wondered why the children couldn't have taken care of their fathers. Complain as they did, Leon got the distinct feeling that freedom was what the roamers wanted and what they cherished most.

Their lives, as the men discussed them, set a familiar tone with Leon. All Bob's known and still living sons and daughters had already jumped the broom and had their own pickaninnies running around. Jesse, it appeared, had a 'shit-house full of girls,' each one a beauty, 'a flower of light.' And Buddy's oldest, out of some number Leon didn't hear, was already foreman and actually getting wages.

Leon heard this and felt proud of his own father. No matter what, Leon had never seen his father be mean to the other men. Leon touched the brim of his hat. He wanted to join in the conversation and say, "My Pappy was foreman too," but he kept his mouth shut. They would never have believed him.

Bob, looked back at that moment and said, "That a fine hat."

Leon shifted his pack so it didn't drag so heavily on his thin shoulders. He nodded to Bob.

"Yo' steal it?"

"It was a gift," Leon said.

"Mighty fine." Bob shook his head and got back to his former conversation. He stumbled and reached out for Jesse's arm. Bob was the oldest by far. He walked as though every step was a struggle, but that keeping up was his lifeline.

Leon wondered whether freedom was worth it to men this old and planned to ask when he got the chance.

A little over half a day's walk, with a few rests, the men quieted and slowed. Cracker-Jack came back along the ranks to Leon. "Jimmy White, you beg for some food."

Leon's eyes widened with fear. "I've never begged for food." His feet moved around as if he couldn't find a comfortable spot to stand. "I wouldn't do it right."

Buddy grabbed Leon's pack. "You got a better chance than any of us."

"What do I ask for?"

"A few day's rations. Tell them you headed upriver for a job." Buddy stroked his beard. "They'll listen to you."

"Can't you just steal what you need?"

"Wham-dammit," Bob said. "We gonna steal whilest you gettin' your rations."

"What if they notice?"

Cracker-Jack pulled Buddy's hand from Leon's shoulder and stepped in to turn Leon toward the farmhouse. He shoved Leon forward. "I show you." After a few steps, Cracker-Jack slapped Leon to his knees. "Git down and follow me."

Behind some bushes, Leon followed Cracker-Jack's finger as he indicated the farmer and oldest son near the far woods fixing a fence, and then two young girls playing around their mother hanging clothes on a line along the side of the house. A chicken coop surrounded by cackling hens stood near the barn, and a pigpen had been poorly fashioned behind the coop.

Cracker-Jack turned to go back into the woods. Leon followed, his hands shaking.

"Listen, boy, we steal a piglet and a couple chickens, what ever we can get without no ruckus." Cracker-Jack gathered his thoughts. "Me, Josh, Buddy, and Jesse do the stealin'. Bob already headin' south to make camp."

Leon looked for Bob and got smacked by a wide hand across his ear.

"Son, pay attention. Whatever happen you go into the woods the same way you comes out. If they thinks you headed North, they won't look South."

Jesse sniggered.

Leon rubbed the pain from his ear. He said, "What if there's a lot of noise?"

"Go north into the woods and circle around. Dat farmer won't track us, He'll stay wit his family, afraid we be luring him into the wood like a pack a wild dogs," Cracker-Jack said. "They mama can't see the coop from where you'll be standin'. We'll be travelin' behind the barn. You act as surprised as they do at any ruckus. You jus' gets your rations and leisurely walk back north where you come from."

Leon held his breath. He couldn't refuse. The plan was set. He gripped his burlap sack. As soon as he walked toward the edge of the woods, the four others took off as fast as four old men can. Leon saw that they had sacks ready for their catch.

Before stepping into the sun, Leon rubbed his fingers along the brim of his hat. He took a deep breath and hummed. He walked into the open. Out the corner of his eye, he noticed that the farmer and his son were too busy to see him walking toward their house.

Rounding the corner from the front porch, the two little girls stopped playing, alerting the mother something was amiss.

She was dressed in a dirty white dress and had an apron tied across her front. She had clothes pegs in her mouth. When she saw Leon, she removed the pins and dropped them into the basket at her feet.

Leon removed his hat. He stood three heads above the woman, so he bent slightly out of courtesy. "Sorry to bother you, ma'am, but I've been traveling upriver looking for work." He swallowed. His mouth went dry. "It's been some days now. I could use—"

"Something to eat," she said, her voice sweet and soft.

Leon continued to look at the basket between her legs. "Yes, ma'am."

She glanced toward her husband and son at the far end of the field. "I think we can spare a bit." She didn't appear nervous at all.

Then, Leon heard a noise and a loud cackle from the chicken coop. He jumped.

The woman said, "That's some chickens fighting out back. Don't pay it no mind."

Then a pig squealed.

The woman turned from the front door to say something else. Her eyes opened wide. Leon jumped back. While the woman spoke, Leon turned on his heels and ran for the woods.

"Don't you want—" Her voice trailed behind him. He hit the woods and kept going, making a wide loop.

By the time his heart slowed and he stopped, his feet had already blistered. Tears ran down his face, and his hands shook uncontrollably. He thought of the woman and two children and how friendly they had been. They took him as white. He sensed it. He should have looked her in the eye. He laughed at his misplaced fear. She probably went back to her clothes line wondering why the hell he ran away. Her husband would learn what had happened soon enough once he returned for the evening chores. By then, it would be too late.

Leon half walked and half ran west toward the river. When it was in view, he turned south.

Leon missed his home regardless of how isolated he had felt there. He missed having a father who would scuff his neck and chase him, a father who told him that he loved him.

A hawk screeched overhead, and when Leon looked up he saw it plummet to the ground toward some small animal. It landed in tall golden grass, but in a moment was back in the air, a young rabbit, gray and struggling, hung from clenched talons.

The hot sun fell lower in the sky. Its color changing as the magical light of twilight approached.

Leon ran. He had no idea how he would find the camp, but decided to enter the darkening woods in hopes that he'd stumble upon it. He was sorry he didn't stay at the homestead long enough to get some food. If he couldn't find the camp, he'd have nothing to eat. He patted the sack hanging from the rope belt he wore around his waist. If he did run into the roamers, he'd save some food in case he got separated from them later.

As the air turned cooler and the night spread through the woods, Leon heard the nocturnal animals wandering a short distance away. A raccoon growled as Leon passed too close to where it sat in the crook of a tree. Deer ran off when he stumbled. Owls hooted. The music of the night sounded much different than day sounds.

Leon tried to be alert to the slightest flicker of a campfire, or the softest sound of men talking. He followed what looked like a trail, where men could have traveled. Eventually, unbelievably, he heard them. It was too dark, by then, to run full-tilt through the woods, but he could jog, so he picked up the pace. His stomach anticipated the food they would surely be cooking. And he kept sniffing the air.

As he approached camp, Leon only counted four men. He slowed and looked around. Perhaps Jesse was collecting wood for the fire. When he took his next step a loud snap came from above. Leon glanced up as a pine branch slapped him on the back of his neck. Jesse stood to the side with his hand on the other end of the branch where he was bending it back.

"Why'd you do that?" Leon yelled.

"I was out scoutin' for you."

"How'd you get so far ahead of me?"

"We walk straight," Jesse said. "We saw you runnin' too. You goin' so fast you probably miles before you turn south."

Leon swatted at the branch and Jesse let it go.

"I smell somethin'." Leon said.

"You runnin' off, we had to cut our work too. Got one piglet and one chicken. You smell the pork."

Leon's mouth watered. He followed Jesse back into camp.

Jesse announced, "Looky what I find."

Leon was amazed to see the men all smile at him as he entered camp.

"A little practice," Cracker-Jack said. The others laughed.

"Sit down," Buddy said. There was a place for Leon to sit with them. "You musta felt somethin' wrong to run as fast as Jesse say."

"I heard the chickens," Leon said.

"She say anything?"

"She said the chickens were fighting."

"See, she weren't worried," Buddy said.

"I know," Leon observed the grease sizzling from the piglet hanging over the fire. "That's a mighty big piglet."

Cracker-Jack pointed, "Big Josh carry that big brother all the way his self."

Leon nodded. Big Josh waved him off.

"The lesson," Cracker-Jack got back to the conversation, "is to pay attention to her. If she ain't worried, you ain't worried. But if she tell one the kids to go look, then you run." He laughed. "But you know how to run. We sees that."

"Next time," Bob added to the instruction, "will ya ask for some lip-lapin' liquor? I could use a drink 'bout now."

"We'll do that juss for you, Bob. Won't we Jimmy White?" Cracker-Jack said.

"They won't give no liquor to no boy," Buddy said.

"I go wit him," Bob said. "I be white, too." He sat straight. "Excuse me Ma'am. I been in the sun too long today. Got terribly brown. I think a little cup of liquor be ding-dong dandy for gettin' me back white."

"You no browner than a cow turd in the sun. She'd scream, "No liquor for you. You black." Jesse screeched like a woman and bounced his hands near his mouth in mock surprise.

Bob straightened again. "Right you are ma'am, which mean I already hallucinatin' without my liquor."

"Your masters let you have liquor?" Leon asked. "We only had it when there a couple jumpin' the broom."

"Don't mock us, boy," Cracker-Jack said.

Leon turned away.

"My Cookie use to bring it to the shack late," Bob said, lips twitching like he remembered the flavor. "We stay up late talkin' and laughin'. I know the children think we didlin' and they pretend a sleep. But we juss playin'." He stared off. "Juss playin' and bein' in love."

"I recall those days," Buddy said. "They no sweeter than now."

"Every day you alive is sweet," Cracker-Jack said.

Big Josh started to sing, then. "Swing low, sweet chariot..."

The others joined in as a quieter background.

Leon knew the song. He'd sometimes sing it when his own words didn't come. He joined in. After a few bars, the others all stopped singing and stared at Leon. "What are you lookin' at?"

Cracker-Jack said in surprise, "You got a strong voice, boy."

"Yeah, you sing alone for a moment," Jesse said.

Big Josh nodded and motioned for Leon to continue.

After Leon sang a few more bars, Bob slapped his knee. "Big-dammit, you sings like a nigger."

Leon stopped singing. "I am," he said.

The men got serious and looked at each other. Bob was about to say something when Cracker-Jack spoke up. "Could you maybe read to us from that there book you got?"

"Yeah, Jimmy White, that a good idea. After we eats maybe," Bob said.

"Eatin's ready," Jesse took up a knife and carved the piglet.

Everyone leaned near the fire to get his share of the meat. Leon wanted to go back to singing where he felt safe, but ate quietly with the rest of them.

After licking his fingers and running them down his pant leg, Leon opened the burlap sack and took out his book. He blew dust and burlap string from it, then opened the cover.

The fire snapped and popped. Jesse bent toward it and poked a log with his finger. The fire settled and sparks flew into the air, floating magically upward into the dark night before cooling and fading.

After Leon read a few poems, the others found their blankets and sleeping spots. Leon curled next to the fire, his back to it. In the woods, fireflies, like loose coals from the fire blinked in the dark. The sounds of animals foraging, grunting, and hissing, came into their camp from the woods. Leon drew the smell of loam, sweet and strong, into his lungs. The fire warmed his back, softening his tense muscles, relaxing his skin until he fell asleep. He woke in the dark with a start. He dreamed that Big Leon had fallen into the muck, bleeding from his wounds. He heard rifle shots over and over again.

The cold had seeped into his back. His arms ached. Leon shuffled to a sitting position. The fire was nearly out, but he found a stick lying nearby and turned the coals until bright red blazed again.

He crawled over and grabbed two small pieces of dried wood and placed them on the fire. In a moment, yellow flames snaked around the wood and the air became warmer.

It must have been close to sun-up because a damp, low fog had crept in. Leon rubbed his arms to get warm, then reached for another log.

"Cain't sleep?" Bob was sitting up.

"No."

"Who you watch die?" Bob whispered.

Leon stared into the fire.

"If you ain't kilt nobody, then you seen somebody kilt. I kin see it in you face. Seen it that first day I seen you eyes in the clear sun."

Leon lowered his head. "My pappy."

Bob pursed his lips, then opened his mouth, but made no sound.

"He died savin' my life."

The fire popped.

"We be your pappy now," Bob said. He lay back down.

CHAPTER 10

Leon woke damp and chilly. The fog held thick to the ground. Heavy dew lay over the leaves. The air was still and quiet except for an occasional crow call. Once again, Leon grabbed a stick and stoked the fire.

Jesse must have heard the fire logs shift. He sat up and reached over to grab a few wood chunks to throw into the coals. Embers scattered into the air. He reached over with his foot and kicked Buddy. "Hey. Egg man."

Buddy stretched his arms and twisted at the waist. Bones cracked. He twisted in the opposite direction and cracking occurred again. "It foggy," he said.

Jesse said, "No? You juss take notice?"

"Watch it, sonny, I still tougher than you."

"That a picture nobody want to see, two old black men wrestlin' over breakfast," Jesse said.

"I'd win," Buddy said.

"Sure, Pappy." Jesse stood and held his hand out to Buddy. "You'd win once I helped you up."

Leon chuckled.

"Don't laugh, boy, it might take both us, but we knock the piss outa you, too," Buddy said.

"I'm sure you would," Leon said.

By this time, the others were awake and preparing for breakfast. Buddy pulled out a folded piece of cloth and laid it on the ground while Jesse got out a frying pan. As Buddy slowly unwrapped the cloth a dozen eggs came into view a few at a time.

"Hot dig-dam," Bob said.

"A little longer we have half a cow, too" Cracker-Jack said while glaring at Leon.

Leon shied from Cracker-Jack's penetrating stare.

Jesse pulled a pot from near his sleeping area. He had put the piglet in there the night before and grease filled the bottom of the pot. He scooped some out using a wooden spoon and slapped it in the frying pan.

Buddy broke eggs into the pan while Jesse shook the pan, flipping the eggs up and back, folding them in mid-air before letting them fall into the pan again.

Leon watched the eggs cook. He could taste them already. Each time they went into the air they looked more solid, closer to being eaten.

At the end, Buddy handed out plates and Jesse carved the eggs into equal size portions and dropped them onto the plates.

Leon ate from a smaller frying pan.

Jesse carved some piglet and handed a piece of ham to each of them. Leon was amazed at their eating efficiency, as if they had somewhere important to be.

A breeze blew through the valley and pushed the fog out of the woods. The sun helped, too, heating the air and blistering the fog away one layer at a time.

When they cleaned up, almost immediately after eating, Leon tried to help. Every time he reached for a plate or pan, another hand shoved his aside. Once he realized that he was getting in the way, he sat back and watched them work.

They were old. They were slow. He wondered how they ever got together, and once they did, worked in such harmony, as if they'd been doing it their whole lives.

Leon observed Buddy cleaning plates and Jesse wrapping leftovers. Leon knew that he didn't fit in. Again, Cracker-Jack had Leon pack the heaviest bundle. Bob carried nothing.

Leon learned about their families and backgrounds. Big Josh was the youngest of the five. He killed a man by accident, while physically and single-handedly holding up one end of a wagon as the man repaired a broken axle. The weight caused his grip to loosen and the wagon slipped from his fingers. The man was crushed and

Big Josh ran. There was a debate among them whether the man died or was knocked out, but Big Josh didn't care. He ran. "Either way, they strap me good," he said.

Cracker-Jack had been the boss of thirty men on some ranch farther west. He was used to being in charge. But when a 'young buck', as Cracker-Jack called him, stepped in to do the job, Cracker-Jack asked to be let go. "It was only a matter of years, anyhow," he said. "Spent time fightin' after gettin' caught stealin' meal from some Yankee troops. Put me in a Negro brigade, they did."

The men told stories, repeating some exactly the same, while others were changed, altered to fit into the present mood. They created their own histories over and over for one another to hear. They wanted every detail brought in, to share the exact picture of the event as it actually happened, even if it were an outright fabrication.

"Tell us again how you asked to leave," Buddy said to Cracker-Jack.

"After I was tol' I no longer in charge, I didn't hang my head one bit. Fact is I was taller that day. Several people tell me that actually true. I growed several inches. I raise my eyes to my long-time friend and master. Look 'im square. 'Sir,' I says, 'would you kindly set me free?'"

"And he say, 'Shoo, boy, shoo.'" Buddy joked.

Cracker-Jack giggled, then got serious. "I wish he had, but he ask me to stay on. He want me to help out. Said he'd feed and care for me. But I ain't no old bull cain't ride the cows no more. I ain't no worthless, sway-back, no sir."

"What he really say was, 'Don' you make me work fo' that boy don' know his job yet." Buddy interrupted.

"Slap-dammity," Bob cut in, "let the Negro tell he story."

"I could stop," Cracker-Jack teased.

Leon laughed to himself.

*   *   *

The day wore on. The sun burned hotter. As the men told stories, Leon daydreamed about the life he no longer belonged compared with the life he now lived. Two sides of the river. Two different lives, but still much the same. He still felt as if he didn't quite belong. Perhaps he never would. He wasn't black or white. He could read like a white man and sing like a black man. Away from his history, blacks thought he was white, and growing up on the Carpenter farm, the whites treated him as if he were black. None of these men even guessed that he was black by birth and upbringing. At best they thought he was foreign.

Sweat dripped down along his sides from armpits to waist. Mosquitoes buzzed around his face and arms. The bugs were especially nasty in open areas. Leon noticed that Bob had ripped off a small bushy pine branch and kept it moving all around his head like a fan. Bob didn't have to swat a mosquito so often as the others.

Leon tried the branch trick and it helped. Except one time when he caught a sweat bee in the crook of his arm and it stung him, leaving a round, red welt.

Leon had always wanted to go downriver and now he was doing just that. Besides Indian paths, there were wagon trails that were not used any more.

An hour after high noon, they found a place near the river where they could sit and enjoy the breeze coming off the water. Jesse cut more meat from the piglet for each of them.

"Are there any towns up ahead?" Leon asked.

"What you need a town for, boy?" Cracker-Jack passed Leon his cut of pork last, after taking it from Jesse.

"I can't keep traveling like this."

"You have to work?" Cracker-Jack said.

"I do."

"You don't work now."

"I know that, but I can't live like this through the winter," Leon said.

"He need to be with people his own age," Buddy said.

"Why the slam-happy hell would he need that?" Bob said.

"He young. He need soft womanly company. You forget already, old man?" Buddy said. "I understand, boy." Buddy turned back to the others. "Besides, what he do after we all die? He know nothin' but liein' and beggin'. And he be alone. This life ain't fit."

"Buddy right in his thinkin'," Cracker-Jack said. "There a nice town maybe three, four days. You help out that long, we leave you there. They's work there."

"It hard work," Buddy said.

"I'm not afraid to work."

"Nobody said you was, boy," Cracker-Jack said. "Besides, we get caught runnin' a white boy, they think we kidnap you. They'd kill us all. Lynch us for sure."

Jesse cut more meat and handed pieces to Cracker-Jack to ration out.

Leon took his and bit a piece off. His fingers glistened with grease. There were fewer mosquitoes near the river-flow, so Leon put his pine branch on the gravel next to him.

"You be good in a town," Buddy said. "You strong. You sturdy enough to work."

They ate for a short while and stared at the wide river going by in front of them. The mesmerizing sound of the water took each of Leon's companions to a different place. Some stared down reaching back to the past; others glanced skyward into the future. The turning ripples of water helped to rearrange thoughts. The ker-plunk of a fish hitting the surface set whatever thought Leon had at the moment into place in his mind, set it more vivid than it had been a moment earlier.

Leon brought his thoughts into words, not recognizing that it was the shock of the fish-sound that forced the words into the world. "You ever get guilty about causing a man's death?" he asked Big Josh.

"Ain't guilty for his death. Guilty for runnin'."

"You pappy do what he done outta love, boy. He give he life like a gift. You don't need no guilt," Bob told Leon.

"What's this about his pappy be dead?" Cracker-Jack asked.

Leon narrowed his eyes at Bob. "It's nothin'. It's a private matter."

"A private matter," Cracker-Jack mocked. "Ain't we speakin' proper now. You a preacher's son or somethin'?" Cracker-Jack stepped close to Leon and slapped the back of his head.

"Leave 'im be. He allowed his private matter," Bob said. "I'm sorry I brung it up, boy."

"We got a right to know what in his past if it might git us kilt," Cracker-Jack said. "Somebody after you? You on the run? We already in danger juss keepin' you along."

"I knowed he runnin'," Buddy said.

"I'm not on the run," Leon said.

"Then who kilt you pappy?"

"Some men. They killed him instead of me. Then they went home. They don't care about me. All they wanted was someone's life." Leon's jaws locked.

"Let 'im be now," Bob said.

"If'n I hears one footfall don't belong to one of us," Cracker-Jack threatened.

"You won't. That's my word." Leon went back to staring at the river. He didn't want to remember his father the way he did, red blood around him, his eyes staring blindly up at the sky beyond Leon's head. Somehow the river sound helped him forget. In the movement, the swirls and slapping, Leon could see Big Leon in the fields, still moving, still alive.

Sweat trickled from the hat band down the sides of Leon's head. He took the hat in his hands and traced the brim with his fingers thinking how he almost got to wear it to another funeral. Had Big Leon known their running would turn into a funeral too?

The sky had sucked up all the fog, turning it into clouds that floated in small groups, changing shape as they meandered east. The black foothills became visible all around them, light glowing off treetops in one area and logged flats in another area. There were signs of men, but no men.

A bald eagle flew overhead, spying on the river trout.

"Wish I had his eyes," Jesse said.

"Wish I had his wings," Buddy said.

"Damn-flammity. I wish we had the fish he gonna catch." Bob said, ending in a chuckle.

"We could stay hear tonight," Cracker-Jack said. "Heard that sometimes the fish gets loose and falls on the ground. Eagle jus' leaves 'em. People finds 'em half a mile from the river."

"We could try fishin'," Jesse said.

"I still got a couple o' Cookie's pins." Bob searched inside his bedroll.

Leon knew where to find the fish if they were there. If the river was any bit like the creek, there'd be fish resting upriver a bit, where the water slows and settles near the flat.

The six of them turned all their attention to fishing. They pulled thread from their own blankets, found long sticks, bent the pins. Leon searched around the edges of the river, where the water stopped, or slowed way down, where it pooled. There were trout and American shad, big ones, lying wait in shallow places, close enough to reach out and touch.

Leon had caught fish with his bare hands before. In late spring after the swell receded, Pine Creek suckers, pike, trout, all slapped their way either upstream to spawn or downstream through the ripples. Leon used to stand in the rocky ripples with his feet planted between a few big rocks, the cool water rushing around his legs and the fish flapping and slapping the water. He'd grab the slippery fellows as they flipped and flopped between his legs. At other times several men would net the fish using burlap or old cotton linen the Carpenters had thrown out. And that's when he thought of his burlap sack.

Leon emptied his knife, book, and revolver, and placed them under some brush, then went back to the river determined to feed the six of them that night. In the distance, fish gulped up the mosquitoes, clump, clump, clump. The sound continued as background music. There were so many fish in the river, they had to be able to catch them.

Near a shallow still pool, Leon stood letting his eyes adjust to the glare beyond the reflection of the river and into its depths. Shad rested near shore.

Leon used two twigs, crossed in the middle, to hold the bag open, then lowered everything into the water. He kneeled on the rocks, which pushed into the bones of his knees. He let his arm enter the water, his fist clasped to one twig and the burlap. He leaned out beyond comfort. Mosquitoes plagued his face, entered his ears, but he rested much of his weight on his other arm and could not brush them away. He blew air up along the front of his face by letting his lower lip push out. That action kept mosquitoes out of his eyes, at least. His head was hot under the hat, and sweat ran down his cheeks.

He waited. Still. The shad, after first swimming off when the burlap penetrated the surface of the river, were back now, and curious. One of them poked around at the front of the sack, one time touching its nose to a crossed twig. But Leon waited. Fish are fast.

The mosquitoes tortured his face with activity, except where he blew with each exhale over the front of his face. He squinted to keep his eyes safe. A breeze rolling blessedly down over the embankment renewed his faith every time it came, providing the needed break in insect activity.

The rocks hurt the bones in his hand as well as his knees, and he shook. He would have to move soon, or fall, face first into the shallows.

The fish were curious. Two others had joined in the exploration of the mouth of the burlap.

Leon barely heard Bob come up next to him. He did not see him, for at the moment his eyes were closed, one wrinkled edge crushing a mosquito that had stepped too close to the corner of Leon's right eye.

As Leon opened his eyes back to a narrow squint, he saw Bob's torn and scarred boots next to him. Suddenly a long stick came down with the smooth and directed motion of a spear. Two shad were forced, nose first, into the sack, recognizing, too late, that it was already moving toward them. Leon pulled his arm from the water, which caused him to pitch forward. Bob grabbed the sack at the mouth to retrieve it. Leon released the sack to recover from his fall.

"Slip-slam, bam, we got 'em."

Once he sat back onto the ground, Leon rubbed his hand, then his knees. He wiped sweat from his face and could feel the poison-filled bumps from mosquito bites under his fingertips. He splashed river water over his face.

"We a team," Bob told him.

The sack pumped like a heart at the bottom end as the two shad fought for breath.

"We done it!" Bob held the sack up so the others could see. Jesse, Cracker-Jack, Big Josh, and Buddy all stared, their bright, toothy smiles flashing in the sunlight.

The eagle screeched in approval, a congratulatory acceptance of life. Then, it dived into the river pulling out its own meal.

That afternoon, Leon and Bob made several more catches, their teamwork satisfactory three times out of ten.

Buddy and Big Josh tried their hand at netting fish by using Big Josh's shirt, the arm sleeves tied into knots that would be difficult to untie later and would result in Big Josh getting bitten so often by mosquitoes in love with his naked skin that he'd be itching for days to come, forcing blood from his own scratches to ooze through his shirt. Still, their efforts were rewarded with several large shad and a pike almost as long and skinny as one of Leon's arms.

Jesse caught two fish, one shad and one trout using Bob's bent pin and a June bug he'd found under a rock. Buddy had no luck with his pin, and after a short while of frustrated attempts, put his stick-pole down and went to collect wood for a fire.

Fourteen fish later, the men spent time talking and laughing in a circle on the ground. Buddy made the fire he'd collected wood for and Jesse got out the pots and pans – all of them – and filled them with edible fish parts. Jesse scooped water from the river, sent Bob and Leon to look for mushrooms and blackberries – Leon on the learning end of the mushroom picking – and boiled the water.

Optimism and joy spread as they worked together.

Sunset brought back into visibility a light haze that must have been transparent during the brightest part of the day. Or perhaps the humidity in the air was already on the rise as the sun dropped and the air cooled. The foothills blurred, but the color of sunlight as it dipped closer to the horizon burst with the colors of a rainbow, first purple, then deep indigo on down to oranges, yellows, and reds. At one point, even light green, as unusual as it was for the sky to be, stood brilliant, backlit by the sun through clouds.

They were a noisy bunch while they were happy, telling stories as they cooked and ate.

Perhaps it was the lowering of the sun, the filling of their stomachs, or only that they ran out of happy stories, but as darkness approached a depressing and sorrowful tone came over their conversations.

"The war kilt my brothers and most of me cousins. Right aside me," Jesse said. "I seed a hole the size of my thumb push into he forehead, then blood flow out matchin' his heart beat. I remember thinkin' he was scared 'cause of how fast the pulsin' blood pushed out." Jesse shook his head as if he were trying to shake the memory out of himself. "The loudness of war make you deaf to music. You ears juss ring like the after-sound of a church bell, but war ain't no church except that it send more people to heaven."

After Jesse fell silent, Buddy said that he lost a brother, too. "But I weren't there to see it."

"You don' know much about loss like that, do you?" Cracker-Jack said to Leon.

Bob gave Cracker-Jack a cold, hard stare. "His pappy shot."

"Shot fer runnin'. And we don know why exactly," Cracker-Jack said.

"Maybe we don want to know," Jesse said.

Bob poked at the fire and sparks burst into the air. "Maybe it not our business."

"We been travelin' together, don't that make it our business?" Cracker-Jack said.

Leon kept quiet and eventually Big Josh spoke up. "We ain't been honest neither."

Cracker-Jack shot him a mean look and the others paused long enough for Leon to realize he didn't know them as well as he had thought. Leon ignored them, staring into the fire as though he hadn't heard Big Josh. Leon's heartbeat quickened. He heard something rustle a short distance away in the woods. His burlap was drying near where he hid his book, knife, and revolver. He adjusted his legs, which were getting sore from being in the same position for a long time.

Big Josh stood up and kicked stones and dirt onto the fire making it spit sparks into the darkness.

"Sit down Josh," Jesse said.

"I kilt that man and you all knows it. We lein' all the time. We lein' to ourselves, makin' up stories of lifes we wanted, not the ones we got." Big Josh peered down at Leon. "Boy, we all runnin'."

"That's it!" Cracker Jack stood up too, now, and the restlessness of the others became an active and wild animal rummaging through their camp.

"I not stoppin'," Big Josh said.

"Damn-dip god-dammity," Bob said under his breath.

"I hated that man. He treat me bad and when his head under that wagon hub, I kick it off the post. I seed his ears squirt blood and one eye push out and land in the dirt. I run and not stop 'til I run into these crim'nals."

"Criminals?" Cracker-Jack yelled.

"Don't never hate a man, boy, 'cause sure enough you kill him. Big Josh finished speaking, then nodded toward Cracker-Jack who had never finished his assault.

Cracker-Jack waited for Josh to sit, then glanced around. "I kilt seven men."

Leon slid back from the fire. He glanced to judge how close he sat from the revolver.

"But they all soldiers." Cracker-Jack pounded his own chest. "I kilt them cause they kilt my family. It was right I kilt them."

Big Josh continued to stare at the man.

Cracker-Jack spit. "I so filled wit noise and anger and fear." He closed his eyes. When he spoke again he whispered. "I start loadin' and shootin' at anybody I sees." He lowered his head and walked from camp into the darkness.

Bob poked Leon with a toe and when Leon jumped, Bob whispered, "He shoot he own son." After a moment, Bob said, "You know, boy, what you try to hide is always there. It never go away. Sooner or later it boil up and make a blister everyone can see."

Leon felt his face flush and his eyes fill with tears. He clenched his teeth and sat still. The killing talk brought unwanted memories of his escape. The men scared him. He had crossed the river. His life was supposed to change.

Leon wished to be free of his own memories without letting go of the emotion. He knew how to make love to the emotion while forgetting the memory. So, in a low voice at first, Leon sang an old song he had heard and cast to memory: *Home Sweet Home*. The sadness of the song gripped his heart, but freed his mind.

The others joined in. Their voices, together, were loud, melodious, clear. Leon imagined that they all let go of their memories as they sang. He imagined that the bad in the world could be changed to good as wood changed to fire and warmth. He imagined nothing but memory ashes would be left by morning. And, then he stopped imagining anything at all and let his heart open to the sadness in the song, someone else's pain. He felt, but no longer connected the emotion to his memories. There were only the songwriter's memories now. And the emotion.

Before long Cracker-Jack came back into the circle, his voice adding to the others as though he too was now pouring out the fires of his mind, reducing his memories to ashes.

CHAPTER 11

Throughout the night, Leon woke to alternate dreams, first of being brutally murdered by the roamers, then of being abandoned in the wilderness. By morning, he set to reality the fact that the roamers were using him. If he were not useful, they would leave him while he slept through the night. Worse yet, now that he knew they had lied, they might slit his throat once his usefulness dissolved through their eyes.

Breakfast was prepared in relative quiet. The tone was somber, which belied the true sorrow they must have felt. They were vagabonds, criminals. Old men with horrible memories and even more horrible pasts. They were unreliable companions.

Anger lifted into the air and appeared to be aimed at Leon. They acted as though it had been his fault that they dragged out discarded memories, that he now knew the truth about them: that they were sad old men who had killed and stole and cheated, that their lives were nothing to be proud of.

Cracker-Jack ordered Leon around all morning, calling him White Boy and, in a sarcastic voice, Big Man.

Leon obeyed in silence, folding bedrolls, dispersing the fire's embers, fetching water in a pan for them all to sip from. With no fish left from the night before and nothing for breakfast, hunger fed the present anger and restlessness.

"Today, White Boy, you best get us enough bread. Don't go runnin' scared." Cracker-Jack motioned for them to get going. Leon scrambled to shoulder his pack and follow them in silence. He couldn't look any of them in the eye without feeling fear rise into his throat.

Already the sky sucked fog from the ground. Moisture from the field and the woods both contributed to the haze in the air. Mosquitoes and deer flies lifted up with the sun, as though being borne from the heat.

Bob leaned close to Leon. "Bet dat hat keeps you head from burnin' in this sun."

"You like this hat?"

"Do."

Leon took the hat into his hands and held it. He leaned as though he were going to hand the hat over to the old man, but his memory of Big Leon reminded him of his attachment to its giver and made him hold to it. He placed it back on his head and said, "Me too."

Bob spit on the ground between Leon's legs and looked him in the eye. "You die, that's my hat."

Leon swallowed and fell back to take up the rear.

That day they walked away from the river. The terrain rose steadily, sometimes so steep they had to crawl up and over a ridge to a flat area. It was difficult for Bob especially, but for all of them except Leon.

Jesse refused Leon's help. "Big Man helpin' the old coloreds?"

Cracker-Jack called out to him, "Damn mule."

"Boney white slave," Buddy said.

The day wore on and Leon climbed ahead, then helped them over a ridge or waited for them to catch up, complaints or not. He rested under pines humming tunes he'd made up long ago, or heard others hum. Martha. Leon didn't feel comfortable leaving the river.

There was little rest for the others. At one point, they stopped to strip the thin bark from a black birch tree and stuff it into their mouths like tobacco chaws.

"Look," Leon said, once he reached a clearing at the top of a hill and turned around to wait for the others. The valley lay below them, the Susquahanna's West Branch sparkling in the sunlight, the dark woods soaking up that same sun. Small puffs of fog rose from black patches in the woods as the heat pulled moisture from the rotting vegetation on the forest floor.

As they all looked at the distance they'd come, at the magnificent valley below, Jesse turned to continue on and pointed in another direction. "Smoke," he said. "Somebody burnin' stumps."

Leon knew that he would feed them that night or be abandoned, or killed, by morning. He would do what needed to be done.

As they descended into the valley, Cracker-Jack forged ahead of the group to evaluate how they would assault the farmhouse.

The valley was narrow, but long even though the hills appeared to slope at the South end, and Leon suspected another creek running perpendicular to the slope. A yellow field spread to their left and North. Corn stood tall on the southern side in long stands going from west to east. They could steal corn, Leon thought, forget asking for food.

Jesse crept up behind Leon and whispered, "That field corn. Tastes empty and gives you the shits."

"I don't want to beg for a handout," Leon said.

"And I don't want to steal. I didn't want to be in no war. I didn't want to be born black." He spit a wad of birch bark that had been in his cheek the entire afternoon, hitting the earth with a soft thud. "You do what you have to do." He walked away.

Leon stared south wishing he were near the water. They could fish again. They could eat berries and mushrooms. The water and woods could feed them.

Cracker-Jack returned with a plan. He gathered everyone together. "They's a stand of sweet corn around the back. Chickens is easy to get at, too. I seed a young man checkin' over the wagon and plow and other equipment like he oilin' and greasin' everything and cleanin' it. We better move fast. See that," he pointed south. "We headed for that flat down there, back to the river." He looked into each of their faces.

Cracker-Jack handed Big Josh and Jesse most of the gear and shoved them off, along with Bob. That left him and Buddy for stealing, and Leon as a distraction. If he could get bread, too, then fine, but mostly he was there to distract.

Leon's stomach ached. He swallowed over and over again. This was it for him. The others had fewer choices. They were old. They were murderers. They were Negroes. He had youth on his side. He had no history that followed him past the river crossing. And he didn't look colored, not even to other Negroes. He didn't know how he did look to them, but it wasn't black. This was it, the last time for him.

Cracker-Jack slapped the back of Leon's neck.

Leon turned in response.

Cracker-Jack's face was stern. "Go ahead," he said.

Leon didn't move.

"Then git to it," Cracker-Jack said. "I know what you thinkin'. Now that you knows so much about us. But you ain't got what it take, boy. So juss git along."

Leon headed for the farmhouse, taking the straightest route, the most visible route. The people inside needed to feel relaxed, as if he were a stranger needing food. As he approached the house, he heard some yelling inside and a woman came out onto the steps. "What you want," she yelled.

"Travelin' downriver and run out-a provisions." Leon held up his sack.

"River a ways off."

Leon lowered his head. He thought hard for something to say.

Suddenly the young man who Cracker-Jack must have seen, came around the side of the house. He had a musket in his hands. It looked old, even at Leon's distance.

"Git 'im some bread, Martha," the man said, and Martha disappeared inside the house.

"Martha's my Aunt's name," Leon said. "Thank you for bringing back that good memory." He took a few steps more. He heard the chickens squabble, but nothing that would alarm anyone. His stomach felt better and his mind cleared. He found he wanted to talk, wanted to be accepted. "When I grew up, Martha used to cook and feed the whole family. She became more of a mama to me than my mama did."

"That right?"

"She never married, herself. Too busy takin' care of everyone else."

The man relaxed his grip and lowered the gun. "I got a Aunt like that."

"It appears most families do. The ones I know. It's like there's a rule that not all the women from one family can marry. One has to stay un-wed to take care of the others," Leon said.

"Don't know about that."

Martha stepped out and walked over to Leon. There was absolutely no concern in her demeanor. She held out an entire loaf of bread and a cloth filled with vegetables. "From the garden," she said.

"Well thank you ma'am." Leon took the food. The woman reminded him a little of Hillary. She had a heavy, child-baring frame. But this Martha also had the prettiest face Leon had ever seen. It was smooth and looked soft to the touch, with patches of almost transparent fuzz on each cheek. Her eyes were brilliant green.

She turned away as though embarrassed by Leon's intense attention. "You are welcome," she said.

"Thank you as well, sir. Your kindness is appreciated. I know you've toiled to receive such provisions."

The man nodded. "You can be on your way now," he said, but he did not pick up his rifle in force.

"Thank you much." Leon looked the man in the eyes, testing his own resolve, and bent into a slight bow. He had already scanned his surroundings and took the shortest route to cover. Once out of site of Martha and her man, Leon ran toward the edge of the woods, turned south and made his way toward the creek.

Once again the sun burned color into the sky as it lowered beyond the hillside. The corn silks turned golden in the light. A hawk screech alerted Leon to the bird's flight, rising on the last thermals of the day. The breeze down through the valley felt cool across his skin, a welcome change to Leon.

He stopped long enough to stuff the bread and cloth filled with vegetables into his sack. The bread poked out the top. He lifted the sack by wrapping one hand around the open hem. He rubbed his head with his other hand. As his hair grew out it became more wavy, looser than when it was cut short.

He hummed and made up words about his adventure. "Crossing the River," had a gospel leaning. He didn't sing very loudly, but did raise his voice to a loud whisper when the chorus came in: 'Crossing the river gave my life new meaning/ baptized my soul 'til I came up screaming/ couldn't walk on water like my man Jesus/ but my life sure change as my Lord God pleases.' He felt it wasn't perfect, but could work on it while he walked.

By the time he entered camp, the sun had slipped behind the mountain and a great glowing haze like a halo along the treetops stood, backlit by the sun. The campfire was ablaze. Buddy stood as Leon approached.

Caracker-Jack asked, "What you standin' for?"

"Leon here," Buddy said, as though it were obvious.

"Ain't no matter," Cracker-Jack said.

"Why you turnin' so mean on him?"

"He think he better 'an us," Cracker-Jack poked at the fire. "And he ain't."

Buddy took the sack from Leon and leaned into him. "Don't you listen to 'im. He mad cause he have to remember who he really be and not who he make himself up to be."

"Ain't true. I tole you why I mean on him and it he own fault. Dammit, you think I cain't hear?"

"No sir, Cracker-Jack, I don't think that," Buddy said.

Cracker-Jack snarled.

Leon sat to the left of Cracker-Jack and helped Jesse and Buddy cut the vegetables into chunks. The others had already slit the throat of the chicken and were nearly finished cleaning it. Its carcass was stuck through with a stick. There were still small feathers stuck to the bird, but they would burn out in the fire.

Leon heard another bird cluck from time to time and saw that it was wrapped in a bedroll and set near a tree a few yards away. It was Bob's bedroll. Bob leaned against a tree trunk, his hand resting on the bedroll.

Jesse cooked up a fine vegetable stew for them. They also had stolen sweet corn and the chicken meat for dinner.

"Was hopin' I'd git that hat today," Bob said.

"I ain't dead yet," Leon said.

"Watch you sleep," Cracker-Jack said.

Leon ducked his head and took a walk to collect firewood.

After dinner, Buddy asked Leon to read to them.

"Yeah, read, smart boy," Cracker-Jack said.

Leon declined.

"I said read," Cracker-Jack repeated.

"I'm tired," Leon said.

Cracker-Jack leaped up and kicked Leon in the shoulder. "You son-a-bitch, you son-a-bitch. You'll God damned sure read outa you book."

Leon fell to his side and took another kick or two. His arm hurt. He held up his hands in surrender and Cracker-Jack backed off.

Leon took the book out of his sack and opened it. His voiced cracked. He read for nearly an hour. All the bedrolls came out and the roamers prepared for sleep long before Leon curled near the fire.

*   *   *

As summer wore on through the heat and humidity of the greater Susquahanna Valley, Leon got better at begging for food. Cracker-Jack's early attacks on Leon escalated into a form of contempt and rage.

Leon sensed that Cracker-Jack felt increasingly vulnerable as Leon's own confidence grew. Cracker-Jack stated his belief that Leon would eventually leave them on their own, once Leon, "...got to thinkin' he could do it all on his own."

The truth was, Cracker-Jack had as much to do with Leon's interest in leaving as Leon's gaining confidence did. Leon was sick of being the brunt of whatever anger Cracker-Jack carried around. Finally, in what Leon could only discern as desperation, Cracker-Jack ordered Bob to go with Leon, to learn some secret Leon might hold to getting the homesteaders to hand over food willingly, along with utensils, and even blankets when they saw that Leon had none.

"Ain't goin'," Bob said.

"You the only one I can spare," Cracker-Jack said.

"You can spare?" Bob shook his head.

"I can spare both you. Now, git. And don't beg fer no Liquor."

Bob smacked his lips and Cracker-Jack pointed at him. "You git you-self in trouble, you on yer own. We leavin' without you."

"Can't do that," Jesse said.

Cracker-Jack shot him a glance and Jesse stepped back.

Leon didn't like the idea of taking Bob with him, but felt better about it once he and Bob were walking toward the house.

Corn stood high against the evening sky, and would be easy to escape through or hide in.

"You teach me what to say, so's Cracker-Jack don't leave me behind," Bob said.

"He won't leave you."

"He show 'nough will. He gittin' mean as a snake."

Leon patted Bob's shoulder. "He's mad at me, not you."

"He raging at his-self." Bob nodded his head, agreeing with his own words.

"I'm familiar with that," Leon said.

As they approached the shack of a cabin, a plump young woman with a ruddy complexion stepped into the yard. "Here for Pa?"

"No, ma'am," Leon said. "We're traveling downriver and ran short of supplies. We were wondering. . ."

"Ain't got no extra. Pa says it gonna be a hard winter."

"Anything would do ma'am. A small amount?" Leon removed his hat and held it in front of his chest. Bob lowered his head along with Leon's actions.

The woman kept looking back and forth at them. Her lips pushed out and tightened as she thought. "Perhaps a few muffins."

Leon bowed slightly.

She turned to go inside and Leon heard a shout in back of the cabin and then the loud crack of a gun. "Git, you thievin' bastards."

Bob turned and ran for the cornfield. Leon skuttled behind Bob with his arms out, trying to urge the old man to move faster. Another loud cry, this time closer, was followed by another shot. Buckshot tore through the corn stalks. Leon stepped around Bob and pulled him along. Another shot and Leon heard Bob let out a puff of air and a huh, like he was asking a question.

Bob slowed down.

Another shot came through the corn, this time in a whole other direction than where he and Bob headed. Leon tucked himself under Bob's shoulder, then placed his arm around Bob's waist for support. They moved slower than Leon wished, but faster than Bob could have done on his own. The compromise suited Leon, since the woman obviously had no idea where they were, as she blasted the edges of the cornfield over and over.

Leon shortened his usual wide circle, and exited the field south of the cabin.

Bob stumbled, but Leon held tight and continued on without thought.

"Should-a asked for liquor," Bob wheezed.

"Next time," Leon said.

"No," Bob said in a trailing voice.

A short distance farther and the other men came out from a stand of trees to greet Leon and Bob. Big Josh took over where Leon held tightly. As Leon backed away he noticed blood running down the back of Bob's head and neck. The other men surrounded Bob, and it appeared to Leon as though the men raised Bob off the ground and carried him, even though Bob's feet were still moving.

An hour later and well away from the farm, Big Josh lowered Bob's limp body onto the ground.

Cracker-Jack slapped Leon hard on the back of the neck, spreading the sting along his shoulders.

"Weren't my fault," Leon said.

"You were with 'im."

Jesse, sitting next to Bob, raised a bloody arm. A series of clotted blood dots spread from his wrist to his elbow. "Leave 'im be. You be with me and look what I get."

Cracker-Jack spit on the ground at Leon's feet.

Leon let the blood rush to his face, but he didn't move. Not this time.

Jesse shot up from the ground and rushed Cracker-Jack. He swung his fists, knocking the leader of the roamers onto the ground. "Enough a you bullying. You got Bob kilt."

Cracker-Jack crabbed backwards, away from Jesse's fists. He turned away as Jesse kicked leaves and dirt at him.

Josh pulled Jesse away.

Leon stepped near Bob.

Buddy scooched to the side to let Leon kneel next to Bob. Leon lowered his face into his hands. "I couldn't help it." He wiped his eyes and looked up. He wished he had not moved to the front to pull Bob along.

"Nothin' anyone could do. Ain't no use in blamin' no one." Buddy glanced over at Cracker-Jack, then looked at Jesse. "No one," he repeated.

That night the men dug a shallow grave in silence. No one ate. Cracker-Jack took his bedroll into the woods and out of the sight of the others.

Leon helped to make a fire, then let himself fall asleep, knowing that he'd awaken several times in the night. Each time he awoke, Leon lifted his head to be sure the others were asleep. As it got closer to daybreak, Leon uncurled his tight muscles, stretched his arms and legs, and sat up making as little noise as possible.

He gathered his sack. On his way out of camp, Leon placed his hat over Bob's grave and left it there. Rather than run, Leon tip-toed as not to disturb his sleeping partners.

Jesse shocked him, stepping from around a tree into Leon's path. "I done blame you," Jesse whispered. He rubbed his arm where the buckshot had penetrated.

Leon wanted to step past him.

"Listen, boy. We go around the town by passin' over the mountain. At first Cracker-Jack want to keep you around 'cause we can use you. But Cracker-Jack turn bad."

"There's a town?" Leon said.

"Follow this creek downstream. At the river, go upstream. It about two days walk." Jesse held out a pot with congealed stew about an inch thick along the bottom.

"You'll get into trouble." Leon pushed the pan aside with his hand.

Jesse agreed with a silent nod and slight grin. "We know you mulatto, but you also carry youself like a white boy. Cracker-Jack be jealous. You keep tellin' youself you white. You look whites in the eye and claim you worth somethin'. You hear?"

"I do."

"Safe travels," Jesse said. Then he turned and headed back to camp.

Leon's stomach ached for the stew, but it wouldn't be good for Jesse had he taken it.

He took a few slow steps toward the creek, then stopped to listen. He couldn't hear Jesse's footsteps. Birdsongs had already conquered the air. The darkness had begun to dissipate into morning, waking the diurnal animals and setting the nocturnal to task looking for a safe resting place where the day's heat would let them be.

Twittering birds increased in number until it was the only sound Leon heard. He picked up his pace, his sack in his hand and his chin up. He felt alert, rested, confident. He imagined a river-town hustling with noise, bursting with work. He could fish the river, farm at the edge of town, fix stables. There would be work for him, and people with nothing murderous in their past, nothing they would need to run from. He could live in a place like that.

CHAPTER 12

The West Branch of the Susquahanna is a winding river, taking sharp curves in one direction and then several miles farther turning in the opposite direction.

Leon couldn't catch a fish without Bob's help. An aching stomach, due to eating nothing but raw mushrooms and blackberries, reduced his ability to sleep. Leon followed the water around one bend after another. Nothing but silence and wilderness spread before him at one turn, then people and noise at the next. The town appeared to have sprung out of the ground.

Leon kneeled in exhaustion. The roaring of the river rushing around the bend muffled the noise coming from the town. For the moment, the sight of people brought him joy. Leon, tired as he was, lifted up onto weak legs and hobbled into town.

Two men heading south in a buckboard stacked with grain, stopped alongside Leon. "You okay, mister?"

Leon looked up and the sun caught his eye. "Tired," he said through a squint. "And hungry."

The man on Leon's side of the buckboard shook his head. "There's work and plenty of it this time of year." He clicked his cheek, snapped the reins, and the wagon kicked back into motion.

Leon watched the wagon go down the road. Work. He changed focus back to the town ahead of him. He'd do most anything for a good meal.

The dust rose from the sun-dried roadbed and lifted into Leon's nose and mouth. He could not will himself to feel white, a fleeting memory of what Jesse had suggested. He stayed in the road unable to enter any of the buildings.

Other men walked the streets. A few said howdy to him. Leon nodded and turned his eyes away. Before long two men deliberately approached him. "You lookin' for work?"

Leon glanced at the man speaking, who stood Leon's height, but carried another forty pounds, which made Leon feel skinny. The man wore a leather hat that shaded his dark brown eyes. Stubble poked out of the man's chin, but not his cheeks, leading Leon to guess that the man was young. The speaker's partner stood six inches shorter and ten pounds heavier, but was older by a few rough years, with a thicker beard, maybe a few week's growth.

"Haven't eaten much either," Leon answered.

"Don't know about that, but the mill needs help."

"Where do I go?"

The young man took Leon by the arm and turned him. He pointed toward the edge of town, not far away. "There." The largest building to be seen had a thin tower-like frame with a fat lower part below that gave the impression of a longhouse. Lumber was piled in front of it.

The young man slapped Leon's back. "That there mill is all this town is." Then he laughed as if he had told a joke, and walked off with his friend.

Leon continued to gaze upriver. There was only the one log pile. As he got closer to the mill, though, the banks became heavy with timber. Even so the woods behind the mill were still thick with trees. He couldn't imagine where all the timber had come from. Upstream, he figured. Leon shook his head assuming he wasn't processing the town properly. Perhaps there was more logic to the town than he could grasp in his present state of hunger and fatigue.

Other men passed as Leon stayed on course for the mill. With each step he heard more people talking and yelling. Then came the clanking and ringing of chains.

He didn't have to say much as he approached the mill. It appeared that no one would go in that direction unless he wanted work. And at the moment Leon wanted nothing more than to earn a good meal and a place to lie down.

"Hey, Harry," Leon heard someone call. Two men came down from the long-house to meet Leon. "Three days work for meals and a bed. After that, you get a daily rate to be determined by how much work you can do. That sound good, son?"

Leon nodded then his shoulders felt light and his knees weakened. He staggered. The two men grabbed him and held him up. "He's fevered," one said.

"Dang-blame it," the other responded. "We take 'im to the bunk house. The others won't like it. Maybe the shed'll do."

Leon slept and remembered little more than lying on the floor. When he saw one of the men again, the burly logger was carrying food. Leon ate slowly. Before long, he felt better. His head cleared.

"You fevered. We ain't got much space for the sick."

"I feel better," Leon said. He looked at the food in front of him. He took a drink of water. "Really, I feel better. I can work."

"No matter. Until you're free of the fever, the other men won't want you around."

Leon nodded as he stuffed food into his mouth. He swathed his plate with a last piece of bread and handed the plate back. His muscles ached. He stood. "I'm ready. Please, don't turn me out."

"Wasn't plannin' to.

Standing required as much will as strength for Leon to accomplish.

The man pulled a crate off a stack. "Here you go. Have a seat. Not much room in here, but you can stretch out. Your sack is over there, but you ain't got no bedroll. I have it deducted from your wages. And the couple meals too. I sure as shit hope you can work once you spry up."

"I can," Leon said. He stepped into the darkness of the shadows and sat on the crate. "Thank you."

The man slapped the door frame with his palm and left, leaving the shed door hang open.

Leon watched him go, then rolled off the crate and lay on the floor where he curled into a ball. He woke in the middle of the night, a blanket over his shoulders. The man must have returned, but Leon had no idea when. He put his palm to his own forehead, which didn't feel hot to his touch. He stretched his arms and legs. The aches were still there, and across his back and in his neck, too.

Leon crawled to the door and swung his legs out over the stoop. The sky spread clear above him. Stars stood close enough to touch. The air was cool. The river rush was loud and the thud, thud, thud of logs bumping together created a rhythm Leon almost recognized. He breathed in the night air. There were no mosquitoes, no gnats. He scratched his arms where he had been bitten the last few days. He rubbed his face with his hands. He didn't know the name of the town nor what type of work he'd be involved with, but he was alive and awake and could feel the sickness leaving his body.

Leon lay back on the floor. His legs hung out of the shed. He reached back and grabbed the blanket and pulled it over his chest and arms, up close to his chin. He had left his bedroll when he left the roamers. This one felt good and warm. He closed his eyes and fell back to sleep. He dreamed of death: Big Leon's and Bob's. The blast and scatter of buckshot through corn occurred over and over again until Leon opened his eyes and his hearing returned. The blast was replaced by the thud, thud of the logs banging together.

Light came into the shed.

Leon's legs were sore, especially behind his knees where they had been bent over the door jam. He rubbed each leg out, starting at his thigh and ending at his foot. After he finished with his legs, he rubbed each arm starting at the shoulder. Then he stretched and twisted his back, holding it in place to let the ache's dissipate. He rubbed his neck, too, and forehead, ears and face, especially around his eyes. When he was through with the massage, he stood.

Across the water, the sun had already lighted the sky. Humidity produced a haze in the distance, obscuring the details of the mountains. The river, filled with fish, frogs, and turtles, stretched gloriously before him, wide and strong. The ker-plunk and plop and swishing sounds rose from the river, a song of its own.

The Susquahanna was fast moving, fed by hundreds of creeks, mountain streams, and small runs. The way it twisted and snaked, the way it cut through the mountains, proved its strength. That morning, the sun lighting the water's deceptive glass surface proved its beauty.

Fish broke the surface everywhere, the pops and plunks penetrating through the constant hiss made by the current as it rushed downstream straight into a sharp bend.

Leon sure wanted one of those fish. Had he thought to steal one of the bent pins and some string from the roamers, he'd be out there fishing already.

He rolled his blanket and sack together. His own bedroll. He rubbed the wool fibers with his hand. The blanket would keep him warm come winter. He stood in the doorway waiting for someone to come for him. He tapped his foot and hummed. He felt much better, like he could put in a day's work.

After a while and no one came by, Leon slapped the floor and stood. He spit on the ground in front of him. He waited another minute and thought about those fish.

When he couldn't wait any longer, he walked down along the bank of the water and around the mill. Heading up toward the bunkhouse, he smelled eggs cooking, and bread. The scent pulled at his stomach as he approached.

"New man!"

Leon recognized the man who had led him to the shed and returned with the bedroll.

"Fever's gone," Leon said.

The man nodded. He held out his hand. "Jack," he said.

"Leon," Leon said taking the man's hand.

Jack cocked his head. "Never known a Leon before."

Leon turned his eyes away from their handshake. He didn't know how to respond. What did Jack mean by his statement?

"That a French name," Harry said from a few feet away.

"My grandfather's name," Leon said.

"They Christian folk?" Jack asked.

Harry answered for Leon. "We ain't none of us Christian after workin' here for a year." He walked up to the men. "You hungry, Leon?"

"I try to live Christian," Jack said.

The other men standing around laughed at him.

"I do," Jack said laughing as well.

Leon followed Harry to a long table made from several cut planks laid across two stumps. Bread, pans filled with eggs, fresh blackberries, and cooked bacon were positioned in a row, ready to be taken.

Leon's mouth filled with saliva.

Harry led him to the end of the table and pushed a plate into his hands. "Spoons at the end."

Leon looked down the table to where the spoons had been piled. The food appeared to go on forever. He followed another man and filled his plate until there was no room for more. He followed the man in front of him to a knoll partway down the bank toward the water's edge. There wasn't much talking while the eating was going on, and Leon was fine with that. He pushed eggs into his mouth and chased them with bacon, then he pushed bread in and chased it with a fist full of blackberries. Sweet juice trickled from between his lips and he giggled with delight.

He had all but forgotten the river and the morning until the sun broke over the hills and a blast of light reflected from the river, making his eyes water.

"Damn," the man next to him said.

"Gonna be a hot one," another man said.

Leon didn't care about the heat. He felt stronger than he had when he arrived. He had food in his stomach, his fever had broken, and his muscles didn't ache.

Several men around him soon rushed through the final morsels of their plates, signaling work was about to begin. It was officially sunup.

He wiped his plate clean and walked back to put it into a drum filled with suds.

Jack and Harry were off under a lean-to talking. They were the bosses, sure and straight, Leon thought.

Harry walked down to Leon while the other men dispersed. "We'll be helping to drive timber downstream. Timber that's been left over after the flood run. We take a percentage for ourselves to build a town here. You might of seen places going up as you come into town."

Harry's eyes were watery and intense. Leon glanced at them from time to time, but couldn't maintain contact for long. Eventually, he stared at Harry's mouth. The man's teeth were yellow and his lips were split in two places like he'd been hit in the mouth by a log.

Harry cocked his head. "You listenin'," he said.

"Yes, sir."

"Well, you can strip the bark what's left from the logs. Help Jake Butler down there. Just ask for Jake, he'll speak up."

Leon nodded and turned to go. He heard Harry shuffling back toward Jack under the lean-to.

Leon felt conspicuous walking among all the whites. Even after he became concerned about the roamers being criminals, he felt comfortable around their mannerisms. These people acted differently somehow, but Leon couldn't put his finger on exactly what that difference was in particular. As he approached the area where Harry had pointed, a thin young man with tight stringy muscles handed Leon a tool having two handles at the opposite ends of a sharp drawknife.

"Ever use one?" Jake asked.

Before Leon could answer, Jake held the blade up by one handle. "Blade's toward you." He grabbed the other handle with his other hand. "You break all the rules. They tell you don't run the blade toward you? Well, not here. Here you pull right toward your own gut."

Jake straddled a log, planted his feet firmly and lowered the blade, then yanked in short bursts. "Don't try to slide the bark off in one long walk backwards. You'll cut your own legs off. Yank the blade through in controlled distances. You want to know where the blade's stoppin'."

Leon listened closely and straddled the log when Jake stepped from it. Leon pulled toward his body in short bursts as he was told. Jake stood beside him watching, then went off to debark his own log.

Leon's log stretched on for miles behind him. He kept looking around to see how close to the end he was. When he looked up, Jake's log had been turned and the man was a quarter length down a second side.

Jake glanced over and laughed at Leon. "You'll get it."

Leon went back to work. He got it, but his arms were already burning. He tried to pull more evenly so the pulsing wouldn't make his muscles ache, but he couldn't even pull through the bark. Then he tried stepping back while his pulsed movement appeared to be separating the bark from the tree, but the blade twisted up, pulled through the bark and freed Leon to fall backward. As he fell, he let go of one handle and the blade came at him. He could see its sheen. The free handle whacked into Leon's chest, then twisted by his shoulder.

"You're lucky, even if you're stupid," Jake said. He came over to help Leon. "Usually men cut their thighs first. Not you, you go for your own throat." He stepped over the log, grabbed the debarking tool and handed it back to Leon. Jake had a big grin on his face.

"It's funny that I almost got killed?"

"It's not funny if you get killed. It's funny if you don't." Jake stepped back over the log and went to his own work station. "Pulses," he said.

Leon worked through the morning and through his muscle pain. He paid such close attention to the work at hand that the sound of the river evaporated, the sound of the other workers faded, only his own breath was heard. Pulse-pulse-wait, pulse-wait, pulse-pulse-wait, pulse-wait. He imagined his breath as the base line of a song, and as long as he kept the base line steady, the work got done. Sweat soaked his shirt and trousers and ran into his eyes. His hands got slippery and slid from the handles of the tool. He eventually couldn't wipe his hands dry on his shirt or trouser legs, so he wiped them in the dirt.

When noon came, there was a silent halt to all work. Like an unspoken yell, the sound of work-stoppage was as loud as the river noise.

Leon let his tool dangle across the log he was stripping. He looked over and Jake had done the same.

The young man headed toward Leon. "You catch on quick," Jake said.

"Thank you."

"Bet you're arms are hurtin' though."

"They are." Leon rubbed one arm with the other, then reversed the action.

"You'll be achin' tonight, but in two days you won't notice. Tomorrow will be your worst day." He patted Leon on the shoulder. They walked together toward the long table next to the bunkhouse.

Once again, the men filled their plates and found their own stumps, logs, and rocks. Then there was the knoll where Leon sat for the second time that day.

Jake plopped down next to him. Using his spoon as a finger, Jake pointed one by one at the other men sitting around, naming them for Leon. "That's Chuck, he's James, then John, and Billy." The men nodded, said howdy, or looked up, mouths full, eyes weary. Billy, though, stared at Leon.

"Billy observes," Jake said.

"Observes what?" Leon said.

Billy answered, "Everythin'." He pointed at Leon. "Like you. I'd say you the quiet sort by lookin' at you. But that not the truth. I seed you walkin' and you ain't a shy walker."

"What in the hell does that mean?" Chuck said.

"Don't know," Billy said.

Chuck laughed and stuffed a piece of bread into his mouth.

"I want to know somethin'," Billy said.

Leon expected Billy to ask about his nationality since he noticed his walk. He imagined they all wondered the same thing, so he answered even before Billy got the question out. "White."

"White?" Billy said. "That don't help."

Leon cocked his head. Did Billy think he was a liar?

"The last name of White don't tell me nothing' about you," Billy said.

Jake said, "Billy has observed that names tell what people should do, or what they come from, like Carpenter, and Butler, and Carrier, and Butcher. White don't fit into his theory."

Leon giggled out of nervousness. "Whites don't do anything," he said. The rest of the men laughed over that one.

After lunch, the silent order went out again, and the men stood and shuffled back to their work.

Leon's legs hurt as much as his arms, but he hadn't noticed until then. His thighs and shins strained to move along. And his back, bent half the day, fought his attempt to straighten up at first. Getting back to work, Leon noticed how he enjoyed being around people even though he felt out of place. While he was growing up, he felt the opposite. People were cruel and standoffish. They were mean even though Leon had done nothing but be born with a different look about him. Even Hillary had used him as if she hated him. It was difficult to understand her motivations. It was difficult to understand any of their motivations.

Leon's pace slowed as he thought, and as his body rejected the shock it had to bare.

Jake whistled at him. When Leon looked over, Jake motioned for Leon to get back to work.

Leon spit and wiped sweat from his face, then went back to the job at hand. He focused on the base rhythm and the labor progressed more smoothly. He hummed to the beat, but it sounded more like grunting when backed by the pain in his body.

He focused hard on his work and on the beating of his throat. From time to time he'd look to his side to see how far behind he had fallen. After a while, he noticed that Jake wasn't gaining on him any longer. In fact, Jake was pacing Leon, apparently hammering away at the pace of Leon's grunting. He had created a machine of two men.

Leon felt proud of his secret accomplishment and began to test it. He speeded up the rhythm and noticed that Jake did the same. Then after a log or two, he slowed his rhythm and Jake kept pace. Leon giggled at the thought that he could control the work with his song.

The idea expanded inside his mind. He recalled how Bob, Jesse, and the others asked him to sing, and how their mood changed when he did. He remembered Martha humming to the attitude in the shack. Or was she creating the attitude with her song?

The debarking tool jerked loose from the log and Leon was able to stop it short of his thighs. He controlled where the blade would stop. Leon glanced over and once again Jake had pulled ahead of Leon, who apparently couldn't think without slowing down.

Wherever he focused his attention that's what got done. Leon placed the tool back onto the log. Jake lifted his head and stared at Leon, or past him. What was so arresting as to get Jake's full attention? Leon turned to follow Jake's gaze.

CHAPTER 13

The river wore a black stripe of timber about a mile long. A raft stationed mid-river floated in position to turn the logs toward shore. Another raft floated three quarters across to the other side of the river, and upriver several hundred yards, ready to accept the logs as well.

Jake appeared to be mesmerized by the log slick.

"Won't that timber bust through those rafts?" Leon asked, struck by the timber's obvious power.

"Nope."

"That river's flowin' pretty fast."

"Look close, Leon. The river runs faster than the logs. The raft men divert some to shore and the rest go downstream to the next town. There are three mills before those logs hit Northumberland. We all do plankin'. Keep some. Sell some."

"Who builds?" Leon asked.

"We all do. Timber don't come down every day." Jake stopped talking and went back to work.

As the first raft got in the way of floating timber, the men scurried to their posts and shoved logs around the raft. It appeared to Leon that the men selected as well as diverted the logs. The agility of the men and their quick accounting of each log fascinated him.

Jake whistled and Leon, without looking over, got back to work. As he worked through several more logs, he listened to the calls of the men. The orders and excitement exhilarated Leon. The sounds of his new companions gave him the sense that there existed an even greater machine for him to be part of. He and Jake were only an axle bearing in the wheel, and the rest of the men, with all their individual duties represented an entire wagon train.

Before the day ended, Jake stopped and waited for Leon to finish the log he worked on. They had worked from two stacks and Leon was proud of Jake having only stripped a few logs more than he had.

"What are you waiting for?"

"When you be finished there, we got to drag these up to the mill," Jake said.

"Why's the mill so far up there?"

"Flood line. In spring we'll be stackin' right next to the building."

Leon, following Jake's lead, grabbed a timber hook. Each of them swung the hook into the first log and dragged it up the hill.

"So, what you gonna do with your wages?" Jake asked.

"Never thought about it."

"I'm gonna go to college," Jake said. "My brother went off to college, then the war take him and me, both, only he never come back. I gonna go to college and help out my mama and sisters. I can read good, and cipher some."

"You're not building a home here like some of the others?"

"Naw. I wouldn't live here. You want to strip logs for the rest of your life?"

"No." Leon was certain of that, even after one day.

"You got a family?"

"No."

"None?" Jake stood straight. "None at all?"

At this point, Leon wished for the questions to stop. After a moment of hesitation, he said, "All dead and that's it." Leon had eliminated his family and his past. Killed everyone off with one shot like the one that entered Big Leon's head. With that memory, Leon erased many others, at least when it came to explaining his past.

"Didn't mean nothing," Jake said.

"Apology accepted," Leon said.

They released the log and went back for another.

Jake stayed quiet for several log-drags, then said what he must have been thinking. "You should meet my sister, Ellen. She gonna need a husband."

Leon laughed. He could feel his cheeks tighten. Sweat trickled into the corners of his eyes. He wiped his face. "Why is she going to need a husband? She ugly?"

"No," Jake said, leaning back as if hurt by Leon's accusation. "I'd never try to pass off no ugly sister. It's just that she's been helpin' my mama for years. She's a hard worker and does a lot of sewin' and cookin' for others is all. She ain't had time for no husband."

"I didn't mean anything."

"She has a pretty face," Jake said.

"How about the rest of her?" Leon said. He really didn't care. He didn't want to have his future planned. He was still adapting to his recent freedom. But it was nice not having to talk about himself.

"She thin like me. Strong though," he said as if apologetic. "She could bare children. And her bosom would swell enough where she could feed 'em too, I bet. My mama said my sister will fill out when her husband and her children need her to. Just like my mama herself."

"What about your other sister?"

"She too young, still. You don't need to think about her."

"Well, it's admirable that you think so highly of your family and that you want to help them out," Leon said.

"I'll get my own family goin' too. Almost did once, but the girl's family gone crazy. I'll find another. Plan on having six little ones." Jake pointed up toward where Jack and Harry made their plans. "I'll be foreman some day. Either that or I'll be teachin' my own college classes. Mark my words, Leon."

"I'll mark 'em."

As Leon and Jake reduced their stack of timber, some of the other men created a new stack. Still others stacked the bark into a wagon. Leon noticed that the mill hadn't put out any planks. "When's this get going?"

"When the river's clean of this run of timber. Maybe tomorrow. Yes," Jake said, looking over the river, "tomorrow."

As they ambled back to get the last log, Leon asked what they'd be doing while the mill was going.

"Strippin' bark." Jake pointed at the timber lying all around. "We got our work."

Leon gazed at his prospective life for the next few months. Hard labor. At the moment there weren't many choices.

When his work was finished, Leon followed Jake to the river and washed up.

"We're lucky men," Jake said.

"Why's that?"

"We get more than beans and crackers."

"Beans and crackers?"

"A lot of wood-hicks don't eat so well." Jake pointed into the river. "That's all they eat. Nothin' else on board those rafts."

"I like being lucky," Leon said.

The two of them meandered up the hill to the bunkhouse and the table of food. Other men had already assembled there. Still others were coming up the bank, some down the hill from the woods, others from town.

The sun, setting behind them, shined its final rays across the river and lighted the tops of the maple and walnut trees opposite them. Leon, sitting on the knoll, stared out across the river.

"Them trees won't be there next year," Billy said.

Leon looked over at the man.

"I was watchin' you while you was lookin'," Billy said in explanation.

"How do you know?" Leon asked.

"Been doin' this a while now. Winter come, we go into the forest and cut. We bank the trees 'til spring floods come along and drag 'em downriver."

"What about these logs?" Leon said.

"These the logs dropped ashore as the flood receded. Crews go up-river and drag 'em in. Not many timbermen left after the first run. All the farmers go home, wood-hicks no more."

"The rest of us either savin' money or buildin' homes," Jake said.

"I'm goin' to have me a feed store," Billy said. "Buildin' it now. When the logs not runnin' and the mill not goin'."

Leon felt happy for the conversation. He didn't talk much, but listened and learned. Apparently he had arrived as the men who had gone upriver collecting bank-dropped logs were sending the timber down stream. The logs had been sitting on the banks of certain creeks waiting for the next flood. There would be three or four summer runs, each spaced out so that the majority of the logs could accumulate for the town. Only a few percent of the original take was left behind. Towns such as this one were built from that small percentage.

Leon wiped his plate clean with the last of his bread.

Billy, as he talked, stared at Leon, but didn't ask any more questions.

Jake talked about saving money for college again. Chuck and James discussed the homes they were going to build when the timber wasn't running. Much of their work was apparently paid them in cut lumber. Others talked about a better life, women, moving on.

Leon got up and dropped his plate into the tub. He had decided he liked sleeping in the side shed, and walked down and around the mill and up the bank. His things were there. His knife and gun and book and burlap bag. And his new bedroll.

On his way down toward the river, Leon felt the intense stare of Billy aimed at the back of his head. But, on the way up toward the shed, no one could see him. His body relaxed once he stepped out of site, but his mind continued its journey. He was a fake. He knew that. But did anyone else? Did Billy suspect it? Was he talked about once out of earshot?

Fireflies lifted like magic from the ground. The darker the area became, the more flickers appeared.

Leon sat in the doorway of the shed. The sun had set. The river sloshed. Fish broke the surface.

A breeze, out of the woods, down the river, announced the end of summer. Already? Leon thought. What would fall bring?

He lay back on the floor. Shelves filled with supplies rose above him on all sides. He couldn't read any of the labels in the dark. He'd try to remember to do so in the morning. If the right things were stored there, he could steal them and be on his way. Most of the men had been kind, but something about Billy bothered Leon.

The days wore on, similar duties, similar meals. Yet little things changed. Fewer logs came down the river and more building went on. The mill started to produce planks. Bark was loaded onto wagons and driven away to be sold somewhere unknown to him.

Whenever he was able to hear Jack and Harry talking, he realized they were somehow making a lot of money from the mill. They were happier and more vocal as the days wore on.

No one said anything about Leon's living quarters in the supply shed. That's where mill supplies were kept: spare parts, grease, oil, even hand tools. If Leon found his sack had been moved he knew no one meant any harm, but that it was in the way when they were collecting supplies.

On occasion Leon read at night, by moonlight. Jake would come over to talk sometimes, too. They'd sit together and discuss what they were going to do with their wages. Leon learned to make things up, to think bigger than he had ever imagined he could. Yet, deep inside, his relationship with Jake gnawed at him. It was based on a false understanding of each other. Lies about family and growing up became easier to make up, but more difficult to live with.

Leon secretly relaxed whenever Jake left for the bunkhouse. One night, before leaving, Jake told Leon, "Billy's been watchin' you and says somethin's up."

"What's he think is up?"

"Don't know. He's as mysterious as he is observant," Jake said.

"Maybe he should pay attention to his work instead of watchin' me."

"He don't mean no harm. Just tryin' to figure things out."

"Well there's nothing to figure. I answered all the questions I've been asked." Leon stood.

Jake looked across the river, then stood beside Leon. He didn't look at Leon. "Well," Jake said, "I'll be gettin' back."

The next day, Leon and Jake dragged planks to the builders. They used mules and ropes to do the job. The work was easier and didn't take the concentration that debarking took. After a while, Leon hummed.

"What's that you hummin' now?" Jake said.

"Don't know it's something I heard hummed once." Leon's thoughts turned to Martha and how she separated herself from the rest of the household. He understood how humming must have resonated inside her head and eliminated many other sounds. As he hummed, the river-sound faded, hammering noises were reduced to the background, and mule grunts and farts disappeared.

Humming did something more for Leon. It kept his mind from wandering. As he hummed, he often sang words inside his head. Even if he didn't know the real words, Leon made them up, as he'd been doing for years. Leon made up songs about building a new life as the other men were building a town. He made up songs about the river, and about sunrise and sunset. He remembered how Martha called sunset, the Lord's sweet song into night, and used those words in a song. And that was exactly how Leon worked. He alternated between holding everything on the outside at bay, by singing songs to himself, and letting everything from the outside in whenever he didn't sing to himself.

When he wasn't humming, he heard the rhythm of the hammers, the swish and hiss of the river's edge, the sliding of wood planks over the dirt, eagle calls, and men's voices.

As Leon settled into one part of his new life, other parts became more difficult. He found that he was doing what the roamers had done. He made up a new life, one that wasn't true, one that didn't fit his shoulders, and one that was too long in the legs. But the most uncomfortable thought was that he couldn't continue living like that. He knew he'd have to go.

"I grew up on a farm," he told Jake one day. "I knew the hands left in winter for logging jobs, and the war, but never heard much more about it. Some returned the next spring and some didn't."

"I'm surprised you didn't go. Or that they didn't talk about it more," Jake said.

Leon couldn't tell Jake the truth as to why that was the case; he couldn't say that he lived away from those men, in a white washed shack in the woods. He couldn't tell Jake that he only worked with the farm-owner's children, and wasn't to talk much with them. There were a lot of things a Negro child didn't learn because he wasn't around the right people, because he was expected not to ask questions.

"Well," Leon said, "they weren't talkers like here."

"Oh, I see."

"So, how many mills are there on the river?"

"More every day, I suspect. There's money in timber. There's train tracks, buildings, rafts, iron factories, furniture. Everything's wood. Pennsylvania White Pine. I hear there's a millionaire made every week in Williamsport."

"Where's that?"

Jake pulled a mule back toward a load of planks, then stopped it long enough to look Leon squarely in the face. "Billy's right about you. Somethin's different."

"I didn't listen when going to school," Leon said.

Jake shook his head slowly. "But you can read. And you speaks nice. You only listen when they teach readin'?"

"Pretty much."

Jake shook his head again. "Williamsport's upriver about a hundred miles. And on the other side of them mountains. They built a boom there that catches so much timber the whole town can live off it for ten years, except that instead some people gets millions and the rest gets jobs."

"Don't sound fair."

"It sound fair if you the one gettin' millions," Jake said.

As they worked, Leon thought. "How do I get across that river?" he asked. The way he had gotten across before was not an experience he wished to repeat.

"Wait, and I'll go with you," Jake said. "We can talk tonight."

For once Leon made a decision on his own. Instead of taking orders or wandering into the next situation, he had the opportunity to plan and decide. And Jake was smart. He would be a good partner for a while.

The rest of that day, Leon imagined all sorts of possible plans he and Jake could come up with, and each one ended in him becoming a millionaire, even though he couldn't imagine what that might mean for him. Perhaps he could save his wages and buy a small mill or start one himself. He could impress the mill owners with his reading ability and rise to be foreman. He could hire men and be a house builder for the millionaires, siphoning off their money as his own. Or, like Jake, Leon thought of going to college and becoming a teacher of reading.

In the afternoon, during the last meal of the day, Leon sat with the other men on the knoll.

The river shined like a mirror in the morning in one spot and fell black as a moonless night in another. The mosquitoes weren't so bad. A slight nip in the breezes pushed through the area. He knew the early signs of autumn as well as anyone. Not only did the air quality change, but its smell, temperature, and direction often made little shifts as if trying to sneak into fall without being noticed. Not so that evening. Leon experienced the telltale signs and that's what encouraged him to expedite his plans for the future.

Billy watched Leon, which made him very self-conscious. As Leon cleaned his plate with a last piece of bread, Billy said, "Somethin' about you."

Leon nodded and pushed the bread into his mouth.

"White's not an occupation."

"Neither is Zimmermann," Jake said.

"That there means Carpenter in German," Billy said.

"So what," Jake said.

"So," Billy said, "if he'd a said his name was Black, I'd believe he was black. Since he say his name is White, he look white. Name of White makes me suspicious."

"What you tryin' to suggest?" James asked. "That Leon here is White 'cause he say he is? And if he don't say it then he's black? That don't make no sense."

"Don't matter," Jake said, and Leon was happy to hear that.

"So what is it?" Billy asked.

Leon lifted his head and looked Billy straight in the eye as he had been learning to do over the past months.

Everyone sitting around fell silent.

"You'll figure it out." Leon stood and went to put his plate in the barrel. He heard the others laughing.

Someone repeated, "You'll figure it out," then sniggered.

Much later, the night fell hard, dark, and cold. There were no buzzing insects. Even the river sounded chilled.

Leon heard Jake stumble in the darkness as he approached the shed. Leon wanted to thank Jake for what he'd said, but didn't want there to be a question about his heritage. If Jake knew what color

Leon really was, Leon feared too many questions would be answered and too many stories would be questioned.

"Hey," Jake said as he approached.

"Hey," Leon answered.

"I been thinkin'," Jake said. He put his foot on the stone step next to where Leon's feet rested.

Leon looked up and could see Jake in the darkness, but not make out the details of his face. He wondered how the man found his way to the shed.

They both waited for the other to begin to speak.

"Well what are you thinking?" Leon asked.

"I been saving longer 'an you."

"Yes?"

Jake's foot shifted next to Leon's. "You know I'm savin'?" Before Leon could respond, Jake went on, "I could match any money you put up, but I need to keep the rest. I want this to be fair and square. I don't need to resent our joining up to get out of here."

"Okay," Leon said.

"You sure?" Jake sat next to Leon.

"I don't need you to be angry with me."

"I guess not."

"And I don't need to feel like I owe you anything," Leon added.

"I suppose that's true too."

They fell silent again, letting their thoughts move as slowly as they needed to.

Jake said, "That doesn't mean you have plans to leave in the night sometime does it?"

"No, but it means I'm free to do so if I change my mind."

"You won't change your mind. I won't give you reason to."

"I didn't think so." Leon leaned back onto his hands. "What are you thinking we'd do?"

CHAPTER 14

Plans have a way of working out once they are made in earnest. Leon and Jake's plan was no different. Focused attention is powerful, it adjusts all the daily decisions that are made, down to how much food is eaten, and how much is stored in a pocket for later. Jerky, when it's available, can last a long while. Both men became cautious while working. Any wound or muscle pull could reduce their ability to travel.

They were not slaves to the foreman. They could choose to leave whenever they wanted. But they were afraid to make their plan too apparent because it would mean that they'd be watched closer. It meant that if someone else came into town, they could be replaced, even if there were a labor shortage.

Whatever their thoughts, whatever their truths, the river called to them. The longer they worked alongside the river, the more mysterious it became. Although the land remained stable, like a man's soul, the river continued to flow. Where did it begin? Where did it end? What adventures lay between?

Some men get caught by the river's promise and others don't. For Leon and Jake, the urge to explore, to move on, grew larger as the days grew shorter in a bizarre but accurate balancing act between the physical and the ethereal.

In early fall, the weight of the scale tipped. Like a line drawn in the dirt, one moment a man is on one side of the line, the next moment on the opposite. A new world emerges. Change happens in the most profound ways once that line is crossed. For Leon and Jake, the scales were not perfectly balanced. Leon was ready to move on.

"I'd like to be settled and with a job before winter," Leon said.

The night sky was clear. The cold biting. Leon recognized the feel of the air, its smell. There wasn't much time to decide now, and he was ready to go.

"A little more money," Jake said. "In case there's no work yet. It's the end of the season. It's cutting time. There won't be timber in the mills until spring floods."

"I can't wait. What's another week, five dollars? A month, twenty dollars?" Leon never owned money and even three dollars seemed like more than enough to live on. He bought a coat and nothing more. He had plenty of money and no interest in things. Money was not the issue, freedom was. He had worked his whole life for other white men and the only real freedom he'd felt was when he traveled those few short weeks with the roamers.

Jake bit his lower lip. He scratched his head. He paced. "Tell you what? I'll go tomorrow after we're paid. We'll meet here. I'll hold our pot, so its together and even. I don't want you runnin' off early 'cause you can't wait. We'll put all the money together in one sack and use it for food as we get to the next town, and room and board while we're in Williamsport. We'll get jobs there and split what's left." Jake grew a beaming smile as if he had the perfect plan.

Leon was glad to go and might have gone alone had Jake not changed his mind and agreed to leave the next night. But as it was, he felt satisfied with the plan. He offered nothing more than a nod in answer.

Jake shoved his hand toward Leon in earnest.

Leon shook it, and the deal was set.

"Let me hold the money, so I can pack up for tomorrow."

Leon cocked his head, but relinquished without complaint. He reached into his sack and pulled out most, but not all, his money and handed it over to Jake.

The following day, both men ate more than usual.

Billy made another comment, but not in front of the others where he could be ridiculed. He said only, "Black or White," as Leon stepped past him.

Leon, gaining confidence in his lie, said, "Billy or William," then continued on. He would be gone the next day. Billy could do little to hurt him now. And being black wasn't a crime. His fear lay in being found a liar.

Neither Leon nor Jake worked as though their hearts were in the job that last day. The two of them ate together but separate from the rest of the crew. Once they were paid, they walked off side by side.

"We'll leave after dark," Jake said. He held out his hand.

"This too?" Leon said.

"That was the plan."

Leon hesitated, then eased his hand forward for Jake to take the money.

"You don't trust me?" Jake questioned.

Leon said nothing.

"Tonight, then." Jake wandered off toward the bunkhouse.

Leon would have wanted to leave before nightfall, but either way was fine. Perhaps Jake was afraid they'd be followed. The woods would be dark, but they didn't need to travel fast. And they'd probably only stay in the woods until they were out of view of camp, then they'd head for the river, their guide on the trip.

In the shed, Leon made sure he had his sparse belongings packed. He fingered his book. The overcast skies had kept him from reading by moonlight lately. He had bought a candle, but rationed its use to make it last.

He tied his blanket with twine. He stuffed his sack and its contents into the bedroll. He felt the extra money there, but did not count it. Security was in knowing its location. He thought about his dishonesty with Jake and wondered why he hadn't handed over all the money. Perhaps because whites had never shown their honesty to him. Yet, neither had Negroes.

Leon sat in the doorway and lay back placing his head on his bedroll. He listened for Jake's footsteps. The sky darkened and the stars emerged. Cold crept from the woods behind him and from the river in front of him. The scent of snow rested in the breezes carried from the north. Only a few weeks left, he thought, before the change in seasons became official.

The stars grew brighter and the air colder. Leon put his arms over his chest and soon dozed off. When he awoke, he recognized the feel of a new day. Morning was near.

Jake had never come for him.

Leon's knees hurt from sleeping with his legs hanging over the shed door opening. Bone chilled, his teeth chattered and his spine had what Martha used to call chicken skin running along it. He thought of checking for Jake at the bunkhouse, but decided against it. The others might awaken. His mind raced, but arrived nowhere. He needed to wake up more, get his wits about him. Then he heard someone coming. Was he wrong about the time? Had Jake fallen asleep too?

Leon grabbed his bedroll with his sack and money rolled inside. When he stepped outside, he saw Billy and stopped dead in his tracks. Only a pre-morning breeze moved as Billy approached.

"He left last night," Billy said.

"Who?" Leon said.

Billy pointed to Leon's bedroll.

"Oh," Leon lowered his head. "How did you know?"

"I observe. I been watchin' you two. Seen you give him your wages. Knew right then my suspicions were right."

"What did you come by for, then? To laugh at me?"

"I noticed him gamblin' on you, but it was too late. You wouldn't a believed me if I told you. Now, you can see on yer own. You don't have much people sense, do you? Never mind, I already know." Billy walked right up to Leon. "Try to be more cautious, more observant of the manners of others. Pay attention."

"I can't trust anybody."

Billy held out his hand and there was money in it. "Can't trust everybody," he said.

"Why you giving me this?"

"Trust don't deserve this treatment. Besides, I know you don't like this work. I don't know what you can do, but I can see this ain't how you gonna spend your life. I will tell you this, the lumber camps is no better. But you'll find out."

"No I won't."

Billy laughed. "That's all the work there is, farmin' in the summer, timber in winter, and buildin'. You ain't in Philadelphia, you know."

Leon didn't know where Philadelphia was exactly. "Maybe I should go there."

Billy laughed harder. "Not now you won't." He nodded toward the woods. "You best go."

Leon shifted his weight as if he were going to run, but didn't move from that spot.

"Black or white?" Billy asked.

"Black," Leon said, and instantly felt at ease. The river sighed. The branches on the trees relaxed. Leon's shoulders rested and his neck softened.

They stared at each another.

"Do I look black?" Leon asked.

Billy cocked his head, looking for something, Leon thought, that could help him with the identification, help him confirm Leon's answer.

"White," Leon said, and the familiar guilt came back. He lied.

"Your choice," Billy said. He waved his hand to shoo Leon. "Now, git. You'll make better time travelin' by day anyhow."

This time, Leon let his body run. He didn't look back. He ran, and for the moment was himself, not black or white, not Italian or Indian. Leon was a child again, innocent and free.

Even in the woods, Leon could feel the river. It had its own weight, its own sound and feel. Like a strong man, the river had presence and charisma.

He felt odd as he pulled away from the river, like leaving home. His love of the river was a true emotion. The river had saved him. It had been there while he worked and while he slept. It was there now, beside him. Yes, he could feel it as he could feel Pine Creek all the while he grew up.

After a while, Leon got angry with Jake for lying. The two of them had become friends and had talked and planned together. Had Jake lied about his mother and sisters? About college?

With each thought, Leon stepped harder and grabbed more aggressively to the tree trunks he used to help propel himself uphill. How could he get along in life if everyone he met was allowed to use him? Even his own family? He stumbled on a protruding root and fell onto one knee. His hand gripped a rock. He breathed in gusts of air. His throat hurt. He had forgotten water. Proof of his stupidity.

Leon sat and put his arms across his knees. He shook his head. The air around him stood still, even though he witnessed the wind playing in the upper branches of the trees.

He had to change. As Billy had told him, Leon knew he had to become more people-sure. He had to observe their every action. As the calm of his own breath returned, Leon sang a song about how he would watch everyone and notice if they lied to others. He sang how he would be the observer of all things dangerous and dishonest. After a while, his throat still scratchy, Leon headed out at a slower pace.

Without someone who knew the area, Leon had no idea where he traveled. The river was his only guide. The roamers had known the hills and creeks and farms. Leon did not.

Yet, he ran across what appeared to be paths, not roads. He couldn't discern whether they were animal trails or Indian trails. He learned to search for scat and prints, to notice hair on branches, rub marks where black bear had scratched or white tail deer had rubbed velvet from their antlers. By focusing his senses on the natural elements, he was amazed at what he knew. Like smelling the river and somehow knowing that it was about two miles off to his right. Smelling the air and noticing that snow was closer than he had imagined.

Rocks and boulders made traveling difficult. His ankles and knees took a beating. His second day out was uneventful, but more wearing on his body. He had eaten a third of his jerky and stale bread. He camped close to a creek that night. He caught two trout in his burlap sack, made a fire, and ate.

The sky filled with clouds. The threat of snow screamed down at him louder than words. Thinking about the snow and imagining himself dying, covered in white, under a tree, Leon recalled what he had learned about the timber camps. How farmers cut lumber in the winter. They dragged the logs to the creek banks to await the spring runoff, the flood that would lift the logs and take them to the river, to the mills.

He awoke shivering. A thin layer of frost lay everywhere along the ground. A sliver of ice had formed near the water's edge. An Eagle screeched. The sun's path across the sky lowered each day. Even so, a single ray through the trees felt warm to the skin compared with the remainders of the night air.

Leon picked at his jerky. He rolled his things together. He stood tall and looked upcreek to where he hoped to find the beginning activity of a timber camp. The first thing he'd do was buy a heavier coat with what little money he had left and some of the money Billy had given him.

With a purpose in mind, Leon made his way upstream, away from the Susquahanna. He had no idea what to expect. When might he run into a camp? Would he hear them working before he arrived? Or see them? He traveled hard that day. The air kept his body dry and cool whenever he stopped to rest. His body stayed warm, the energy coming from the workings of his legs and arms, from the speed of his movements.

More than once, Leon came upon deer and frightened them into escape. The deer surprised him with their speed and agility. The animals had apparently congregated in a particular part of the forest, as though this herd was the largest in the world. He had stumbled onto them by accident. They teased him. He knew how deer muscle tasted dry and gamy, the jerky salted to bring out the tang.

Leon rested against a tree and listened. More deer rustled around in the leaves ahead. Or maybe not. This sound was different. Something was wrong with the weight or pattern of movement. He crept up to a clearing. Jake held a fallen branch and raked over the area where he had built his camp. Fire burned in Leon's stomach and chest. His eyes bulged, taking in everything they could. He reached into his sack, felt for the cold metal, and pulled out the revolver.

Jake looked up when Leon stepped from the brush. "Don't shoot."

"I should kill you right now," Leon said.

"My family needs it. I had no choice."

Leon walked toward Jake and told him to sit. "I trusted you."

The fear in Jake's face turned to disgust. "You weren't honest. As soon as Billy noticed somethin' wrong 'bout you, I seen it too. I should-a telled the boss. You ain't nothin' but a nigger. Them other men, they cain't see nothin'. But Billy knowed and then I seed it too. You ain't deserved this money. Go ahead and shoot me if you want, but there's the truth of it."

Leon boiled. "I'm not a nigger," he said. "I'm a man like the rest of you. Billy doesn't know shit about me. You don't know."

Jake appeared to question his own words. "It's 'cause you don't say nothin'. Everything's a secret with you."

"A man's allowed his privacy." Leon stepped right up to Jake and shoved the gun not three inches from his nose.

Jake's eyes narrowed. "You ain't Leon White. If you anythin', you Leon with no last name. You got Hillary Carpenter with child, then run off." He tightened his lips.

"Jacob," Leon said.

"I knowed that you."

Leon squeezed the trigger until it went off on its own.

Click.

Jake's mind appeared to register the sound instantly. He slapped the gun out of Leon's hand. The useless metal flew into the leaves a few feet away. Then Jake brought his boot up and kicked Leon squarely in the chest, knocking him down the hill. "I'll git you." Faster than a frightened rabbit, Jake ran away.

Leon's chest hurt and it took him a minute to stand again. He went back to find the revolver. He should have asked for his money back. He should have pistol-whipped Jake. Nothing appeared to be the right thing to do.

The money had been gone the day before and it was still gone. Hillary was with child. That's why he'd been chased out.

Leon sat on the ground and rubbed his chest. He hadn't fooled anyone. Billy was right. He needed to transform himself, to observe and copy, or he would surely get lynched one of these times. Or he could be black. But Big Leon had died for Leon's chance to change his life.

It wasn't until later in the day that Leon learned the truth of the deer's migration. While he walked a ridge along one of the hills that paralleled the creek, the tree line thinned, letting more of the sun splash into the woods. Direct sunlight warmed the area regardless of the altitude. The insect population grew. The deer sightings subsided, but squirrels were everywhere, birds squawked, crows warned of Leon's arrival, flying together, noisy black clouds heading toward the river.

When he broke from the woods, he expected to see the remains of a harvested field, a farmhouse where he could beg for food and directions, but that was not what fell before his eyes. Leon came upon a graveyard. The death of a wide patch of forest stretched for more than a mile. Tombstones of tree stumps lifted from the ground. His heart sank at the same time his stomach celebrated. Somewhere near he'd find work, but he would have to kill the trees to get paid.

Leon had grown up in a shack nestled among trees. The trees had protected his family from wind, rain, and snow. Many of the songs he created as a youngster praised the trees. Here, they had been torn from their magical place and left soulless. He could feel the lack of trees as strong as he could feel the presence of the river his first day out.

It was unbelievable what men could do. It was powerful and sad. But it was work. Billy had laughed when Leon suggested he wouldn't work in a lumber camp. Billy had been right. Leon knew he had to settle that battle inside himself. Sensing the loss before him, he could only imagine what the war had been like. This expanse would be littered with human bodies instead of wooden ones. Perhaps his five friends had been right to make up their lives, to create new stories for themselves. After all, that is what Leon was about to do, too, unless he ran into Jacob. Then there would be trouble.

Leon searched the area for activity, for sheds, wagons, tools. Brush and bark littered the area. He headed downhill along the standing trees, planning to camp near the creek once again. From there, he'd go up creek until he hit the forest and go uphill until he found where next the cutting would begin.

As he made his way back to the creek, the two worlds called out to him, one in sadness and one in life. A family would wait another year or two, then move into the flat at the top of the hill. They would work hard to remove stumps and clear the land. They'd be sure to build next to the woods for protection, yet grow their crops from the cleared area. Leon knew that was how many of the farmers began their lives, by homesteading a cleared woodland area. He no longer wondered why their lives were sad though. How long would it take to wear the sadness out of a butchered forest? How many laughing children would it take? Squawking chickens? Squealing pigs?

The mosquitoes appeared to lift from the earth in the mild temperatures the sun brought to the clearing. Near the creek, Leon noticed a few logs and could see why they had been left behind. One was split. An uneven gouge twisted along its entire length leaving no visible appearance that a single board-length could come of it. Other logs were hollowed, having been the dying older branches of trees.

Leon did not fish, but ate the last of his bread and jerky. He decided that if he didn't run into a camp, he'd walk down over the slope and search out the river again. Snow hung in the sky, even though the sun's warmth tried to hide it during the day. Leon was not convinced. Once at the river, he could easily walk the riverbank for a few more days. He could walk at night as well, not getting the distance he'd like, but keeping his body heat up.

He fell asleep, shivering, once the sun dropped. He awoke several times to sounds that stopped once he woke up. Before dawn, Leon rose, rubbed his arms to warm them, tucked his mouth under his bedroll to breathe body-warm air over his chest and arms, then swore and got up. Packing his few things, and placing his hands flat into the warm coals that were left from the night's fire, Leon felt sufficiently ready to head out.

This would be the day. The gurgle and bubble of water relaxed his mind. The creek spoke to him, conversed in the language of water. He'd travel half the time upcreek and if he found no signs of an early logging camp assembling, he'd jog his way downstream toward the river. Every wrong decision stole a day from him.

Few insects buzzing about, continual bird-songs and squirrel-chatter, and the background tinkle and tuck of flowing water, kept Leon hypnotized. He stopped and focused on the power and strength still left in his legs. His stomach tightened, folding into its own emptiness. His arms felt numb, his hands sensitized. After he let out a long sigh, new sounds echoed through the woods, ones that didn't belong there. Had he unconsciously followed those sounds? He ran upstream where the water slowed, fanning out into a deep pool. Boulders lay visible under the clear water's surface. Trees bent into the pool and would soon become weighted down by snow and fall across the water to create a bridge that led only halfway across the creek. It would land on the submerged boulder and await the spring thaw when it would be dislodged by cut timber. The creek would be cleared again.

The sound of people talking grew as the sound of the creek and forest animals blended into the background. Leon jogged toward the voices stopping to listen every fifty yards. As the voices became louder, Leon was surprised to find that he got happier. By the time he left the creek bank and traveled uphill toward the conversation, he was humming and making up songs.

The land opened into a small clearing. Several small cabins sat in the open. All around them, the ground lay bare and muddy. Short logs created a path around the buildings. A group of men cleared brush, talked in loud voices to one another, and generally cleaned up.

Leon observed the men for over an hour, looking for Jacob. The coast clear, Leon stepped into the open. Two men dropped the brush they dragged and met him halfway into camp. One had black hair and the other red hair. Both looked to be Leon's height. "You're early," the black-haired man said.

"I felt snow coming," Leon said.

"Get your harvest in?" the man asked.

"I'm not a farmer. Worked at one of the mills downriver."

"That so?"

Leon nodded. "Several days downriver."

"Well, come-on in. You can help get camp ready. Built the long-house, you'll be staying there with a few of the men until we get a crew going. The cabins got built last season. Red here chased a clan of 'coons out yesterday and a family of skunks the day before.

Red produced a broad and toothless grin. "'At's the foreman's cabin."

"I don't mind a skunk once in a while." Leon said.

"Don't think you'll be staying in the bosses cabin though. You'll find the long-house just fine, I'm sure," the dark haired man said. He held out his hand. "Name's Jeb."

Leon reached forward. "I'm Leon."

"Welcome Leon. We can use some help getting ready."

CHAPTER 15

Leon paid for his first meal by the sweat of his brow. Not wanting there to be any doubt about his enthusiasm, he cleared branches, underbrush, and hollowed logs from the area long after the others had quit for the day. Jeb had to convince Leon to stop. "There'll be plenty to do tomorrow," he said.

With a satisfied smile, Leon dropped the log in his arms and followed Jeb back into camp. The men introduced themselves that first evening. Jeb and Red, Leon knew, then there was a Bradley and a Horace, a William and Sam, and Buck and Walter. They were all sizes and all ages, yet each looked as though he could outwork Leon in an instant.

Leon had never thought of himself as weak or thin, but these men made him feel like the lesser hand. They opened a place for Leon to sit. Sam on his right and Walter on his left. Buck served beans and bread. "Get used to it. This is what we eat." He pointed the serving spoon at Leon. "I take it you've never worked in a camp before?"

"No sir," Leon said.

"If you had, you'd a stayed longer with the mill."

Leon didn't like the sound of that comment. As he ate, the others talked about their families, their plans. Leon understood that these eight were not farmers. They worked for the Lasser-Fitzgerald Timber Company. They had hauled food and supplies to the camp, those that they could, and awaited another shipment soon.

Once the sun dipped behind the hill, Leon shivered with the chill. The air temperature, with all the green around, slipped down a good ten degrees in a half hour and would continue to drop as night bore down on the small group. The birds quieted, but the raccoons and squirrels protested the presence of the men by chattering and scolding from nearby branches. An owl hooted. The wind picked up.

"You might of been right to show up early," Jeb said in reference to the chill.

Leon told them what they knew. "Creek water froze last night. Along the edges. A deep frost settled in, too."

"Gettin' cloudy," Buck said.

"We'll get goin' in a few days when everyone shows up," Sam said. He cleaned his plate with the last of his bread. "Spring comes faster than you might think out here."

"Right now I want to be ready for winter," Leon said. "I need a heavier coat."

"We can fix you up," Jeb said. "Morning good?"

"That's good." Leon helped to clean up. He listened as the conversation waned and settled.

After a while, one of the men left the group to make the bunkhouse fire. Later, Leon followed as most of the others found their place in the bunkhouse. Leon selected a wooden cot that, in spite of the cold, for the night, seemed to get a lot of the heat from the blaze. He unrolled his bedroll onto the cot, then sat and read by the light of the flames. The men got quiet for a moment when he first pulled the book from his pack. He hesitated, wondering if he should slip it back into his pack, then the men started chatting amongst themselves and Leon relaxed. He read for practice as much as to learn. Reading separated him from others. Not many people he'd met could read as well as he could. He had no idea about this crew, but no one else leaned near the fire with a book in his hands.

Walter walked over to Leon. "Hey?"

Leon put his finger where he had been reading and lifted his face to Walter. The fire made him look even younger than he had originally appeared. It brought out the smooth features in his beardless face. Walter had his arms folded in front of him, holding closed a gray wool coat that Leon admired. Walter's hands were broad while his fingers were thin and delicate.

"I brought a couple of books if you'd like to borrow one," Walter said.

Leon closed his book on his finger and stood. "I'd enjoy that."

"Okay, then," Walter said.

"Yep." Leon turned to look into the fire.

"Well, think I'll go get some shut-eye for now."

"It's going to be a cold night," Leon said. He sat back down. The fire popped and spit steam in a hiss.

"In the morning," Walter said.

"Good night." Leon set his book down after bending the corner of the page. He tucked his legs up and held his blanket close. One man snored and others breathed heavily in sleep. Walter rustled around for a minute or two, then fell off to sleep as well. Although Leon lay awake for a longer time than his fatigue might suggest. He felt secure and safe inside the bunkhouse – and warm. A light rain fell outside, the varied sounds of drops hitting leaves; the ground, and the bunkhouse roof added comfort to Leon's soul. The fire hissed when rain made it through the hole in the bunkhouse roof where the smoke from the fire escaped. Leon thanked the Lord he slept inside tonight. Before slipping all the way into sleep, he heard a rustle of noise and growls stir behind the cabin. The winding down of his mind and the fullness of his stomach teamed together to draw Leon into a deep sleep where he dreamed of his mother touching his face and shoulders. Martha hummed so loudly that he couldn't hear his father, who watched what Bess was doing to Leon. Big Leon's eyes showed a terrible anguish, and he yelled undecipherable words toward Leon. Bess's strong arms pulled Leon from behind into her. Leon couldn't escape even though he knew he was stronger than she. His strength had somehow been drained. He tried to peel her fingers from his tightened stomach until suddenly there was a shot. A bead of blood appeared on Big Leon's forehead. Bess squeezed Leon and pulled him even tighter into her so he couldn't run to his father. Martha stopped humming immediately. The silence hurt Leon's ears and he screamed out again and again. "Let go! Let go!" He awoke.

The inside of the bunkhouse was black. There was some stirring and a formless, sleepy voice said, "Now, go back to sleep."

Leon rolled onto his back. He was sweating even though cold air had replaced the warmth of the fire.. The evil of his birth followed him everywhere. He held his eyes open, yet there was nothing to see. Several hours later, light came.

Leon was the first one outside. A thick fog lay over the area. Although there was no frost, the damp ground and air penetrated his clothes and chilled him to the bone. Work would help to warm his body. He collected wood to build a fire. He lit the first dry wood he found.

Buck rested a pot of beans over the fire. He stirred the bubbling mass with a wooden spoon that looked hand -carved. His hair stuck out in several directions. A three- or four-day beard scarred his chin and neck. "Another fire wouldn't hurt." Buck pointed to a second pit five feet or so from the one he leaned near.

Leon foraged for more wood. He sang an old Civil War song he had heard, "When Johnny Comes Marching Home", until he forgot the words. Then he sang, "Amazing Grace", which Martha used to sing to him on occasion. Dropping wood onto a pile and going back for more, Leon cycled through a number of familiar and unfamiliar tunes, then made up his own: "Run from my pappy/ run from my ma/ find myself in a wooden hall./ Axing the timber/ stacking it tall/ don't think I'll be home till fall."

The other men paraded from the bunkhouse one or two at a time until all eight were milling around. Walter and a third younger man, Horace, collected firewood from inside the forest, bringing it in armfuls to the clearing, and letting it drop onto piles near the fires.

Horace came from behind as Leon looped around camp. Horace stood like a rock, short and thick and grizzly. His arms were stumps. His teeth showed pits of black, like stars in a pale white sky. "When the cuttin' starts, we'll put up wood for the winter. That bunkhouse could use some all-night fires."

"I noticed the racks along the cabins," Leon said.

"We'll fill 'em to the brim soon."

"You work here before?"

"This my third year." Horace said while the two walked. "Come from Ohio, clear across the Western half of Pennsylvania to get here,"

"Why?"

"My daddy and two brothers dead in the war. I's runnin' from that memory, plain and simple. Found myself here. Jeb and Red took care a me, let me work."

"What do you do the rest of the year?"

"Odd jobs. Sometimes mill work, sometimes farm work. I like that nobody owns me.

They dropped their loads and Buck told them to stay. "Beans is ready."

Leon sat next to Horace. Buck filled a plate and handed it to Leon.

"So, Leon," Jeb said, "you a singin' man?"

"Suppose I am."

"You learn those songs from home or from war?" Jeb had some gray in his short beard and his eyes were big, wide slashes across his face.

"All over," Leon said. "I have a memory for sounds. Hear a tune once and I own it. Not always so lucky with words though." He met Jeb's eyes. Leon let a calm step into him.

"Wondered," Jeb said.

Leon knew Jeb wasn't finished. He didn't know what it was Jeb was getting at but waited for the next comment.

Red spoke up, though, blocking what appeared to Leon to be a purposeful pause on Jeb's part. "It's good singin'," Red said. "I, myself, could never carry a tune in a bucket, but I can hear a good one. My ears is smarter 'an my voice."

Jeb said to Leon, "Some of those songs from Negro workers, you know?"

Leon wiped the last of the bean sauce from his plate with a piece of bread. He stuffed the whole sauce soaked lump into his mouth. When he saw that Jeb was about to speak again, Leon held up his hand as though he would answer once he swallowed. It stopped Jeb long enough for Leon to think.

Leon gulped. "A lot of the songs I learned from Negro workers." He swallowed a second time. "Then there's the war songs I heard, even though I didn't go to war, and love songs. I don't like them much."

"He got the singer's memory," Red said.

Jeb sat back. "Well, you sure got a pretty voice. And I don't mean pretty like a woman, but pretty like a man."

"Thank you," Leon said.

During the long work-day, Leon kept discussion to a minimum by singing. Once in a while, when a tune was learned, Walter would sing along. Sam too would sing from time to time. They even learned Leon's made-up songs like they were real ones. It wasn't until several days later, when the camp filled up that one of the men, Bradley, produced a harmonica and let it cry out a tune at night, usually as everyone settled down to sleep.

In no time, winter dropped by for an extended visit. The routine of hard work brushed the days away two at a time. Wages accumulated but the men had nowhere to spend it but in the camp's supply store. And there wasn't much there. Leon bought a wool coat and a second blanket, an Indian blanket that a trader had brought through.

The forest makes new sounds in winter, not merely muffled, but new. As the trees were cut down, "... in their sleep," as Jeb said once, the clearing made a different sound altogether.

Leon had saddened at Jeb's words, almost to tears. His repeated dream with Bess and Martha and Big Leon made him want to die in his sleep, but he always woke. Did the trees have nightmares and never wake from them?

To Leon, the sound of a tree falling stretched through the forest like a scream. Every time he heard that scream, he saw his father's face lying in the grass and mud. Like a sledge hitting a fence post, that image pounded into Leon's head a hundred times a day. Big Leon's face reminded Leon of his heritage. Half black, half white, all the rest a lie.

The loud screech and scream of the trees, the crack, crack, crack – like shots from a musket – breaking limbs as it falls and hits the frozen ground. Snow, leaves, and dust burst into the air, and a great pain backed by muscle hammered into Leon's memory.

Every day Leon dreamed of getting finished with this segment of his life. Every night he dreamed of his mother's attack from behind, taking her guilt out on Leon, taking her hatred of Big Leon out on his son, who wasn't really his son at all. Everything a lie. The world built from lies and cheating, from revenge and hatred. From evil. And Leon was that evil, and he couldn't run from his dreams.

Some days he sang all day making up words to fill all the space inside his head for memory and to burst the song loudly enough to cut short the screaming of the trees. Leon lived a dead life by day and at night dreamed a living death.

The work in a lumber camp could be varied daily. It took eight to ten men to stack tie, buckle, and mule-haul logs down the hill. Another half-dozen stacked the timber ready for the spring floods. Cutting trees were done in stages, trimming them, hauling brush, debarking. The camp maintenance for all those men was organized by a rotation of four. Fires, meals, medical care. The camp was a city of muscle and sound, a metropolis of activity geared toward death. And for Leon, it was a fearful and dangerous world where the work at hand was destruction. Every man's death or slash indicated how the forest fought back. Leon sang to the forest. He apologized to the logs as he obediently stripped the bark from the smooth wood.

Leon did a thousand jobs in one season. He didn't know whether Jeb moved him from job to job because he lacked the skill for any or because he could learn each easily. Or did Jeb move him from duty to duty because the man recognized Leon's difference, his separation, and the job-switching made it easy on Leon?

Sucking in the frozen air as he worked kept his lungs clear, dry and in pain. Debarking became more threatening because the cold numbed every inch of his body. Leon witnessed a man slice his own leg and not notice. Fingers were cut completely off, arms gouged. The kickback from a tree knocked one man back twenty feet and into another tree, killing him. Every day that Leon worked reminded him that he had made it through the previous day. Some of the men claimed to be 'too mean to die' and that led Leon to thinking that he was too evil to die.

He couldn't explain the evil any more than the others could explain their meanness. None of the men appeared to be overly mean, especially those who claimed it.

Leon decided that it was a personal meanness, like his evil was a personal evil. Only the person himself could know the truth. Leon had enough evil happen in his life that he often felt he fit easily into its palm. He vowed never to do this work again. He didn't know what he would do, but he knew what he'd refuse to do. Song was the only thing that helped to reduce the emotional or physical pain.

Horace and Walter sidled up to Leon on many occasions.

"I love this work," Horace once said.

"I love the pay," Walter countered.

Looking at Leon, they waited for what he loved about the camp, the work. "I'll love it when it's over," Leon said.

They all laughed, including Leon.

"I believe you," Walter said. "It don't feel like you belong here even as I watch you do the work. I don't really belong either," Walter said. "I do it because it's good payin' work."

"Do you like farming?" Leon asked.

"I do. I like growing things better than cutting things down."

Horace slapped his knee. "You wouldn't be groin' nothin' unless we cut the trees first."

"That's not true," Leon said, surprising himself.

Horace didn't like the comment and Leon could see it in the man's face. "What land is there?"

"Maybe you're right," Leon backed down.

"Don't stop there," Walter prodded. "I agree. There're valleys and flatlands all over this country."

"Flood planes you mean." Horace spit into the fire and it sizzled. The night sky threatened a third night of snow, perhaps the last until the spring onion snow.

Leon looked forward to the end of winter. Perhaps he could leave early.

"Help me here, Leon." Walter put a hand on Leon's shoulder.

Leon didn't care to help Walter uphold his view of the land, even if Leon agreed. "Don't know for sure," Leon said.

"You said it singer-man, now back it up. You think I don't know nothin' 'cause I don't read every night like you?" Horace said.

"I can't back it up," Leon said.

"Won't," Horace said.

"Let 'im be," another man said from across the fire.

Horace shoved Leon with both his stubby arms, then stood up.

"Fight!" someone yelled.

"Not a fight," Leon said.

Horace shifted back and forth as if he were getting ready to box.

Leon looked away. If Horace wanted to fight, it would have to be behind Leon's back.

Then Leon felt a solid slap to his ear. The sting intensified in the cold air. His eye hurt too, where a finger had wrapped around and poked it. He fell to his side and stayed there.

"Coward," Horace said.

"Shit," Walter said.

Leon sat up slowly. It was quiet except for the snap of the fire. "You win," Leon said.

Horace bent down next to Leon's ringing ear. "No, you lose." Horace walked away.

Walter patted Leon's shoulder and shook him gently. "You all right?"

"I'm fine."

"Why'd you let him do that? You were right."

"Right or wrong wouldn't change him," Leon said.

"I don't understand you," Walter said. "You should stick up for yourself and stop running."

Leon never thought that he was running, but now, in reality, he saw that was exactly what he'd been doing.

CHAPTER 16

The change in weather shifted slowly, then one day the sun felt hot. At night, the bunkhouse stayed warm longer. The soft morning air relaxed instead of sharpened the skin. Robins and wrens returned to the area and chattered in the morning. The odors turned organic. The creeks filled. Spring thaw and mixed rain and snow filled the runs to brimming. The water cut new paths into the soft ground.

The men got grumpy. They tested one another. Leon found he couldn't hide from the general din of anger and stayed out in the rain until many of the men fell asleep. It wasn't so bad. He could do it for a while, but he felt he couldn't stay in camp much longer. In private, he told Walter about his plan to leave.

"So, up-river?"

"Yes. I need to get to a bigger place where there are more jobs."

"I'm going back home. I need to get crops in. We'll have one or two more snows at the best. Rivers will stay up, then floods will come."

"I know the routine."

"Now's the time to cross," Walter said. "Get to the other side of Bald Eagle Creek, stick to the river until you see a river raft. They'll take you across for pay. But not when the flood comes." Walter held out his hand. "Ever in White Deer, look up my farm."

Leon shook hands, the feeling of rough skin and raw muscle surprised him. Walter's softer personality didn't fit his rough body. "I'll stop by for dinner," Leon said.

"I'll make sure it's a hearty one. None of these beans."

For reasons he couldn't determine, Leon didn't want to let go of Walter's hand. He held tightly until they both became uncomfortable. Their eye contact and handholding turned suddenly from friendship to erotic, and then discomfort.

Leon thought to tell Walter that he'd miss him and that he was sorry about Walter's disappointment when Leon backed down from Horace. But he said none of it. That would have created too strong a bond between them. That would push against the handshake, the extended eye contact, the traditional way a man interacts with a man. The fragile connection could turn as easily into contempt or anger as it could deepen the friendship.

Leon released his grip and turned to head into the bunkhouse. By morning, he would be gone.

The sky darkened. It had broadened by the lack of forest. Its heaviness, too, had grown with the expanse and lay sadly over the clearcut.

Leon rubbed his hands together. They too were rough and callused. A hundred splinters had been pulled from them over the winter. The numbness of his skin had allowed great holes to be excavated by the use of his knife. Tender meat lay exposed in the bared skin of his fingers and palms all winter without notice.

Leon lay on his bedroll in the dim light. Heat from the dying fire spread through the bunkhouse. Walter had not followed him inside.

Sleep came smoothly and quietly to Leon's body that night. He awoke before the stir of another man, ready to go. Only his bedroll needed to be tied into a bundle, wrapped around the rest of his belongings. He paused next to Walter's bunk. He almost reached out to touch his friend as a last goodbye.

Outside, the touch of morning brushed against his face and arms. Leon knew the way. He had asked directions from several men over the course of the cut and held tight to the details. It was easy really: cross a creek, keep walking north, and cross a river. There were a few terrain problems that would take him away from the river, but north wouldn't change directions on him.

Leon passed several stacks of lath and shingles and had to stay above the log line next to the creek. They had cleared a lot of acreage, and it was hard to believe that the floods could carry that much timber without clogging and damming.

Morning turned to noon, and Leon stopped to eat bread. He thought to fish, but the creek mud and fast currents kept him from doing so. He brought enough bread for a few days. He could eat mushrooms as well, and birch bark when he ran into it.

The water ran beautifully and dangerously this time of year. Leon couldn't see bottom in most places. The swift currents churned even the rockiest bed to brown. He ran across a deer that had gotten snagged by errant tree roots and drowned. It's sinew and hide stretched downstream like a wiggling snake unable to escape. How many times had he seen that image in his life? The carcass was too many days old to be edible.

He continued on and before long got to a place where a great pine had been toppled. Its branches held to another tree on the opposite side of the creek, not eight yards away. He'd have to climb up the slope of the trunk. It was either that or continue upstream and pray for an easier crossing. This might be his best chance. Being less than a day out, crossing the creek now would allow him to cut across to the river.

Leon inspected the tree and then pushed against it to assure its secure hold in place. The branches at the top were tightly embraced with another tree's branches, which would make the final transfer from one tree to the other the most difficult part of the crossing. The pine branches he used to keep himself stable were rough to the touch. The needles had already begun to dry. They poked at his hands and forearms and even through his trousers. Leon put his knife into his mouth in case he needed to excavate a few branches while crossing. His footholds became thinner forcing him to squeeze the side of his boot into tighter and tighter spots.

The river raged below. The current rose and fell in great swells where huge rocks below the surface stood firm. He had no choice but to make it across. Each push through thick foliage got Leon more fatigued. The foliage was so thick that cutting the branches wasn't a viable option after all.

As he fought his way in and around the branches of both trees, something snapped. He held his breath. The tree dropped three feet and twisted before it held again. Leon gripped anything his hands could grasp without dropping his things. Luckily his foot shifted but didn't dislodge from between two branches. His face got scraped badly and the knife, torn from his mouth, plummeted to the bank next to the brown water. He leaned out of balance and struggled to right himself.

He had not thought about how his weight would affect the tree's stability. He couldn't make himself lighter, and was afraid to test the stability of the tree now that it had already appeared to be unsafe. The trees could twist apart from one another and dump him into the creek or drop him thirty feet to the rocky bank.

He looked back to where he'd come from. Returning was not an option.

Leon's grip tightened. His palms hurt. He held with one hand as the other searched for a secure hold. He'd rather hang upside down than fall. In this hand-by-hand manner, Leon worked his body through the entwined limbs until he reached the trunk of the upright tree, at which point he hugged to its trunk and rested. Then he climbed down.

His knife gleamed on the dead leaves and needles amid the dull colors. Leon retrieved it and took a moment, while standing on the embankment, to fill his mouth with bread to remind the rest of his body that the threat had ended. He walked Northeast, cross-country, toward the Susquahanna.

A prideful success swept through him. He could have died there. Hell, he would have died fifty times over the winter, but he hadn't. Living got easier after a few serious scrapes. It got sweeter as his journey edged on.

Leon didn't travel much farther before he stopped to make camp. Trees stood all around him. Even after the cutting that had gone on there were thousands more still standing. While working in the camp, it was easy to assume that the rest of the state had been pulled up by the roots or cut short as quickly as the area that he worked. It appeared natural that a clear path would lead to the next town, the only obstruction being the hills between them. But there were still trees, acres of them, as if the trees had fought back by shear number. In the forest, a calm lifted from the ground, a blanket of security rose. In contrast, cut areas became abrupt and scarred. This was true even though farmers like Walter pulled the stumps, raked out the rocks, cleared and plowed and planted the ground. By harvest the graveyard of stumps would be turned into golden grain, then bread. Livestock would grow fat. One crop would replace another. Even as the people grew old and died, other people would bud and grow in their place.

Leon traveled smarter than he once had. He built a small fire and boiled a tin cup of water. He collected peppermint leaves for tea and pulped them with a stick until the water turned dark. In it he dipped his bread for flavor.

After his light dinner, Leon readied his roll and leaned back against a tree trunk where he gazed upward at an angle and watched, 'The Lord's sweet song into night.' The colors streaked, depending on the density of the particular cloud the sun attached to. Amid the green of forest life melted the display of dusk. Eventually color faded, night arrived, and stars speckled the sky a sweet sugar between the clouds.

Leon stoked his small fire and built it up to last halfway through the night. His stomach asked for another morsel, but he went to sleep knowing that morning food would be better used.

His nightmares prevailed. They had become more regular through winter, but woke Leon quickly and with little noise to bother the others. Alone in the forest there was no one to bother. As if his dreams knew of his solitude, they allowed him to scream out. Leon awoke with the echo still reverberating around him.

The fire crackled. It leaned toward failure, so Leon uncovered himself and built it back up. He sat close to it, facing away. Once his back warmed, he turned. He wasn't tired. His stomach ached. He decided on one bit of bread and a small sip of water from the canteen he had bought early on in his employment. His bedroll, extra blanket, and wool coat kept him plenty warm while sleeping. The fire drove out the dampness. The trees provided a false security, the feeling of being closed in and safe. Leon slept once again and awoke to morning light and loud birdsongs. He had not dreamed a second time.

After tea and bread for breakfast, Leon killed the fire, covering it with dirt, and packed to leave.

Rather than travel directly over the hill between him and where he believed the river to be, he mounted a small ridge and followed it around the mountain.

The bread was not supplying the energy he had hoped. When he ran across an opossum, he grabbed a fallen branch to use as a club and chased it up a tree where, after a short climb, Leon was able to knock the animal over the head. When it looked stunned, Leon stabbed the opossum in the back of the neck, held it with his foot and dragged the knife around to the soft tissue at the animal's throat.

He let it bleed out by knotting its tail around a thin tree branch. His mouth watered and his body got ready for the nourishment. Leon defecated in a hole he dug. The acid already building in his body to digest the opossum had given him a mild case of diarrhea.

He built an early afternoon fire, aware that he was not making very good time. Eating meat would help to strengthen him for the next day's journey.

He skinned the opossum and buried the entrails along with the skin, head, feet, and tale. The fire spit flames up to meet the juices. The meat browned. Leon turned the hand carved spit and waited patiently for the meat to darken, for the blood to stop oozing when he poked at it, for the smell to turn from the raw scent of uncooked meat, to the sweet scent of a meal. He charred the outside. There were at least two days worth of food on the bones. That night Leon ate the heart and liver first. He disliked the taste, but knew it provided great energy and strength.

The meat didn't taste anything like the venison that often made its way into the beans at the camp. The opossum meat tasted sweeter and felt tougher than the venison.

Leon lay the leftover meat into the fire to be sure it cooked thoroughly through. With a full stomach, he sipped at his tea. He sang while one more night bore down on him.

The meat kept Leon warm all through the cold night. He awoke to see that a light snow had fallen, the last of winter, he was sure. He brushed his top blanket free of the snow. His body felt hot except for his face, which had poked into the air from the hood he had made of the blanket.

Leon let the mid-March morning creep into his clothes as he prepared for his next day's travel. He needed to continue around the ridge and eventually that path would lead him to a place that would overlook the river valley.

Despite the onion snow, the whip-o-wills and chickadees knew that spring had arrived. They sang spring's praises to the world. The deciduous trees would soon bead with new life, each day a million buds popping from the ends of branches like magic.

But for now, the sky spread a dark blanket over the area. The air warmed inside the room of clouds. Rain would bring water to runs and streams, which in turn would produce runoff to accumulate in the creeks. As the ground thawed and the water level rose, the river would begin to fill with timber.

Leon felt an urgency to travel faster, to make better time, but he didn't know Indian paths from deer trails. Underbrush became dense at times, especially close to creeks. The forest breathed with alternate clearings and dense underbrush. Opening to another stump graveyard, Leon circumvented the camp by traveling barely inside the woods, up the slope, and around the workload.

Leon stopped for a late afternoon meal. His legs hurt, and he breathed heavily from the near vertical climb he had been enjoying. He wiped his brow and hunched down to remove the opossum meat from inside his bedroll. He heard an eagle squeal, and peered into the sky.

Although he couldn't see the eagle, he noticed a thin tree line that indicated a ledge. Curious, Leon got up, grabbing his bedroll as he did so, and worked his way toward the opening. He stood in awe.

PART III

CHAPTER 17

Even with the clouds obscuring far hills, the valley spread for miles in browns and greens, brilliant yellows. The textures varied from mounds of fields left fallow, to the softness of sprouting grains. The river reflected gray from the sky. A breeze through the valley drove south, cooling the air. A combination of forest grove and farm field alternated across the land. Then there were the towns, one small and to the south, the other larger, much larger, and to the north. The northern town perched at a bend in the river and spread to both shores.

Leon sat on a rock and ate from his leftover meal. Alone on that rock, Leon felt relieved of his past for a while. The lying he had done fell away like caked dirt from his boot. His childhood, his father's death, and his mother's craziness, slipped over the edge of the long embankment, away from him, down, down toward the river to be washed away in a moment. His memories blurred and faded, replaced by the hope he saw in the panorama below. He wished desperately to be a new man. A white man perhaps. He had already taken on the lie for a year, why not hold onto it? Live with it? The longer he felt white, the easier he accepted the reality of it. And then there was his real father, his real blood, that meant his lie was already half true. Why hadn't he seen that before? He could live that life. He could be white. He was as much white as black.

Shale trickled down the embankment set loose somewhere below him. A chipmunk emerged, scurried into some brush and another trickle of stone rolled downhill.

Leon rose from his perch and gathered his things.

Before nightfall, Leon hiked a sloping ridge around and down for several hours, making little progress toward what he knew was his destination. Yet, somehow, before night came down hard, Leon walked into a flat clearing where he could rest for the night. The rain he had expected had not arrived. Even though the air had warmed during the day, the temperature dropped considerably after sunset. Leon built a small fire and bundled himself in his blanket before curling his body on its side to prepare for the cold.

In the middle of the night, a light rain fell. Leon woke, dragged himself and his gear into a grove of pines where he felt better protected, even though it was away from the fire. The hush of raindrops falling throughout the forest soothed him. The trickling reminded him of his childhood, snug in his own corner, near the back door of the shack. The peaceful patter of rain helped him to dose once again.

He woke several times to the warming air and stared into the night, listening, breathing slowly. As the light of day advanced, Leon finished the food he had left. The sun peeled layer after layer of fog from the valley floor, from the river, and from pockets of trees, which made it look as though smoke rose from the woods. In time, the sun hit Leon directly. The humidity stuck to him.

At the base of the hill, the brush got thick, briars reached out to entangle and strangle poison oak, sumac, and choke cherry. Leon walked along that wall until he found where animals, probably deer, had created a tunnel through the brush. He could only hope that the cut-through went all the way to a clearing rather than end in the middle.

He held his knife out and cut away small man-shaped areas where the briars encroached on the tunnel. Birds flitted all around him in and among the brush. The loudness of their voices kept out the sound of the wind.

He proceeded for nearly two hours, wondering every fifteen minutes whether he should retreat and find a creek to follow. But he continued through, never slowing more than it became necessary for him to cut his way farther in. Leon followed the animal's trail even though it turned and looped back more than once. He pricked his fingers often. His clothes got caught by the briars, which pulled on him like tiny hands trying to keep him from going on. But he broke through time and again until he poked his head, and then his body, through a final thicket to a grassy field, long and damp, leading to what he knew were trees lining the riverbank. Although the air had warmed the topsoil, under the dampness the ground stood frozen.

Leon skipped and danced and twirled his arms careful not to slip. He hooted with joy to be through the brush. The sun leaned heavily into noon. The loudness of the birds had remained in the brush. Leon smelled the clean river-water air.

A few hours later, Leon glimpsed a road on the other side of some brush. Where that road came from was a mystery, but where it headed was the south bank of the Susquahanna River opposite the great town of Williamsport.

He jogged, twisted his ankle and halted. His ankle ached. He rubbed his briar-pricked, timber-scarred hands together. They were rough and tender at the same time.

The late afternoon sky began to cover over with clouds. Breezes from the north chilled Leon's skin. This night, he was sure, he'd be inside.

Leon leaned into the road. Grass grew down its center and choke cherry grew at its edge. He limped. He couldn't place all his weight on his ankle. Occasionally he'd skip on his other foot to propel himself forward a little faster. That is how he made his way into town.

Five children saw Leon. They ran out to him. The two oldest looked to be ten, while the other three, ragged and energetic, were somewhere between four and seven, Leon guessed.

"Mister? Mister?" A dark haired boy with bowl-cut hair said.

"Yes," Leon said, but he did not halt his progress.

The children followed.

"You in the war, Mister? You get wounded?"

Leon slowed to reduce the need to limp so noticeably. "Nope. Twisted my ankle."

"Naw, you joshin'. You was in the war weren't you, Mister?"

"Ah huh," one of the smaller kids said.

"Why would I josh you?"

The five of them looked around at one another as though some silent communication took place. Then the spokesperson said, "You don't want no pity." He said it as if it were the most logical reason, as if the statement rang true.

"Well, I'm sorry to say it, but it's not true."

"Ah huh," one of them said again.

"Nope," Leon said. "I wish I could claim some pity, but I can't do it and be honest."

"Twisted then," the older boy said.

"Twisted. It'll be fine in the morning."

"Oh." That disinterested response was followed by, "We best be going." Then all five of the kids ran down the road, turned off into an alley, and were gone from sight.

Shacks and houses were set back from the road. Some were well-built while others were barely standing. Little paths broke off from the road and led down skinny, weed-lined lanes or into a small cluster of buildings.

Dogs barked. Crows cawed. A woman came out a doorway and threw a pail of water to the side of her shack. She looked tired. She looked right at Leon and then went back inside. Evening followed Leon into town.

When Leon got into the heart of South Williamsport, he passed several men who nodded. "Howdy," Leon said to each one in turn.

Another few people stood along the street and Leon asked for directions to where he could buy something to eat and maybe get a room for the night.

One man, dressed in a wool suit with a wool overcoat, pointed diagonally across a few streets. "About there. Go two more streets and turn left. Five more streets and you'll see the Timberline Pub. They got cots in the back you can rent, and food you can eat."

"Thank you sir." Leon held out his hand and the man took it reluctantly. Leon shook the man's hand hard, then went on his way.

Leon surprised himself when he got to the Timberline Pub and couldn't get his feet to take him inside. He'd never been inside a pub. He'd never been anywhere that he had to ask for a room and a meal even though he had the money to pay for both.

Another thing stopped him too. There was a sign, written plainly, the first word underlined. Still, he thought, after the war. It read, "Negroes use back entrance." So, Leon hesitated.

All things black and white ran through his head. Another man stepped past him and walked inside, then two more came up. One said, "Can't read?"

Leon pulled out of his daze. "No, I can read. I just. . ."

"I know. It's hard to believe, but there's still folk with an odd opinion as to who is part of mankind and who ain't. And here, in this Quaker-built town, makes it even odder. I figure it's their opinion. The food's still good." The man stepped back and waited a moment. "You goin' in?"

Leon stepped forward, white once again. White with a black heart and a black family. White with a black memory and a black father who died to save his life.

Leon didn't know what to do once he stepped inside. The man who had gone in before him sat at a table along one wall, while the two who came in behind him ambled over and sat at a more centrally located table.

Leon shuffled into the room, then made his way to the side and bumped into an empty chair. Embarrassed, he sat down and placed his bedroll on the floor under the table.

A middle-aged woman brought two steaming plates of food to a table, then walked over to the man who entered right before Leon.

"Biscuits and gravy," the man said.

The woman nodded and walked toward Leon. "Dinner?" she said.

"Biscuits and gravy sounds good," Leon said. His mouth rushed with anticipation.

The woman nodded at him as if he were a regular customer. Then she checked on the two men who came in after Leon. One of them ordered biscuits and gravy, but the other ordered chicken and dumplin's.

That sounded good. Leon would enjoy chicken and dumplings much more, but he couldn't urge his hand to wave the waitress over.

He couldn't moisten his throat enough to get sound out. He really wanted that chicken. He hadn't had chicken in a long time. Growing up they often had chicken. There were chickens cackling all over the place now that he thought about it. He had never noticed how many chickens there were in his life. It was too late, though. There'd be no chicken tonight.

Over the bar, three meals were listed on a slate. The chicken bore the most expensive price, then the biscuits and gravy, then beans and bread. A few tattered-looking men ate beans and bread, more who had biscuits and gravy, and only a few with chicken and dumplings. Leon could have been one of the few.

A moment later his meal came out. The plate emptied steam into the air. Leon reached out and took the plate from the waitress before she could set it down in front of him.

"Hungry?"

"Yes, ma'am."

"Want a beer with that?"

Leon had never had a beer, but had seen enough drunk farmhands to dislike the idea.

"Water, then," she said before he could answer.

"Yes, please." He looked at her, something he had to do consciously. "And, do you have a room I could rent?"

She laughed, then got more serious. "Ain't got rooms to rent, but we got a cot in a room you can rent."

"Then I would like one."

"You ain't asked how much?"

"How much?"

"Half-dollar."

"I'll take one. In fact, how about I stay two nights." Leon didn't want to stay two nights. He wanted to find his way across the river.

"Pay the bartender when you pay for your meal."

"Yes, ma'am."

She brought his water and set it down. She lingered a moment as though she were trying to figure something out and the answer was written all over Leon. When she deciphered the code, she shook her head and walked away.

Leon only stopped lifting the fork to his mouth for that moment the waitress hesitated. The rest of the time he managed to chew and swallow long before the next forkful entered his hard-working jaws. He scraped the plate the best he could without lifting it up and licking it. Then he downed his water. He sat back in his chair and glanced around the room. He took a few deep breaths and reached for the money from inside his bedroll. He pulled out what he needed without exposing what he had. He counted it out. He stuffed the rest back farther inside the pack, deep into his burlap sack. Leon grabbed his bedroll and stood. The chair squealed across the floor. Several people looked up for a moment, but didn't linger. It had been nothing but noise. Leon wasn't different. He wasn't anyone to be watched or concerned about, and he felt better about that than ever before.

As he paid for his cot and meal, the bartender said, "Cot's in the back. Room three. You can sleep anywhere there ain't already a body."

"Thank you, sir."

As Leon gathered his pack, the bartender looked over his shoulder and said, "Hey, you ain't left nothin' for Mary. You get bad service?"

Leon didn't know what the man meant, but he met a set of flaming eyes stuck into a square head with a week's beard on it.

"Left what?" Leon managed to say.

The bartender leaned closer to Leon's ear. "A tip for her good service." The man nodded toward the table.

Leon turned in time to see another customer leave a coin near an empty plate and got the message.

"I forgot," Leon said. He reached deep inside his bedroll and grabbed two coins. Without looking at them, he walked back to his table and placed the coins next to his empty plate. He stepped away quickly and went past the end of the bar and out the back door.

A dark hall led him ten feet where there were four doors, two on each side. A number was painted on each door. At the end of the hall was another door, which stood open. Leon guessed that it led to the outhouse.

He opened the room three door. Cots lined each wall. The center of the room opened to enough space for another three cots if needed. Not one window breached the wall space. Three cots were occupied. Leon took an empty one to his left. Next to each sleeping area lay a candle and three wooden matches. The well-swept room smelled of food cooking from the pub in front. One man's candle flickered in the half-dark.

Leon unrolled his bedroll in a careful manner, tucking his wages deeper into the burlap sack and shoving the sack against the wall. While maneuvering his collected wages, Leon pulled out his book and placed it on his cot. He sat and bent to light his candle.

The room was the most comfortable and clean space he had ever occupied. He had a full stomach, a cot to sleep on in a clean room, and a candle to read his book by. The air inside the room was chilly, but not cold, not in the open weather. Leon settled back on his cot. He raised the book above his head and turned slightly to catch the candle light across the page. He read.

"You. What you readin' there?"

Leon turned and the man in the other cot with his candle lit, across the room, had a newspaper in his hands.

"Henry Longfellow."

"A fine poet," the man said. Then he snapped his paper and returned to his reading.

Leon returned to his reading as well.

As the evening wore on, the room filled with boarders. Before Leon blew out his candle to go to sleep, he grabbed his sack and went to the outhouse. The acrid smell lifted from the pit. He sat down, protected from the rising wind. After finishing his own business, Leon stepped outside and around to the back of the building. He took a deep breath. Down over the bank rolled the Suquahanna River. The water sparkled as if there were stars in it. The familiar smell, the familiar sound, rose from the strength of the never-ending movement of water. Trees overhead stood black against the cloud-covered sky. A bright spot where the moonlight tried to creep through the clouds intensified the contrast between the black of the trees and the white of the clouds. It intensified Leon's feeling of being grounded in his blackness and also in the whiteness he had been forced to reach for in the clouds. The trees knew no more of the white cloud than the cloud knew of the trees. Always visible to each other, they could never really touch.

Leon went back to his cot, blew out the candle, tucked his sack next to his chest, and fell asleep.

The next morning, he woke to the sound of an argument.

"You stole my money!"

"What the hell you talkin' about?"

One man shoved another against the door.

Leon checked his own stashed wages and felt satisfied to find it in place.

The man with the newspaper broke up the fight pretty quickly. "Take this outside. It's between you two, not the rest of us."

Leon could tell that the accuser didn't want to listen, but the newspaper man stood over six and a half feet and was as broad as the door. He didn't look threatening, not in his demeanor, but he could have ripped both men's arms off if he had wanted to. The two arguers could see the big man's potential and decided to take their argument outside.

"Well, that's a night," the newspaperman said.

The others laughed.

Leon pulled his things together. The smell of bacon and eggs filled the air. He put his bedroll under his arm and went out back to the outhouse. It was occupied, and Leon could hear someone groaning inside, so he stepped to the back of the outhouse and peed down over the bank. The river seemed to have picked up speed even from the night before. Leon felt a stronger urge to get across where he felt there'd be more opportunity for work.

The noise that occurred in room three must have awakened the rest of the place. As Leon came back inside the other room doors leaned open and the men inside milled around packing their things and leaving to go into the dining area.

The pub was as much a dining hall as anything. Mary was back on the floor taking orders. Only a few people had food. The tables filled quickly. Leon sat against one wall, taking his seat before anyone else could. The newspaper man came through the back door, looked around the room, and headed for the same table where Leon sat.

"Mind if I sit here?"

"Not at all," Leon said.

The man strained the chair when he sat down. The groan of the wood sounded deep and gutteral.

"Name's Hugh. Hugh Richardson, 'cept my pa's name ain't Richard." He laughed and held out a broad hand.

Leon reached across the table. Hugh's hand was big and rough, even to Leon's battered palms. Hugh wore his dirty-blond hair a little long and shaggy. He fashioned two intensely deep blue eyes. His look intimidated, but his manner did not. Hugh opened a broad smile that cut through his oddly square head and showed off his mixed bag of multi-colored teeth, everything from white to black and most colors between.

Looking at that smile, Leon wondered what his own teeth looked like. He ran his tongue over the back of them and they felt rough. He rubbed at his face and felt the soft texture of a beard past prickly.

"I come here to work," Hugh said.

"The same," Leon said.

Mary stepped up to the table. "Breakfast, boys?"

Leon looked to the slate at the end of the bar.

"Ain't no specials. Just two breakfasts. Meat an' eggs," Mary said, "or bread an' coffee."

"Meat and eggs," Leon said.

"Bread and coffee," Hugh said.

Leon looked at the size of the man in front of him, then looked at Mary. "He'll have meat and eggs, too. I'll pay."

She turned away.

"Much obliged," Hugh said.

"That's all right. You look like you need the energy."

"Read in the paper there's jobs all over. Gettin' ready for the flood time," Hugh said. "There'll be timber flowin' soon."

"If you can read, you don't have to work with the other men, do you?" Leon said, his hopes exposed.

"Lot of men can read. Besides, hard work don't hurt nobody. Wages are good. Jobs is plentiful."

"There must be something else."

"I hear the mill owners bring their own men to the job, but the paper says there's openin's." Hugh paused, then added, "Bet you can get one."

Leon felt his face brighten. "I bet I can."

Mary headed for their table with two plates of eggs and bacon. "Coffee be right up," she said.

Both men dug into their eggs and each had two cups of coffee.

Hugh sat back in his chair at the end of his meal. "Easiest way to cross the river is to walk the tracks a little ways east of here."

"You thinking we'll go together?"

Hugh looked hurt right as Leon said that.

"I'd be proud to," Leon said.

Hugh's disappointment slipped away. "I'd like to travel with somebody smart for a change."

"You can read."

"I'm built for hard labor, nobody ever goin' to see otherwise. I'm used to that and don't really mind, truthfully."

"Well, if you don't mind, that's fine, but I'd rather not wrestle with dead trees."

"You be the right size to go either way. And you talk smooth enough to get what you want."

"I never thought of myself as talking smoothly," Leon said.

"Well, you do." Hugh slapped the table and several people looked up.

Leon liked the idea of himself as a smooth talker in the educated sense. Leon felt healthy having eaten, and felt qualified even though he didn't know in what. He got up and paid a dollar for breakfast and told Mary as he handed it to her that the rest was hers. She smiled broadly. Leon had no idea what breakfast really cost, but he was sure it was less than a dollar for the two of them.

He felt a little bad about paying for a second night in room three when he had no intention now to stay the night. But he felt rich and he felt lucky, and only the day would tell where those feelings would lead him. Traveling with Hugh, even for a short distance felt like the right thing to do.

Outside the Timberline, Hugh asked Leon for his name.

Leon thought back to the friends he traveled with through the woods. He thought about Jacob and wanted to end that memory. He didn't want any more questions about his name or what nationality he was. "Bob," he said. "My name's Bob White."

"Proud to be travelin' with you, Bob." Hugh patted Leon's shoulder as they headed for the railroad bridge.

CHAPTER 18

A chill air stirred songbirds to life. A cloudless sky called up insects from wherever they sit through the night, whether close to the ground or under leaves, against the stems of weeds.

The newly christened Bob White followed Hugh Richardson, single file into increasingly thicker underbrush. It wasn't long before the idea that Hugh could easily rob him that Bob thought to turn back. He slowed.

"You ain't tired already?" Hugh said. He stood twenty feet in front of Bob.

"Just thinking. How far is this bridge?"

"Not sure. Half mile maybe."

Bob rose onto his toes and stretched his neck hoping to see down-river.

"It's there. Bartender told me last night."

"I could pay for a raft."

Hugh walked back toward Bob. "Save your money. There'll be plenty to spend it on if that's what you want. The bridge will be just fine."

Bob stiffened.

Hugh must have noticed. He shook his head and turned back around. "I won't do nothin' to you. Just wanted someone to travel with."

Bob hurried forward. "Let me lead for a bit. It's difficult to see past you."

Hugh stepped to the side and Bob took the lead. In short order, his pack under his arm and the morning light dancing over the dew-moist underbrush, Bob began to hum, then to sing. His mind focused on his song.

Hugh hummed along with Bob's song.

A deer jumped from a place in front of them and both fell silent and stopped in their tracks. Hugh began to laugh. "That thing scared the hell out of me."

Bob led Hugh farther into the thicket where the deer had been and two more bounded off. Another hundred feet and a clearing opened to gravel and hard steel. Bob's heart raced. The bridge was there. Five hundred feet from the river, a road entered the area where the tracks lay black against the brown soil. "We could have taken that road."

Hugh stepped up beside him. "We could have, I guess."

The railroad bridge was open-sided, dropping into a cloudy, rushing river. Ice chunks sat piled along the banks and into ground protrusions. Some had jammed and locked themselves into tree roots.

Bob placed a tentative grip on a steel track, and the cold attacked his fingers. He pulled back as if burned. He stood and looked at Hugh.

"Don't worry, we can do this," Hugh said.

"There has got to be another bridge," Bob said.

"Probably, but we here now."

The gaps between ties were wide enough to fall through. "I'll go first," Hugh said.

The steel burned so cold that crawling might freeze their hands.

"I don't like this," Bob said.

"You want across?"

"I know. I know." The menacing river licked up and rolled under the bridge with great force.

"Don't look at the river. Don't look through the ties, but at them. They're about one stride apart. If you watch them, you'll step on them," Hugh said.

Bob shifted his bedroll. Then he put his arm through the twine that held it together. His hands were free. He put them out to his sides for balance.

Hugh laughed. He held his bedroll in one hand and stepped onto a railroad tie between two long steel tracks. "The first few steps there's no river." He began to walk.

Bob began to sing. "The river's my friend and savior you know/ it cries like a baby in winter snow./ It moves like a serpent all the way home,/ let it be kind and gen-tle." His voice rang steady until punctuated with each step. Hugh walked far ahead of him. Halfway across, a strong wind – cold as the ice along the rising riverbank – pushed hard against Bob's body and he thought he might slip. His voice got louder and his legs spread across two wide ties. Bridge planks ran under the steel, but there wasn't enough space for safe footing.

Bent like an old man, his legs crouched as if he were trying to sneak across the bridge, Bob stepped and sang an even motion across the wind-torn width of the Susquahanna.

Hugh held out his hand at the end of the trek and Bob shook it as though they had just met. The river roared behind him.

"Good job," Hugh said.

"I damned near pissed myself," Bob said, forcing them both into laughter.

"You got quite a bellow in you," Hugh said.

"It keeps my mind busy."

"Ain't never heard that river song though."

"Made it up."

"No?"

"Make a lot of songs up. In the moment. Then they go away." Bob rambled. "When things get bad or scary, I sing. If I'm making up songs, I'm not thinking the worst and somehow the worst doesn't happen."

They walked from the bridge, the river song waning as birds chirped loudly in nearby trees.

"Sounds like a philosophy to stick with."

"Perhaps it is," Bob said.

"Where you grow up?"

Bob stopped walking.

Hugh turned and nodded without stopping. "Don't need to tell me. I just wondered."

Bob caught up to Hugh. "I don't like to think about where I come from. I got out. That's all I know. Like I died and was born new. My whole life's new. I'd like to start with now."

"I suppose a man don't need to look behind him. Can't retrace where he come from. Can't change it none. I suppose a man can look ahead his whole life if he wants."

"Where are you from?" Bob asked.

"All over. Left home at thirteen just after a solid beatin'. My mama was cryin' but I never looked back. My pa threw an axe at the back of my head. Handle hit me square and bounced off. That's the last of it."

"I'm sorry."

"I take care of myself pretty well. No need for you to be sorry. If you ain't talkin' then maybe you had it worse."

Bob didn't respond.

Hugh didn't force the issue.

Bob and Hugh followed the tracks into a turn, then west into town. They veered off to a road with a sign that said Fourth Street. "I've never seen one of those," Bob said, stopping to read the sign.

"A sign?"

"A street sign. I've seen road signs pointing to the next town, but never a sign 'in a town' telling you where you're standing."

Hugh spit into the road. "Well shiny shit balls, you are an odd one. I'd a thought you learned to read in a big city to hear you talk."

"I don't know how I picked it up, I just did. The language, I mean. I just know what sounds right most of the time and what sounds wrong." He shrugged and moved along. Hugh fell in beside him.

A lot of shacks and boarding houses – some on the verge of collapse – stood along the eastern side of Fourth Street. A mile or so up, they came to a crossroads. Looking toward the river, Bob noticed a bridge. He poked Hugh's arm. "The bartender didn't tell you about that?"

Hugh laughed. "He did not. I'll bet he's laughin' all day today."

Bob shook his head. "Had one of us fallen into the river, it wouldn't have been funny.

After walking past several cross streets while heading west, some big houses lifted out of the ground like giants in a circus. Bob's eyes bulged and his head swiveled on his neck as he tried to take in the whole town at once.

Hugh did the same. "Wow," he said. "I only heard about this."

"Some of these people are rich beyond what you can imagine," Bob said.

"And we're goin' to grab some of it." Hugh's face lighted up like a huge square lantern, his teeth wet and colorful. "Why I bet there's more work than there are people."

"I bet you're right," Bob said.

There were general stores downtown, and restaurants, and dance halls, and more rooming houses. There were shacks and mansions, building supply stores, and even a news and bookstore.

The closer to the center of town they got, the more people they encountered. Bob and Hugh must have made an odd pair because people would turn as they walked past. Bob watched with interest and smiled only if he made eye contact.

He wasn't sure what the people thought, but Hugh sure appeared to like the attention. He would turn and say howdy. He'd nod his head, or wink at a lady or child.

At the far other end of town, the boom built into the river took on its own industry and enterprise. Bob could feel the weight of it before they reached it. Saw mills stood back from the riverbank, stacked lumber made piles everywhere. The railroad tracks passed near the stacks and into the wilderness beyond town.

Hugh led the way up the hill to an office over the mill shed. Once there, Bob knocked on the office door.

"Come in," a nasty voice said.

Bob and Hugh entered the room. A man sat behind a wooden desk. His bushy hair curled on the ends. He wore a face full of freckles so dense that in some areas they merged, making brown patches. "Lookin' for work, are you?" He shoved some paperwork aside and folded his hands in the center of the desk, feigning patience.

"Yes, sir," Bob said.

"Not much yet. Maybe another week, maybe another month."

"Looking at the river, I'd say sooner than a month," Bob said.

"You a rafter?" The freckled man perked up, one eye shaded in a dull red blotch like a hunting dog might have.

"No, sir. I just watch the river."

The man laughed. "I thought you wanted work?"

"He'd work out in the office," Hugh said.

"Oh?"

"He's a good reader and a good speaker. He might even make a good shift foreman he's so organized."

"Shift foreman?" the man said. He waved the idea off. "Too young. I have a steady crew that shows up. Farmers livin' all around here who done this before." He motioned beyond the city boarders. "And my three brothers' all the foremen I need and more. I can use log rollers, mill handlers, and flatbed loaders, but not today."

"Can I sign up today?" Hugh asked.

The man opened a notebook and turned it toward Hugh. "You can."

Hugh bent over and signed his name below several others. There was a space for an address. "Ain't got a place to stay yet."

"Fill it in later. I got your name. That's all I need. You'll be back."

The man slid the book over to Bob.

"I'll think about it," Bob said.

"You do that." A freckled hand reached out and closed the signup book.

Hugh left the office with Bob behind him. "What the hell you thinkin'?" Hugh said.

"I don't know. I stepped inside and my whole chest and throat tightened. I couldn't imagine working there. Something inside me wouldn't let me sign that book."

"He won't sign you on now. Not unless he gets desperate. The list could drag on for pages before the one I signed. He might not even get to our names.

"Your name."

"My name, then. What do you think you're going to do in a lumber town if you don't want to touch wood?"

Bob paused on the decline toward the river. "Look at this town. There're stores that need help, shipping clerks, bartenders."

"You know anything about any of that?"

"I can learn," Bob said.

Hugh shrugged his shoulders. "Even if you'd a signed, you didn't have to take the job when it was offered."

"This way I can't take it."

The light from the sun had lowered and the early dark of spring headed into town. Even more people appeared in the streets, some obviously tired after a long day of hard work.

Bob smelled food cooking and his mouth began to water. "Let's eat," he said, "and find somewhere to sleep."

"I'll buy you dinner, since you paid for breakfast."

"That's okay," Bob said.

Hugh looked indignant. "I can do it. I got money."

"Then why..."

"I'm careful is all."

"You got me here safely. Let's call it even."

"Deal. I'll eat what I want and you do the same."

"I don't want you being upset," Bob said.

"Then let me take care of myself."

"You've been doing it long enough to know how. I suppose you can keep doing it," Bob said. Out of courtesy, Bob chose a place that looked inexpensive. Hugh appeared to be fine with it. "There was a place I saw that had a sign said, 'Thirty Bunks.'. We can stay there tonight."

"That's okay for now." Hugh stepped into the restaurant Bob had suggested. "Let's pray for rain," Hugh said under his breath as he walked inside. "And a fast thaw."

Bob was concerned for his new friend, but no more concerned than he was for himself. Why he refused to sign in for a mill job was a curious memory now. The thought came with doubts about what else he could do. At least he knew wood.

Bob glanced around the room and there wasn't one black face. He didn't remember seeing one in the streets either. Yet he was there. Why? How could he be there and no other black man could?

He dug into his mashed potatoes and gravy. He had decided to order whatever Hugh had ordered. Although he would have wanted meat with his meal, Hugh did not spend the extra amount. Bob went along, but now wished he hadn't. He also wished he hadn't looked around the room. He felt separate. He felt black. Not black like Big Leon was black, but black like Bess. Black like the pickaninnies he grew up with. Black like Martha. He turned to look outside. The air coming into the restaurant brought a chill. A glimmer of light reflected off the railing. *The Lord's sweet song into night*, he thought.

As quickly as he felt separate, Bob's shoulders sagged. He wasn't himself, didn't feel as though he could be himself, whoever that was.

In a day, Leon had disappeared and Bob White had been born. But who was Bob White? It was a confusion he had lived with his whole life regardless what name he went by.

Hugh tapped a spoon against Bob's plate. "You goin' too deep in there. Your whole face change right before my eyes."

"I was thinking."

"You were traveling. Probably somewhere you didn't belong."

"Why do you say that?"

"Your look. Wasn't good."

Bob put a glob of potatoes in his mouth.

"You looked defeated," Hugh said. "You looked sad. It made me sorry I asked about where you from. I know you were headin' there."

Bob looked up at Hugh's big head. "I was thinking."

"How about we sleep outside for a few days?" Hugh said.

Bob shook his head.

"Maybe not tonight, but in a week if there ain't no work."

"There'll be work. I can feel the river rising. I can smell the ice melting."

"What will you do?"

Bob shook his head. "Don't know yet. But there's work here. I just have to find it."

"I believe you will, Bob White, I believe you will."

After dinner the two men took their bedrolls and packs and hit the street again. The air belted them at every cross street, clapping against their ears in a fury. Cold and warm at the same time, the air brought rain. The clouds thickened, then darkened with dust particles. The leaves on trees turned up. Those few in the street hurried somewhere with a purpose. Bob and Hugh were no different.

At Campbell Street Bob led the way to the Thirty Bunk sign. They climbed a few stairs and walked in. A man in a black wool coat and beaver-fir hat said, "Three bunks left." No greeting, no introductions.

"Two," said Bob. "For the week."

"Two dollars each. 'Til next Wednesday."

Hugh and Bob paid the man.

"In the back. No fightin'. No arguin'. No pissin' inside."

Bob wrinkled his nose and followed Hugh. The room wasn't very big. Straw bunks were built into every wall space except where the door stood. A second shelf of bunks was built above the lower ones. There were two candles lit in the middle of the floor. The three available bunks were all bottom bunks, two of which flanked the door. Hugh and Bob took those two.

The room smelled like urine. In the dim flickering, the floor appeared stained. Most of the men were lying in their bunks staring above them. One man struggled to read a newspaper in the near darkness. Two men, both in top bunks, lay head-to-head whispering and letting out with quiet laughter from time to time.

Bob unrolled his blanket and placed his burlap bag next to the wall. He curled next to it. He had almost fallen asleep when Hugh grabbed his shoulder. Bob jumped.

"Hold up," Hugh said. "I was thinkin'."

"What about?"

"About you can sing."

"So?" Bob wondered where Hugh was headed with the comment.

"You can sing. That'd be your work."

Bob made a face and rolled back over. "Nope."

Hugh kneeled there for a few minutes as if waiting to continue the conversation. Then Bob heard him get up and go back to his own bunk.

CHAPTER 19

Rain pelted the bunkhouse and saturated the roof. Bob woke to the sound of dripping on several occasions. Once he woke to the sound of someone leaving the room and a few minutes later returning. He dreamed of Bess touching him and awoke hard. Guilt overtook him, and sorrow. When he tried to replace the image of Bess with thoughts of Hillary, his body reacted by going flaccid, all adding to his confusion and disgust. He slept again only to awake from another dream. This time, he sawed timber, slept under trees, and sang. In each vignette the background reverberated with a continuous humming. Morning arrived much too suddenly. The door to the bunkhouse had been left open and the smell of rain-soaked wood and weeds poured into the room stirring the residents.

Bob stretched his legs and felt for his sack, which lay beside him. A few men grumbled as they woke. One man shoved another who got too close. "No fightin'," someone said in a gruff morning voice.

Bob rolled his blanket while lying in his bunk. He packed his sack inside the blanket making sure he could reach in to grab money if what he had in his pockets wasn't enough.

Hugh wasn't in his bunk when Bob peered around the door. Had Hugh abandoned him? Bob stepped into the morning, tired from the fitful night. "Hey," Hugh called from near the outhouse door. Bob nodded and walked toward him. The outhouse had a terrible stink coming from it. "I think someone was deathly sick last night," Hugh said.

"I heard someone go out."

"Didn't hear nothin' myself."

A man left the outhouse and Hugh stepped inside.

Bob stepped up into Hugh's space. Two other men now stood behind him.

Once inside, Bob pulled his shirt over his nose and mouth. Someone had gotten sick and the odor practically made Bob sick as well. He did his business, held his breath, and walked out, stepping quickly to put distance between him and the outhouse.

Hugh waited. It had been two days and Bob wondered why Hugh had attached to him. Bob wasn't used to having someone with him all day like that, at least not when there was nothing particular going on. If they were working together then it would be fine. If they were traveling, on the move, it would be fine. But wandering around town with little on their minds gave Bob the oddest sensation he had ever had in his life. Like he had picked up a stray dog. Bob didn't know what to say to Hugh much of the time. He'd already learned that Hugh had been on his own for years, and either enjoyed labor or felt that was all he could do. Regardless which way Hugh felt, he had come to terms with it and appeared satisfied.

Bob considered his rebirthing in the river where he had essentially died, going in black and coming out white. There was his new name, now. Where had that come from? Bob White had been born in an instant. Already the story of Leon faded as though it were only a story. Except in his dreams, his past became foggy and thin, weak and elusive.

Hugh focused on work and encouraged Bob to, "Go in and talk to the man," whenever he noticed a possibility.

Time and again, Bob listened, went into establishment after establishment, and was turned down over and over again. His first interview was short. A stubby man with greasy hair stood at the counter of a feed store. The words on the sign were misspelled. The sign said 'Halp Wantd.'

Bob, on Hugh's insistence, stepped to the counter. Before the man could say anything, Bob said, "I'm here to help." He pointed to the front where the sign hung.

"You know feed?" the man said.

"I know it, but I never sold it."

"What you know?"

"Animals eat it," Bob said.

The man looked at his own shelves – bags, boxes, buckets, and bins. "You know the difference between oats and barley, between hay and straw?" the man asked.

"Grew up on a farm," Bob said, then he looked at Hugh to see whether he took that bit of information in.

The man behind the counter also glanced at Hugh, then back to Bob. "You lyin'?"

Bob turned back. "No. I'm not."

"Then why you give your partner that look?"

"What look?"

"I don't need the help right now," the man said. "I'm thinkin' I'll need help in a week or so. When the town fills."

Hugh grabbed Bob's arm and pulled him around. Bob followed without resistance.

"The place was filthy," Bob said. "Did you see it?"

"Sour grapes," Hugh said.

"What?"

"You ain't never looked for no job, have you?"

"I've worked on farms and logged all winter," Bob said.

"You ain't never 'looked' though, have you?" Hugh said again. "'Cause if you have, you're no good at it."

Bob gritted his teeth.

Hugh slapped Bob's shoulder hard, sending a sting through his arm and into his neck. "Listen to me," Hugh said. "You got to first introduce yourself. Look 'em in the eye and say, "I'm Bob White. Glad to meet you, sir.' Then you tell 'em straight out. You say, 'I'm lookin' for honest work.'"

Bob pulled free of Hugh's lingering hand.

"Okay. It's fine if you don't want work," Hugh said.

"I want work."

"Then why do you refuse work yesterday and act like a damned ass today? I'd say you're not wanting very hard."

"I don't want to be a logger any more. Or a rafter or a roller or a stacker," Bob rattled off just in case Hugh didn't hear in his voice how he felt.

"And here we are in a loggin' town. Where in hell do you think all this money comes from? Why do you think half this town is here?"

"Half," Bob said.

"Well if you want to be part of the other half of the town remember where the money comes from. Lumber. And remember whose payin' you in the long run. Lumbermen."

Bob felt a few drops of rain land on his arm. He looked up. "It's going to rain again."

The two of them walked silently until Bob cleared his head. "Jobs have just been there. I never had to talk my way into one."

Hugh spit on the ground. "You're in a new world. Once the floods hit, this town will be totally different. Maybe then someone will drag you off the street and beg you to work, but you won't have no choice in it, all the best jobs will be filled."

"I'd like a choice," Bob said.

"You want me to teach you?"

"I'd appreciate it."

"Then you do as I say."

The rain was intermittent and sparse. "We have a little time," Hugh said. "We'll pick places you don't want to work."

"Why?"

"So you can practice." Hugh walked Bob through the important interview steps as he saw them. After he tested Bob a few times, they entered a cobbler's shop. There was no sign for help.

One man stood behind and off to the side of the counter. He pounded a tack into a boot sole. The man looked up. "Be with you," he said. After several more nails were forced into place, he pulled the boot off the anvil-like fixture it was draped over. He grabbed the boot's mate and placed the two together on a shelf next to him. "What's the problem?"

Bob held out his hand. "Name's Bob White and I'm looking for some honest work."

The man stared at Bob's hand. He wiped his hand over his apron, then placed the fingertips of each hand in a pocket along the front of his apron. It looked as though he were scratching his own belly. "Barely enough work for me. You don't see no sign do you?"

"No, sir," Bob said. "But when the town fills up, you might need help."

"When the town fills up I'll have a full day's work." The man nodded. "Thank you for comin' in. If you ever need yer boots repaired, I'll be here."

Bob lowered his hand. "Thank you, sir." Back on the street, he said, "You make me nervous. Watching and listening from behind."

"I have to see what you're doin' or I can't help."

"Well, what the hell was wrong with that?"

"Nothin' except he didn't ask no questions."

"Two more times," Bob said.

"We'll see."

They visited five more places before Hugh let Bob go in alone. They walked up and down the streets looking for help-wanted signs, of which there seemed to be plenty. The first one Bob visited alone – Hugh waited in the drizzle – he was asked to write down his name and where he stayed while in town.

"Be needin' help soon," the man said.

Bob felt confident after that even though only about half the places he went into appeared to be interested in hiring him. None needed help right away.

CHAPTER 20

Bob slept in a room that increasingly smelled like urine as the men decided not to visit the outhouse. The rain continued. The snow melted. The river rose.

He lay on his cot imagining the water screaming down through the creeks and streams and runs. Eyes closed, he watched piles of timber lift from the banks, turn into the flow of liquid, and get propelled down stream, a battering ram so massive and so powerful that it would rip creek-side trees out by their roots. So angry would the spirit of the timber be that men caught having the wrong footing along the banks would be killed. The stories were everywhere. The river gave and took life with equal assurance and disinterest.

Bob loved the river. He loved its power and strength. He loved its fish. What he feared was the wrath of the trees. The floating logs with a mind of their own. He knew that the timber would use the angry and vengeful part of the river, and he wanted to be away from it.

After some weeks spending much of his time indoors, the stench of bodies and excrement even permeated Bob's clothes. The men became agitated with one another. Bob kept to himself.

He took a short walk down muddy streets and alleys. He sat alone at breakfast. Then he walked to the edge of town and curled next to the trunk of a densely leafed tree where the rain was less likely to soak him. Under the tree, Bob listened to thunder, far off on the other side of the mountain, but coming closer.

Bob did not hear Hugh coming into the woods until branches were pushed aside and a hale of drops fell with the sound of hands clapping. "What are you doing here?"

"Did I interrupt a private party?" Hugh said. He sat near Bob. "I'm sick of smellin' piss and sweat."

"There're just too many people there all the time." Bob and Hugh both leaned against the trunk of the tree, their legs stretched straight out, pant legs damp, boots muddy.

"You don't like people much, do you? I notice you don't talk to no one unless you have to. You don't engage in no conversation."

"There isn't much to say. I don't know them. I don't know their families," Bob said.

"You don't ask no questions," Hugh said.

Bob shrugged.

"You got secrets. I know men who got secrets and they stay quiet. They talk a little. They ask questions. They learn about people, but they don't let too much of themselves out. Only a little." Hugh fell silent.

Bob listened to the distant thunder.

"You got big secrets. I see it in your face. So can some of the other men. They talkin' about you. They curious."

"Let them be curious."

"Damn, Bob, I'm trying' to tell you that they get nervous about you. They don't like it. The more they feel you got secrets the more they don't trust you. They watch you. They blame you for stealin'. Hell, they blame you for the rain comin' and the jobs being slow. They'll blame you when the river drives the lumber to the boom."

"What can I do?"

Hugh slapped his thigh. "Now you talkin'. You got to open up. You don't have to tell yer secrets, but you got to be interested in what's goin' on."

"I am interested. I listen to them talking."

"You got to participate."

The wind blew and the tree dropped collected rain all around them. The smell of spring rose from the ground. Bob took a deep breath. He didn't belong there, yet he had to learn to belong.

"What is your secret?" Hugh asked.

Bob thought back. He had been born, then reborn in the river, then reborn again in the town where he now lived. He didn't know whether he even knew the secret he held inside. He knew dreams.

He knew memories, but none of them could be articulated. None seemed to be important enough to matter. He could lie, but what would that matter? He knew only one secret, and it was nothing. It was from long ago, in a dream, long before two rebirths. At the moment, under the tree beside Hugh, Bob hardly knew whether he was black or white. Neither felt real to him, even when he remembered Big Leon's bulging, begging eyes. He remembered blood pushing from Big Leon's chest up through his shirt. He remembered Edna's words, the... 'blood and gush...' of his own birth.

Bob lowered his head. "My Pa was killed right in front of me and I don't want to remember."

"I see," Hugh said.

The thunder boomed closer. The rain let up.

A trickle of wet ran down the side of Bob's neck.

"What'd your pa do to get kilt?" Hugh asked.

Bob heard the question as accusatory. Had he said too much? Big Leon had done nothing wrong. He had done something right, something thoughtful, unselfish, and loving. "It was an accident. Hunting. There were too many of us in the woods."

"I'm sorry, I thought it might have been in the war.

Bob said, "No, not the war." But he wished he had said that. That might have made Big Leon a hero at least, which was much more fitting than getting in the way of a bullet.

"I didn't fight in the war either. But don't tell no one. Sometimes I lie about it so they don't think I was scared."

"Why didn't you go?"

"Not everybody was called to. Me, I was deep in the woods. Part of the time I was livin' with Indians. Part of the time I was just walkin'. Truth is, I don't know why I never walked in that direction."

"It's okay," Bob said. "We all walk in our own direction."

Hugh looked into Bob's eyes. "You could lie and I wouldn't say nothin' about it."

"That's kind of you," Bob said, but he knew he had already lied.

In a moment, Hugh lifted up to go. He crouched so that he could crawl out from under the tree branches. "I got work," he said, then laughed out loud. "It's a good thing, too. I'm broke. Ate my last meal this mornin'. Got a letter said I'm hired so I can get a tab."

"You leaving the boarding house?"

Hugh shuffled his legs to get comfortable. He stared beyond the tree's canopy. "Be gone tonight." He looked at Bob. "Yours is comin'."

"I know."

"Been lookin'?"

"Not today."

"Now's the time."

"I know. I just couln't."

"You must have a shit pile of money if you ain't worried," Hugh said. "Shit, I'd be thinking about this summer. You know, once them jobs is taken there ain't no more of 'em?"

"I realize that."

"Don't act like you know. Damn, Bob, even niggers is gettin' jobs. You don't want no nigger doing your work now, do you?"

Bob tensed. He gritted his teeth. "No. Don't suppose I do." The words hurt more than he expected.

"Mill's callin' in all they can get. If you don't like mill work, there's raftin'. The river'll be black with lumber soon. Money will be flyin'."

"Told you before. I'm not working with timber."

"Don't get mad. I'm just helping, is all. You don't seem worried, yet mid-summer you'll be starvin' and sorry. And once they start hirin' niggers they won't want to replace 'em. Niggers come cheap after the war."

"I wish you'd stop calling them that. They're Negroes. They've got a heritage too."

"Touchy are we?"

"No, it's just not respectful of people."

"At least now I know somethin' about you." Hugh crawled out from under the tree. "You want to let them wooly-headed niggers have your job, go ahead." Hugh stepped into the clearing and walked away.

Bob watched him go. He pushed his chin out. He was as much Negro as he was white. More, once he considered who raised him, who he could rely on. His next thought negated the first. Bud and Tunny had been as insensitive and mean-spirited as Hank and Earl.

Hugh blended into the mist. His footprints remained in the soft leaves dropped the prior fall. The weeds had, but were already gaining their composure, lifting back up to fill the space Hugh had opened. Bob inhaled deeply. The scent of rain and rotting leaves filled his head, reminding him of his childhood. He had been thinking too much about the opposite sides of the road he had grown up on.

Bob didn't feel totally white or totally black. He spit onto the ground next to him, as angry with himself for not knowing, as he was with Hugh for suggesting what he couldn't know. Hugh had been a disappointment, but could he be blamed for it? Bob's own mother had been a disappointment as well. Both his fathers were disappointments until the very end when they both came through for him in their own way.

Sadness settled over Bob's shoulders. He let the cool, wet air bring him to shivers. He wished he could just cry out in sorrow and in pain, but there were no tears in his eyes. His chest thickened, his throat closed, but there were no tears.

An opening in the sky let the sun splash over the weeds and hit the tree, bringing it into amazing brilliant color. Bob laughed at the sun. He laughed at his sad heart. He was alive, after all, alive and living as if he were a white man, even though he grew up in a black house. His life suddenly seemed funny.

At mid-day, Bob, wet and clammy, strolled through the downtown streets then up and down the square blocks. He looked for work, but ended up bypassing every help-wanted sign. Mud collected on his boots making them heavy. He did see several Negroes, but they didn't make eye contact. They walked past him, heads lowered and turned away. The white men said hello, or nodded. Even women looked at him. How could the Negroes not recognize him as one of their own?

Bob sensed a renewed confidence in himself. Perhaps recalling his past also let it go? The next help-wanted sign he came upon, he stepped onto the stairs, walked through the door, and up to the counter.

A big man with fat, wide hands came from a back room. "May I help you."

"Your sign says you need help." Bob turned to point out the door.

"Ever bake bread?"

At that moment, Bob recognized the sweet odor his thoughts had drowned out. He looked around. He was in a bakery. "I've watched enough times," he said.

"What's your name?"

"Bob White." He held out his hand.

The man's chubby cheeks tightened into a smile. His flower-dusted hand reached to take Bob's. He gripped firmly, the strength due from kneading and rolling. Heat poured from the back. "Somebody did you no favor giving you a name like that."

"You learn to live with it," Bob said.

"I suppose you do. Come on back, we'll talk a bit."

Bob followed the man into the back. A block of heat hit Bob squarely and his face burst into sweat.

"This here's the hot-house. Ingredients." He pointed along one wall. "Water buckets." He pointed along the floor in the back. "Kneading table."

Bob noticed the hollowed area of the huge wooden table, its worn-smooth surface, flour-white with a huge glob of dough sitting in the middle of it.

The man pointed to himself. "Jasper." He laughed out loud. "Town's fillin' up. Don't need a second baker, but I do need a runner can get water, meal, flour, all my supplies. These shelves will run empty more than full when I get to bakin'. Then you might do some mixin' one day and kneadin' dough another. Deliveries start early, too. Need to keep the fire burnin' not too hot and not too cold. But most of all, Bob," Jasper pointed at him, "you got to be happy. Don't want no stiffs around here."

Bob laughed at Jasper, not so much from what was said as from the big man's appearance. The way he wore flour in his hair and on his hands. The way Jasper talked and how he moved, his belly going everywhere first. How could someone work there and not be happy? "I can do that," Bob said.

"Well, I like your smile and I like your lean looks. If you can keep up, we got a deal."

"When do I start?"

The door creaked behind Bob. He hadn't even heard that noise until now.

"Don't need no bell," Jasper said explaining the noise. "Excuse me. I got a customer."

Bob nodded. He heard Jasper say, "Mr. Billingsford." Bob stepped to the back of the room. Another door was propped open. An alley opened to scattered trash, barrels of waste, and the strong stench of rot. When he stepped outside, a cat scurried off.

Jasper came back into the hothouse. "Got to get back to work. Just sold my last wheat loaf." He wiped his hands on a rag hanging on a nail sticking from the table's leg. In a few steps, he peered into an oven. With a long paddle he poked around inside. "Comin' along fine," he said. He began kneading the dough that lay on the table.

Bob watched. It was as though Jasper had forgotten he was there. When Bob walked around in front of the table, Jasper glanced up. His hands and arms were working the dough, pushing, lifting, rolling, slapping. "Seen the river today?"

"This morning."

"You check it tonight. Then again at sunup. Let me know when you think the lumber's coming. You worked with lumber, right?"

"How'd you know?"

Jasper held up his hands, turned them so Bob could see them. "You ain't got a baker's hands."

Bob looked at his own nicked and scarred palms. "He laughed. I know wood and I know water."

"River of dreams," Jasper said. "That river's fed more families and made more men rich, it's almost unnatural. Like it's alive. Some kind of mysterious force. All you got to do is ask it for something and it delivers. It delivers until it can't. Know what I'm sayin'?"

"I think I do."

"That's what we do. Men. We give to this world 'til we can't no more. That river's alive. It's like any good man."

"I never thought of it that way," Bob said.

"Better start. 'Cause just like a man, if it gets angry it can kill you. Don't cross it or that river will show you what anger can do."

"I won't."

Jasper began to roll the dough out flat. "See them buckets."

"For water."

"There's a well you draw from. Back in the alley." He stopped rolling out the dough and lifted his face to Bob's. "One bucket of water comes straight from the river. I got a strainer for when the lumber's runnin'. Each of them other buckets gets a cup of the river's soul."

Bob laughed.

"That the only thing's *not* funny. That river's part of everything I bake here. Each loaf, every muffin, has been blessed by that river. Understand?"

"Yes, sir."

"You can start an hour before sunup, tomorrow. First bucket is river water."

Bob got serious for Jasper's sake. "I can do that."

"Hired a young boy one time. Couldn't give like the river. Thought he was goin' to trick me. I seen him piss in the bucket to make it look more like river water." Jasper folded the flattened dough into a ball, picked it up and slammed it onto the table. "Do that and I'll kill you."

"I'm an honest man," Bob said.

"Just sayin'."

Bob nodded.

"Start tomorrow, son."

Bob left the bakery. He had a job and it had nothing to do with lumber. He thought ahead. Perhaps Jasper would teach him to bake. He'd make a good baker. He lifted his palms. The dough would feel soft on his hands. It would wear the calluses smooth and smooth out the nicks as well. Bob made a little skip as he walked back to the boarding house. That was the worst of it. He'd have to continue to live in the boarding house for a while. He checked his pockets where he had begun to keep his money. Before the end of the day, he decided to get a bath. He could do that behind the saloon in the middle of town. He'd start work with a clean body.

CHAPTER 21

B ob learned the limits of his own body. The hours at the bakery were long. The more he picked up about the art of baking, the more Jasper let him do, not out of laziness, but commerce. Jasper spent much of his time in the front selling the baked goods. Someone had to keep the dough mixed and the oven filled. Bob had never negotiated his pay, but found Jasper to be a generous man.

Bob could smell the river rising. A deep soil scent, muddy and thick as it crept over its banks. Days ahead he heard the lumber running.

The day before the boom began to fill, Jasper closed the bakery at noon and became a hawker for the day, soliciting business from the mill. He planned to deliver bread and muffins right at the mill first thing in the morning, during lunch break and shift changes. The men could bring fresh bread home.

When the flood hit and the lumber rumbled into the boom, Jasper told Bob that that was the first year in the life of the bakery that he was ready for the rush. "Men eat more when they're working."

Bob made most of the daily deliveries for the baker, loading the baked goods into a small mule-driven cart, and leading the animal through town. He kept his promise of working hard, retrieving one bucket of river water each day, and being in a good mood. He sang much of the time he worked.

The town lived for lumber. Noise and excitement bombarded the streets. Stores became busy. Restaurants, hotels, boarding houses, and theatres were frequented. Mornings came early and evenings never ended.

Although Bob disliked the boarding house where he slept, there were few places in town to stay as cheaply. He had a bed and was happy for that.

In July, Jasper's hothouse became unbearable. Even Jasper stood at the doorway that opened to the counter, obviously avoiding the heat as often as he could manage. Bob stepped to the back entrance praying for a breeze to curl down the alley or through the shop, although shop breezes were also hot.

At the height of the heat wave, it seemed as though no one in town could sleep and the saloon collected the men like snakes in a bag all curled together. Bob learned to step into the saloon with familiarity, like his own house, even though there were never any Negroes inside except him. It wasn't that they weren't allowed, only that they didn't frequent the place. Bob imagined himself wearing a mask. He was an actor with pale makeup. On other occasions he didn't know whether he acted or had become someone else altogether, someone different than who he started out to be.

He slept very few hours. He didn't talk much because he worked long hours, ate, and slept or walked the streets in the coolest part of the night. He and Jasper talked business. How many loaves sold? How many muffins? What did Bob think they'd need the next day?

Then one night while Jasper and Bob cleaned up, a melodic sound rang through the alley like a dream. Bob turned an ear to it. Two men sang in mid-tones as they walked down the alley.

"Pretty sound," Jasper said. He stood behind Bob who had stopped to listen.

"It is," Bob said.

"Not as pretty as your singin'," Jasper said as a matter of fact.

As the men got closer to Bob and Jasper, they stopped singing. One of the Negroes stood as tall as the doorway and looked rather skeletal, the other stood broader, heavier, and a foot shorter. They carried instruments. The tall one held a guitar by its neck. The short man carried a banjo over his shoulder.

The short one smiled at Bob and Jasper. "Hey dare," he said.

"Hello," Jasper said.

"We told there a alley shed we can stay in. Dis the alley?"

Jasper stepped in front of Bob. "Down there." He indicated a structure that appeared to have been added to the back of one of the buildings. It leaned into the alley and was held to the side of the main building by nothing more than a pair of two-by-eight studs tacked between the two structures.

"I thought that was a storage shed," Bob said.

"McGregor rents it out. A favor to his uncle Jimmy Finch."

"The man who owns the saloon?"

"That's the one." Jasper watched as the Negroes walked by. "Not much room in there."

"We be fine," the short man said.

"Let's finish up," Jasper said. When he and Bob were back inside, Jasper nodded his head toward the door. "Don't worry about them. They'll be gone by the end of summer."

"Why would I worry?"

"Havin' niggers in the alley," Jasper said as though that were reason enough.

Bob shrugged. After cleaning up and locking the doors, Jasper and Bob went out the front. Bob never knew and never wondered where Jasper lived, only that the man always went the opposite direction on the street. Bob looked over his shoulder to see whether Jasper looked back. He dodged down the alley. He stepped as quietly as he could. He could hear the Negroes rustling around in the shed, settling themselves. At the back entrance to the bakery, Bob sat on the stoop.

In a few minutes, he heard the men talking in low, undecipherable tones. Then the sound of strumming came. And then some banjo picking. In a moment the men were singing. Bob listened first to Civil War songs such as "When Johnny comes Marching Home," then gospel, then tunes he couldn't place. Eventually, the men were laughing and just playing their instruments, no singing at all. The sound relaxed Bob. His mind wandered back to a time when his innocence had not been compromised. Even as the Civil War raged in other parts of Pennsylvania, little Leon knew only six shacks and the landowner's house and barn. Fred Carpenter, as Bob learned, had moved from Virginia long before the war. What he considered himself in relation to the war never entered Bob's thoughts, and only a slight curiosity nagged at him now.

He dozed off. When he awoke all was quiet. The Negroes had stopped playing and the shed door was closed. Groggy and sore, Bob rose with caution, letting his neck and knees crack and readjust to movement. He walked to the roominghouse and slipped into his bedroll careful not to disturb anyone.

Early the next morning, he exited as quietly as he'd arrived. In after dark and out before light. He pulled a bucket of water from the river and delivered it to the bakery. Jasper had already begun work, mixing vats of flour and walnuts for a walnut loaf. He also had a batch of butternuts, a special treat.

Bob pitched in by first straining the river water and portioning out a cup to each of the other buckets. Then two-at-a-time, Bob carried the buckets to the end of the alley and filled them. He hummed as he walked. On his third trip, the short Negro sat on a turned-over bucket outside the shed. He smoked a cigarette. "Hey dare," he said. "I know dat tune."

"I'm sorry if I woke you," Bob said. The light of day glowed over the mountain, but the sun wasn't quite up yet.

"Cain't wake me. I sleep through cannon fire. Sleep so deep I forget my own name when I wake up." He sat straight and turned his head to look up and down the alley. "Who am I," he said while twisting his big head. Then he laughed.

Bob laughed with him.

"Dat's why I don't know dat tune. What is it?"

"I don't know either. My aunt used to hum it. She sang it sometimes too, but I can't remember the words."

"Pone," the big man called. "Pone, what dis song?" He began to hum.

The thin man stepped from the shed. It was magical that they could both fit inside. He cocked his head, then picked up the humming. "Woodman, Spare dat Tree."

"Damn. Dat's it."

They both began to sing. Their voices merged as one melodic voice.

Bob recalled the words once they started. He nodded his head.

Pone waved his hand for Bob to join in, which he did, adding another harmonic to the already smooth sound. Singing with the two of them freed Bob of any lingering embarrassment he may have had. He belted the song out.

Jasper yelled from inside the hothouse. "Ain't payin' for singin'."

Bob quieted and picked up his buckets to deliver them. Once the lyrics played in his head, they came back easily. He sang on his way to make deliveries.

He ran into Hugh from time to time, and on this day they met up on Arch Street heading toward the river.

"Bob," Hugh said.

Bob still struggled slightly with his name, so it took a moment for him to turn around. "How are you? You liking the mill work?"

Hugh raised a bandaged hand.

"What happened?"

"Got slammed. Down to half pay, for half a man. Working in the sawmill though. I can stand my own ground even with one hand." He raised his right hand, the arm strong, the fingers and palm thick with callus and muscle.

"I'm sure of that," Bob said.

"And you, deliverin'. I seen you a lot. Called out once, but you never heard. Like now, I'm thinkin' you're hard of hearing." He glanced at the muffins. "Headin' to the mill?"

"First, then to a few places in town. They make the stew, Jasper makes the bread."

"Any day-olds?"

"Nope. All fresh."

"Look, I'm good for it. You can trust your old friend, even if we ended on a bad word."

Bob hesitated.

"You stayin' the same place?" Hugh said. "I'll come by with the money tonight. I been thinking about what I said."

"You know where the bakery is?" Bob said.

"Yeah."

"I'll be there tonight."

Hugh smiled, green and glowing. "I'll be there."

Bob handed Hugh a muffin.

"Two?"

"Tonight, or it comes from my wages."

"Don't you ever drop any by accident? I don't mind the dirt."

"No," Bob said. "And I don't plan to."

"Thank you for these. Tonight. You'll see me."

Bob nodded.

As soon as Hugh had his muffins, he hurried off to work. Bob put in a full day, rushing some jobs. He was eager to talk with Pone and his friend that evening, but by the time the bakery closed, the men were gone.

Later that evening, Hugh arrived. Bob leaned against the porch post.

Hugh's slow movements belied his fatigue. "I didn't forget." Hugh stood in the street staring up at Bob, the last light of day being replaced by moonlight.

"What is it?"

"Nothin'. Been hearin' things is all."

"What things might that be?" Bob stepped easily from the porch into the dirt and mud of the street.

"Nothin'." Hugh held out his hand to place coins into Bob's palm.

"Thank you."

"Want to go for a drink? Tavern's just down the street."

"Sure," Bob said. He dropped the money into his pocket and strolled with Hugh.

"You like sellin' bread?" Hugh asked.

"It's better than logging. Better than cutting lumber at the mill. For me, that is. I had my fill of lumber long ago."

Hugh held up his damaged hand in the fading light. A lot of people were on the street. A few glanced at Hugh's sudden motion. "I'm beginin' to know what you mean. I have to work longer and harder to make up for this. I keep thinkin' what if it never heals? What if I'm crippled my whole life like them soldiers that come back with missin' parts. I think I can lie and say it was a war wound, and get a pity job. But I don't want no pity job. I want my hand back."

"We all have our wounds."

"Do tell, Bob. What's your wound? I know about your pappy. What else you wounded for?"

"Here's the place. Shall we?" From outside, the din of conversation stood against a background of piano music. Bob motioned for Hugh to enter the saloon first, then followed him. Suddenly, the piano demanded attention, and the din receded into the background. Individual conversations came and went as Bob and Hugh walked through the tavern to find an open seat at the bar.

"Two beers," Hugh said.

Bob seldom drank beer. He drank wine once during a jump-the-broom ceremony when he was thirteen.

Hugh grabbed his mug and took a long drink. He smiled broadly.

Bob had never seen him so happy.

Hugh nodded and Bob drank from his mug. The beer tasted salty and bitter, but Bob didn't let on. He glanced around the room, an uncomfortable feeling coming over him with that many people in one place. There wasn't a Negro to be found. Bob wondered where they met, where they drank beer and laughed?

The piano player banged out tunes that Bob had never heard, then came upon one Bob did recognize. He hummed along with the tune.

Hugh knew some of the other men and they laughed together. Bob didn't listen much to what they said; the conversations all appeared to have started at the mill.

After a while, Hugh's friends and Hugh turned to Bob. He leaned close and Bob could smell Hugh's breath of beer and tooth rot. "Sorry about what I said before."

"What did you say?" Bob wondered whether he should have listened to the conversation more closely.

"Not just now. Long before. About you lovin' Negroes."

"Negroes? Don't know if I remember that."

"I'm sure you do. And I'm sorry."

"It's done," Bob said.

"You accept my apology?"

"I do."

"They got some good singers here. They're Negroes. You'll like 'em."

"Maybe I will." Half of Bob's beer rested inside his mug and already his head felt foggy.

Hugh ordered two more beers, pushing his empty mug toward the bartender. He motioned for Bob to finish his. Two more were set on the bar. Hugh winked at Bob, "You get this one."

Bob paid and took his first sip. The bartender had whisked the other mug from the bar.

Hugh pointed to the back of the tavern where Pone and his short friend strolled onto a small, makeshift stage. When Pone started playing his guitar, the room quieted down.

Bob recognized Jimmy Finch as he walked onto the short platform. He could hear the planks creek.

"A special treat tonight," Jimmy yelled. All this week and next, we got Pone and Shorty. You won't be sorry you come. And, hey, tell yer friends, cause they only got so many performances before they movin' on."

All the time Jimmy Finch spoke, Pone put in background harmonies and even picked a few notes to emphasize certain words. After Jimmy stepped down, Pone's music became louder. Shorty cleared his throat and said, "First thing we do is thank the Lord for our talent and for bein' able to share it wit you fine folks."

A lot of the men sitting at tables shook their heads. Others nodded approval.

Pone and Shorty sang a gospel song ending in "We thank you Lord." Then the music got livelier and more complex. Shorty dragged his banjo over his shoulder and it appeared almost as though it started to play itself before his fingers ever reached the strings. The crowd of men hollered and whistled as the Negroes sang Civil War songs.

Bob noticed how Pone and Shorty would play a few ruckus tunes or patriotic war songs, then drop into a serious, sad song about lost love or lost sons in the war and the whole crowd would drop into near tears right along with the song.

"Damned right," one of the men would cry out, as if unable to contain himself. "Lost my two boys," another yelled.

Right after a few sad songs, Pone and Shorty would raise the crowd's spirits again, and get the men yelling. At the end of the night, their last song was to thank the Lord once again.

Bob had hardly noticed how late it was, how many beers he had, or how many he paid for.

Hugh patted him on the shoulder. "Them's talented niggers," he said, then looked up at Bob. "I mean Negroes."

"What's 'at spose a mean?" Bob drawled. He had trouble standing as well.

"Nothin'," Hugh said. "Here, I'll help you back to the boardinghouse." Hugh walked close beside Bob, shoving him whenever his stagger grew into a strong lean.

Bob hummed and sang under his breath as they headed to where his bunk waited. Hugh took Bob under the arm to help get him through the boardinghouse door, then dropped him into his cot just before Bob passed out.

CHAPTER 22

Bob woke in a cold sweat, alone in the room. The sun had been up for hours. He vaguely remembered crawling outside during the night to vomit behind the building. When he rolled onto his side, his head hurt. He gritted his teeth and rubbed the back of his neck. Forcing himself to sit up, Bob opened his eyes into a sliver, letting light seep in like flour through a sifter. As his eyes adjusted, he continued to open them bit by bit. All the while he rubbed his temples and neck. Tongue fat, mouth dry. He stood, moaned, but remained standing. He stumbled outside and went straight for the outhouse. After relieving himself, he walked into the restaurant and ordered a late breakfast, eating only half before getting up to leave. No one tried to talk with him. He set his money on the table and left.

The food and coffee helped to ease his sick stomach and clear his head. His pace picked up. The sounds he encountered outside – people talking, crows cawing – appeared to be louder than normal, but didn't hurt his head as much as the clanking plates and silverware had a few minutes earlier.

He walked through the alley to get to the bakery.

Jasper was busy at the kneading table, his back to Bob.

When Bob's foot knocked against the floorboards, Jasper swung around, gave Bob a look of disappointment, then turned back around and began working the dough over even harder, slapping and pushing at it.

Bob approached Jasper at a distance until he stood in the man's peripheral vision. "I'm really sorry. I got sick."

"You got drunk." Jasper stopped whacking the dough and stepped right up to Bob. "I don't give a shit if you want to get drunk as long as you do your job." Back at the table again, Jasper slammed his fist into the dough. "I lost time and money this morning. There was no water from the river, no water from the pump. You know what that meant? Well, I'll tell you. I had to get it myself. That put my mixing behind, which put my kneading behind, and my baking. Even after my first baked batch was done, you weren't here." He slammed his hand on the edge of the table. The crack made Bob jump. "I couldn't leave to make deliveries."

Bob knew what it all meant, but hadn't realized how extensive the damage would be until he heard it laid out like that. He lowered his head and glanced away. "I was with my hurt friend. He needed a few drinks, and..."

"And nothin'. I'll take my loss out of your pay. Do it again and don't come back."

"Yes, sir."

"Now load up and see if you can sell anything at lunch." Jasper shook his head.

Bob loaded his cart and headed for the mill, hocking and selling baked goods along the way. He arrived at the mill early. While straightening his goods and setting the cart in a level spot, he happened to look up and see Hugh talking with someone. Bob recognized the man, but shook his head, refusing the image. When Bob looked up again, the man was gone and Hugh was walking toward the cart. As he approached, Hugh grinned at Bob. "How'd you fair last night?"

"You know damned well how I faired. Poorly." Bob said.

"Maybe we try again tonight? Get you used to it."

"It's not for me."

"Don't like beer? We could try whisky." Hugh glanced at the muffins.

Bob picked three up and handed them to Hugh. Other men were headed over. Bob needed to sell a lot of bread and muffins, even if he had to buy them himself.

"Thank you," Hugh said. "Didn't see you this morning."

"I got sick."

Other men selected items and paid for them while Hugh and Bob talked. As the crowd dispersed Bob asked, "Who were you talking to?" He indicated where Hugh had stood with the other man.

Hugh turned to look behind him, then twisted back around. "Before you come?"

"Yes. I saw you with somebody. Who was it?"

"Just another mill worker. I don't know all their names. Most of 'em ignore me now I got my hand hurt." He raised the specimen into the air. "Know him?"

Bob bit his lower lip then said, "You appear to have new friends is all. I'd be careful if I were you. You don't know how trustworthy some men can be."

"You mean like they make up a new name?"

"Like they make up stories about other people that aren't true. Stories that sound true, but aren't." The veins in Bob's temples pounded at a faster pace. He hoped Hugh wouldn't notice.

"I'll watch myself," Hugh said.

"You do that," Bob yelled as Hugh headed back to work.

Bob packed up and started toward town. He thought about who he'd seen Hugh talking with. It was Jacob. Bob figured Jacob would have been long gone, back with his family, in another town, anywhere but working at a mill in the same town Bob had landed. Maybe Jacob would be with Hillary. Bob closed his eyes. She would have had her baby by now. Could it be black?

Bob needed to find out what Jacob had said to Hugh. The whole Negro thing for sure, but did Jacob really know the truth?

He should have pistol-whipped Jacob in the woods. He should have killed him. He had been mad enough.

Bob slipped back into thinking about his work. His head cleared more as the day wore on. He ate several walnut muffins that afternoon when his appetite returned. He promised Jasper over and over throughout the day that he wouldn't get drunk again and he wouldn't be late for work. Yet he hadn't decided whether he would be working for long. He also feared for his life. A black passing for white could be lynched, beaten to death, or shot outright in the street.

"If you get drunk again," Jasper was telling him, "make it Saturday night so you miss church instead of work." By the end of the day Jasper's mood mellowed. "I have a suspicion that God might forgive you easier than I will."

Bob tried to smile politely at the joke, nodding in agreement.

"You're acting nervous," Jasper said. "Don't worry. I'm okay now."

"Still not feeling quite right."

"I'll clean up tonight. But be down here before daybreak."

"I will." Bob went to look for Hugh that night. The mill had its own set of barracks, several on either side. The closer to the flood line, the lower the level of worker. Bob didn't have to go far to find Hugh's barracks. Stepping up to the door, Bob smelled the odor of hard work and wood. A mixture of sweat and pulp, sawdust and bad breath. It was nothing like the sweet smell of biscuits. His nose curled before he walked inside. He asked the first man he saw where he might find Hugh. The man seated on an upturned log stood, towered over Bob. The man's thin, farm-hand muscles didn't look as though they could handle logging. They were meant for scything a field, stretched out, swinging in a cool autumn breeze, laying hay. The wrinkles around the man's eyes were from squinting in the bright sunlight.

"Hugh ain't here," the man said. Even his voice sounded high-pitched rather than low and rough. "He's probably drinkin'. That where he goes now he's sufferin'. And I'll tell ya, it ain't helpin' him none."

"I should have known." Bob thanked the man and headed for Jimmy Finch's bar.

Once again, the rise of conversation filled the streets long before Bob walked inside. His hands shook. His jaw ached from being tight the whole way over. He stood staring at the doorway. If Hugh had wanted, he could have told everyone whatever story Jacob was spreading. Bob's heart pounded. This could be his last night alive.

He had no idea what he'd say to Hugh. The subject of his life was broad and deep with faces and names and acts. There wasn't enough time to explain it all. He stepped through the door and no one seemed to notice. Safe, so far.

He recognized Hugh at the bar. Bob half-expected Jacob to be sitting with him, but Hugh sat alone. His head bent over as though he were looking for something in his beer mug. As Bob crept up to the big man, he noticed Hugh's tired eyes, drooping eyelids, and slack facial muscles. A visible depression lay over the man's head and shoulders. Hugh's hands lingered near his mug as if he were about to grab it, but had forgotten mid-act.

"Hugh?" Bob said.

Hugh turned slowly until he saw Bob. "You got nothin' to worry over."

"I'm not worried," Bob lied.

"You so tense I could play you." Hugh said.

"We need to talk a bit," Bob said.

The crowd quieted. Pone and Shorty were coming on. Bob lowered his voice. "Let's go Hugh." Bob grabbed Hugh's thick arm. Even with one arm, as strong as it was, Bob figured Hugh could out work him physically.

Hugh rose to his feet and followed Bob into the street. In the background Jimmy announced the Pone and Shorty act to loud howls, stomping feet, and pounding fists.

Outside, the night air soothed Bob's muscles. The smell carried the scent of flowers and wood, of night air, crisp and clean.

Hugh followed a few steps behind Bob. "You got no worries," he said again. "That man's gone. He high-tailed it."

Bob stopped and waited.

Hugh put his hand on Bob's shoulder. "I don't care who you were. I might be a big lug, with a big head and big hands, but I'm a good judge of people. And you ain't bad. You just ain't like other folks."

"Why'd he leave?"

Hugh held up his injury. "One less person means one less chance they'll get rid of me."

"What do you mean by that?"

"There a lot of reasons. That's just one. I tell 'im if he don't high-tail it, I'm goin' to hurt 'im. Maybe there be an accident one day." Hugh shook his head. "Suppose he believed me."

"Thank you."

"Let's walk to the edge of town. You owe me a story now. And I suspect it's a good one." Hugh winked and held his gaze for a long time.

Bob had no idea where to begin or end his story. He had no idea which parts to leave in and which to skip over. What was worse, though, was that he couldn't account to the accuracy of his own memory any longer.

Hugh, apparently impatient with the silence, said, "Jacob said he stole your money."

"He did."

"He said you had the chance to kill 'im, but you didn't."

Bob nodded. Let the story make its own way out, then, he thought.

Hugh said, "I told 'im you was going to finish the job, but I stop you. He didn't believe me. Said you too coward. Jacob said when you first come into camp you act like a Negro. You act that way so much the men started believing it. They needed the help. Some didn't care and some did. But Jacob, he said he didn't want no Negro takin' full pay. He said it was his duty to take some of it back." Hugh walked with Bob a little farther. They neared the edge of town. "He said the name Leon is what you used then, but he was sure you the same man."

Bob waited. He walked. He purged his own memories, thoughts, beliefs. What did it matter now? What would it mean? He could move into the black section of town. He could do odd jobs. Hell, he could sing alongside Pone and Shorty. He knew he could do that.

"So, am I right so far?" Hugh had given his information freely and openly.

Bob knew it was his turn to speak. "The facts might be close," he said. "It's the why's that aren't."

"Jacob didn't offer none."

"I know." Bob thought back and decided he didn't need to tell the whole story. Somehow that story didn't fit him any more. The realization freed him for the moment. "I never told them anything about myself, but my name. They assumed I was Italian, not Negro. Jacob brought that on later. I was too scared, too quiet, and maybe even too stupid to try to change their ideas. Once I let it go, it was done. I didn't know their suspicions or I would have come clean."

"The dilemma of the quiet man."

"You sound like you're familiar."

"Where did you learn to read and talk all educated?"

"It seems like a long time ago. I hardly remember. But I know now that reading kept me alive and safe. It gave me a new identity."

The two men turned around to walk back into town.

"You can keep your identity for all I care. I don't need to know no more," Hugh said.

"Why?"

"Told you. I'm a good judge of character. If not, my whole life would change. Look, Bob, we're all alone in this world and we all make up what doesn't suit us. Every story I hear has got as much untruth as truth when it comes to facts: how hard a worker one man is, how good a lover another claims to be. None of the stories are true all through. Facts bend too easily around a man's tongue. But there's one thing for sure and that's that once they bend they're real. Our stories change according to how we tell them."

Bob knew Hugh was talking about his own story as well. They walked on. "He tell anyone else?"

"He tried, but nobody believed it or cared. He a mouthy man. Nobody listen. I didn't except I tried it out on you."

"So now what?"

"You ain't changed in my eyes. I'm just sorry about some of the things I said to you, not knowing what you are."

"What I am?"

"Didn't mean it like that," Hugh said. "I never enslaved no one."

"Maybe not."

"Everyone's free now."

"No one's free unless they're set free. There are plenty of slaves. Besides, I see how whites live. I see that blacks, most of them, don't live the same. The Indian's have been shoved out of the way too."

"It takes time. It could of been the other way around. I know that don't make it right. But there's Negroes all over who live like white men. It can be done."

"If people knew, how would they treat me?"

Hugh lowered his head. Some would treat you the same. Some different. Like Jacob. He's a southern boy in his heart."

"They're not just Southern. What about the men who don't want to sit with a Negro at a table, but will listen to him perform on stage?

Pone and Shorty, you know where they live? In a shed. Two grown men living in a shed. That bar's filled every night and I'll bet they get very little pay for their time."

"Don't get angry with me. I see the same thing every day. It didn't matter when I was whole and able to work. I admit that. But now I see it clear. They look you up and down searchin' for a reason to treat you different. To put you in a hole and then leave you there. I'm big, so I got big pay and the hardest work. Now, I'm not the same. I work next to skinny farm boys and Civil War amputees. My pay's cut in half." Hugh kicked the dirt in the street, turned his head, then looked Bob squarely in the face. "Them mansions still being built, but ain't a one of us is seein' any of *that* money. We all slaves, God dammit."

Bob shook his head. "I've seen what people can do to each other. I thought being white would change that, but it doesn't. It only changes the type of pain one man puts on another. It only changes the extent to which they do it."

Hugh's eyes turned up as though he were addressing someone in the sky. When he spoke, his calm voice stuttered slightly. He spoke for more than just himself. "I just want to be able to live this life out to its end. Have a good job and a place to stay."

"I just want to be left alone." Bob started toward the alley that led to the back of the boarding house. "I don't like the way people treat each other. I just want to be away from them."

"Why don't you change it then?" Hugh stood in the street. "You're smart. You could write for the papers. You could talk to people. Make 'em understand it ain't right to treat everybody bad just 'cause you can get away with it."

"They won't listen."

"Dammit, Bob, they wouldn't listen to a little kid. They might not listen as well to an ex-slave. But you're a man now. You're a smart white man. You can make a difference."

"Why are you saying this?"

Hugh held up his hand. "I want equal pay. I give my hand to this business. We gotta start treating each other better."

"It's for you, then." Bob left Hugh in the street.

"It's for all of us. You think about it."

Bob lifted his hand and let it drop next to him, a farewell gesture. He'd heard enough. He'd said enough. Perhaps too much. He went into his room and curled up on his cot. As a boy, he'd never slept on a cot. Here, the room was half filled with transient men who came to town for a quick buck before moving on, and half filled with men too cheap or too poor to find a more hospitable place to stay. Bob fit neither category. He wondered then why he stayed there. Familiar? To help feel alienated? Assure that he wouldn't have to get to know anyone? That he could be left alone as he had told Hugh he wanted? Was that how he wanted to live out his life?

Bob rolled into the wall. How long could he hide from himself? He clasped his hands over his ears to keep out his own questions. He consciously tried to relax and bring on sleep, but throughout the night was awakened by the groans of dreaming men or the distinct sound of someone pissing in the corner. During his interrupted sleep, Bob dreamed of a better life for himself, and by morning was thinking differently. Why couldn't he change the way he lived? Why couldn't he help others? He jumped from bed and got ready to go to breakfast before getting water for Jasper's day of baking.

He was the first person in the restaurant. He could smell coffee. A stout woman he'd never seen before appeared to take his order and in less than five minutes brought it out to him. Bob ate and left money on the table. Daylight already brightened the other side of the hills, a glow hovering above the tree line and falling over the ridge. In less than a half hour, the tip of the sun would be screaming morning's call.

Bob rushed to fill the water buckets. He readied the first batch of flour, sifting it into a giant bowl.

Jasper whistled when he came in. "Don't think this makes up for your being late."

"It wasn't meant to."

"Good. Thank you just the same." He grabbed an apron and tied it around his waist. "You could start a fire in the oven while I'm mixin' things up here."

"Yes, sir." Bob headed for the wood pile. His mind raced with thoughts and questions. He felt his options were broad and he needed to narrow them.

If he really could do anything he wished, what did he wish? Bob lifted his own hands and pulled them close to his face. There were creases cut deep into them, but the roughness had been worn away.

"Ain't never seen you own hands afore?" Pone leaned against the shed door, a corn cob pipe glowing as he sucked air through the stem.

Bob walked toward Pone. "Tell me something."

"Got plenty to tell. Whatcha wanna know?"

Bob's pulse quickened. He had second thoughts about talking with Pone. But he spit out the words anyway. "Am I black or white, Italian or Irish?"

Pone pulled the pipe from his mouth. The noise from the street slipped down between the buildings. The air stood still, and the sunlight burst into the alley. He looked Bob up and down. "Turn around."

Bob turned.

"Now walk away, then back."

Bob did as he was told.

"Bend over then stand straight," Pone said as he pushed his little finger into the pipe bowl and re-lit the tobacco.

Bob bent over and straightened.

"Now jump up and down," Pone said.

Bob's seriousness ended. He laughed and Pone laughed. "Damn you," he said.

Pone pulled on his pipe, a wet sucking sound came with the brightening embers.

"So, what do you think?"

"Don't know." Pone tapped his pipe on his boot and reached into his pocket for more tobacco. "They's so many different people in towns like this, I juss can't tell one man from another. Unless you talk like a foreigner, I don't know where the hell you comes from."

"What if I told you I was Negro?"

Pone laughed. I seen you walk in the front door of Finch's without even droppin' you eyes for a second. I seen you grab a white man by the arm and he follow you outside. If you a Negro like I knowed Negroes to be, then you a strange and dangerous one for sure."

Bob looked at the backs of his hands then turned them over.

"You had one bad dream lass night mister. You waked up all confused." Pone packed tobacco with his little finger.

Bob loaded his arms with wood.

Pone sucked on his pipe.

CHAPTER 23

Regardless how much rain fell or how high the river rose, nothing could lower Bob's positive attitude. Business for Jasper boomed. Bob took to delivering bread in the late afternoon – fresh and warm from the oven – to the mansions along Third Street. Walking the street that close to the great Susquahanna, river of dreams, he could hear her singing. Bob knew that river sound, different than the sounds of the creek, more powerful, more determined, but still the same, still water.

He imagined all the creeks feeding the Susquahanna. He remembered how they rose during the thaw and rain, how they licked at the stacked logs until they lifted them enough to dislodge one and the rest came rolling into place, rushing toward the river. And if the water took its time, the woodhicks unleashed the logs into the creeks.

But the river, strong and true, could handle the backbreaking abundance of hemlock and pine. All the logs did was push the water higher, make the river stronger.

Bob found that he could talk with the help as well as the master and lady of the houses he delivered to. He found that he could look any of them in the eye and speak as though he were their brother. Just like interviewing had been, the more often he spoke with the people he delivered to, the easier conversation rolled from his tongue.

Each night he read. There was a library in Williamsport, and he signed out one book after another. He read poetry and fiction and philosophy, science and politics. Several nights a week, he sat at

Jimmy Finch's and nursed a beer along with Hugh, whose hand was healing slowly.

They talked about logging and books. Bob urged Hugh to read more, telling him it was the true path to freedom. He also told Hugh that reading would clean up his English, which Hugh decided wasn't a bad idea.

"If I speak better, I could work different," Hugh said.

Pone and Shorty had passed through and Finch was hosting three more Negro musicians. One night, while talking with Bob and Hugh at the bar, Jimmy Finch told the men, "The sound those black folk make just goes straight to a man's soul. We're all suffering, but not like them. They're suffering for more reasons than I like to think. And they can sing it. Hell, we all come from somewhere else. We all miss our homes. We've all been touched by pain and war. But them," he pointed to the stage, "they can bring those feelings home."

Later that evening, walking to the boarding house, Hugh said, "What do you think about what Jimmy said tonight?"

"About the singing?"

"And about the pain?"

"He's probably right."

"You feel that pain again when you hear the songs?"

"Sometimes," Bob said, staring into the dark.

"I'm sorry," Hugh said.

"Do you feel it?"

"More than you might know."

"I wish that it wasn't true for you," Bob said.

"White men treat you pretty bad?"

Bob thought for a moment. "Black or white, I've been treated about the same."

After walking a short distance in silence, brushing away the occasional mosquito, Hugh said, "Jimmy Finch should know about a Negro's pain."

"Why do you say that?"

"He's been part of the underground railroad all his life. I wonder what he thinks now that things have changed? I wonder if he feels relief or lost purpose?"

"How do you know about Jimmy?"

"Things like that get around. Haven't you ever wondered why all his acts are Negroes?" Hugh said.

"They're cheap pay for good talent," Bob said. "And what about those two living in the shed in the alley behind the bakery? There's no heart in that."

"Pone and Shorty had their whole family in town and they all stayed at Jimmy's except those two old coots. I hear they wanted some peace."

"Well, well. I never thought. I guess I figured it brought in money and that was that."

"Some folks won't go there 'cause of who he brings in and lets sleep in his home."

"I can only imagine." Bob glanced at Hugh. The moonlight fell into the dusty street in blotches, blocked by clouds. "Isn't Jimmy a little young to be part of the railroad?"

"He grew up with it. His Pa and Ma worked to save slaves all the time he was growin' up. He's a good man."

Bob slapped Hugh on the shoulder. It was still difficult for him to do that without feeling at least a twitch in his frame, wondering whether it wasn't just too familiar. "Tomorrow we meet at the library."

"You gonna make me an honest man, ain't you?"

Bob waved and walked down the alley. Before entering through the back entrance, he used the out building. On his slow stride back, he heard a scraping sound, like a boot against the dirt. He swung around and advanced right into an oncoming fist. He felt the blow of a stick as well. Then two more punches, one squarely on the back of his skull. He rolled into a ball, but as soon as he hit the ground, he was out.

He dreamed it was dark. He stood alone, not because he wished to, but because no one wanted to stand with him. He tried to see into the dark, straining his eyes until even darker shadows began to appear. This frightened him even more. He whipped around and attempted to find a familiar shape. His head twisted back and forth. There were many shadows overlapping. Then the shadows began to move as though they didn't want to be recognized. So Bob picked one out and tried to follow its movements, but the shadow blurred.

Bob waited. He had no choice. The sun would soon rise. He could feel it. He could hear the river. When he stopped worrying, the shadows stopped moving about. One at a time they faded and the darkness lightened. Color came into the dream. The color of sunrise and sunset. He watched the horizon. It looked familiar. When he realized where he was, he looked down at Big Leon only he wasn't dead. He was just lying down. He winked. Laughter came from behind. When Bob turned, Fred Carpenter stood over him, pointing and laughing. Big Leon sat up. Fred Carpenter held out his hand and helped Big Leon get to his feet. They both laughed, leaning back until they almost tipped over and bending forward until their chins almost touched their knees. Bob looked from one to the other. He held the gun. It went off on its own, into the ground. Dirt leaped into the air. The color on the horizon got splattered with mud. Bob's heart raced. He heard voices, opened his eyes, and saw Hugh standing over him. "The gun," Bob said.

"They didn't have one," Hugh said. "Lucky for you."

"What happened?" Bob felt sharp pain in his side and all down his neck to the middle of his back. "Where am I?"

"You got jumped. That's what. And now you're here. The back of Jimmy Finch's. Where he lives."

Bob grabbed his head. "Who was it?"

"Don't know for sure. I heard an odd thumping that didn't quit. Bein' around wood and people, you get used to the sound wood hitting flesh makes. You're not supposed to hear that sound come from an alley in town." Hugh laughed. "I ran after that sound and whoever it was run off faster than I could chase them. You were all crumpled on the ground so I pick you up and bring you here. It's the only place I know was open."

"That was the kindest thing anyone has done for me."

"You been good for me, my friend." Hugh put a hand on Bob's shoulder. "Rest. I'll be back after work." Hugh left the room.

Bob saw curtains on the window, a dresser against a wall. Candles had been lighted and placed around the room. There also stood a small stand next to the bed. A bed. He was lying in a real bed. He had never done that before. He stretched his arms out to his sides. His ribs had been bandaged and his arms were sore. He rolled his head to the side. A pillow, too. The room smelled fresh and clean. There was also the scent of flowers, but he couldn't see any in the room. On the stand next to the bed was a book lying on a small white piece of cloth with holes in it. But not just holes as if worn through, but a pattern of holes, a star-like pattern or a snowflake pattern. Bob picked up the book. He read the title: "The Spy,," by James Fenimore Cooper. He opened to the first page. His head hurt, but it was a physical pain, outside his head, not inside like when he had gotten drunk. He could read with this kind of pain.

In a short while, the glow of sunlight came through the window, lightening the curtain and the room. He stared, the book folded over his index finger and held close to his chest.

A slight knock came and the door opened. "You're awake." The woman appeared to be around Jimmy Finch's age and had the same dusted blond hair and straight, prominent nose. She wore a gingham dress and walked smoothly and elegantly across the floor. She blew out each candle.

Eyeing the book, she said, "You shouldn't try to read in such little light." She opened the curtains and let in the morning. She opened the window, too. Clean, fresh air burst into the room. "How are you feeling?"

Bob widened his eyes. "I'm—"

"Your head must hurt. There's a huge knot back there. At least there was when they brought you in."

"I'm better," Bob managed to say.

The woman stepped near Bob.

"I'm Jenny Finch, Jimmy's sister. I know, Jimmy and Jenny. I've heard all the rhymes." She winked and pulled the edge of the blanket tight near his shoulder. "There's a Jerry and a Josh. Jimmy got the best of the deal, being first. The rest of us just repeats." She laughed a quiet, high-pitched laugh almost like a giggle only lasting a bit longer.

Bob couldn't help laughing with her.

"So, you're better? You want a little breakfast?"

Bob wasn't hungry at the moment, but said yes, just so Jenny wouldn't leave and not return.

"Good. I didn't want to bring it if you weren't awake yet." She pointed to a chair that Bob hadn't noticed before. "Your friend leave?"

"I suppose he went to work."

"You suppose?" She laughed again. "Well, I suppose you're right about that. He sat here all night Jimmy said. I'm not sure he's going to get much done."

That reminded Bob. "Jasper," he said and tried to sit up. The blanket fell to his waist and he realized he was naked. "Oh. Who?"

"Not me, I can tell you that," she said with a sly grin and a slight flush of her face.

Bob smiled. She was the best humored woman he had ever met.

"If you mean Jasper Snipe." She stopped. "Oh, that's where I've seen you." She waved her finger at him. Then she placed her hand on his bare shoulder and pushed him back. "You lie down. I'll ask someone to let Jasper know. Now, let me get your breakfast. You drink coffee I suppose," she said with a wink.

Bob nodded. He pulled the blanket up to his chest and watched her leave As the door clicked, he relaxed, realizing that his entire body had tensed up when she came into the room.

He stared out the window a little while longer, then began to read again. He smelled breakfast cooking long before it arrived. Jenny stepped into the room with a tray balanced on her hand. "Sit up," she said.

Bob slid up so that his back leaned against the headboard, a finely whittled set of hemlock planks. He couldn't see the exact design, but could feel it imprinting on his back.

Jenny set the tray on his lap. "You don't look all that comfortable." She pulled on the pillow. "Lean forward."

He leaned and she stuffed the pillow behind his back. "There." She lightly patted the pillow so close to his bare skin that he could feel the warmth of her hand, then she backed away.

Bob leaned against the cool cotton. "That feels good." He picked up his fork. "Thank you for breakfast." He didn't want her to think he was ungrateful, so he lifted a forkful of egg into his mouth. As his elbow rose, he felt the muscles pull in his rib cage and winced.

She walked over to the window. She stood an average womanly height. Had an average build, too. She wasn't skinny and wasn't healthy, but somewhere between. She did move nicely under her dress, graceful and strong. And her breasts, Bob noticed, appeared to be firm.

While she walked around the room, he ate and watched her. Finally, she sat in the chair where Hugh had waited throughout the night.

"You haven't been in town very long, have you?" She sat straight, but relaxed, alert.

"A few months."

With a curious look on her face, she asked, "Where'd you come from?"

"The hills mostly. I spent some time as a wood hick and mill worker downriver. Built some homes down there, loaded wagons and trains."

"How'd you come by working for Jasper?" She leaned forward, reached up with one hand, and played with the ends of her hair as they talked.

The sun made her hair appear more blonde than brown. Where the sun wasn't dancing over it, her hair darkened. He imagined that at night there'd be no sign of yellow in her hair at all. As the color changed, her face changed. Her lips lightened and darkened opposite from her hair. Here eyes were brown, but sparkled in the light. And they appeared damp at all times, as though coated by Bob's beloved river water. "Jasper had a sign out: Help Wanted," Bob said once he swallowed. "I didn't want to work around dead trees any more."

Jenny laughed her giggle-laugh. "Dead trees," she said. "Why without those dead trees where would this town be right now?"

"I know. But I grew up near, well, in the woods and it pains me to see them all cut down."

"More will grow back."

"You're probably right."

"Jimmy said it's just another step in progress. It isn't always pretty, but that's what happens."

"Then where is this town when all the trees are gone?"

"There'll be something. There's already been mining and fishing, something will come along."

"I'm not so sure," Bob said.

She jerked her chin forward. "You can be that way." There was silence in the room for a few minutes. Jenny looked out the window. Bob finished eating and drank down the last of his lukewarm coffee.

"I've been right here pretty much all my life," Jenny said, after some thought.

"You sound as though you resent it."

"No, but I would like to see more. Jimmy said all of Pennsylvania looks pretty much the same. Some towns are bigger and some smaller and that's all."

"I wouldn't know," Bob said, "but he's probably right."

"Well he's not." She clipped her words. "New York ain't just bigger, it's different. I've read about it. Even Philadelphia is different. Now you go farther west into Kansas and it gets flat and on to Colorado there are mountains that would make Bald Eagle Mountain across the river look like a mole hill."

"He said Pennsylvania."

"Well, I'm not staying in Pennsylvania."

"Where'd you learn about all this if you've never left town?"

She pointed to the book on the stand next to him. "Same as you. I've read and I've seen drawings and even pictures."

"I'd like to go someday," Bob said to his own surprise.

"I'm going to take a train straight across the country and stop in any town that looks the least bit interesting, whether the buildings are different, or the scenery, or the people just plain feel friendly." She laughed louder than before, seeming to be delighted with herself.

Bob laughed with her. "We could stay in hotels and sleeper cars, under the stars and under the trees."

When he looked at Jenny, her head was turned and her hand held over her mouth. Her red face grew dark with blood and the moisture in her eyes made it appear as though she were crying. "Is something wrong?" he asked.

"No. I don't think so."

"What did I say?" He wished he could go over to her, but remembered his nakedness. He reached out. "Was I talking too much?"

Then she burst out laughing.

"Am I funny? Am I stupid? What did I do?"

"No, please." She laughed. "You're getting upset over nothing. I just felt embarrassed."

"Embarrassed?"

"When you said 'we.'. You said *we* could go."

Bob sat back into the pillow. "Oh. I'm sorry. I got caught up in the idea of getting away from here. I didn't mean anything."

"It's all right. Nobody ever really means it." The smile left her face for a moment, then came back, fake.

"No, I didn't mean that either. I'd be glad to go."

"You don't have to say that," she said. Her eyes turned down as though she no longer wanted to see him.

Bob set the tray aside and slid down in the bed to hide. He was sorry about what he had said, but it was too late. He pulled on the blanket, and as his legs straightened, his feet pushed into the open.

"Now look," Jenny said. She stood to help pull the blanket over his feet. "Oh, you're feet look like they hold a lot of stories."

"Would you like to hear a few," Bob said not quite knowing why.

"I would some day." She pulled the blanket down.

The motion of the blanket across his naked body, and the look in Jenny's eyes when she said what she had, made his penis twitch. The blanket jumped and Bob bent his knees to try to hide the movement and to get his feet covered quickly. He winced again. He couldn't tell whether she had seen what had happened or not, but something inside him hoped she had.

"You'd better lie back down."

"In a moment," he said.

"I'd better go."

"You'll come back? For a story?"

She picked up the tray from next to him. "Later, I suppose, to check on you."

They stared at each other for a moment. Bob's body tensed in fear and lust.

Jenny turned and left the room with the tray.

When Bob was sure she was gone, he inspected his feet. Deep creases moved down the center of his souls and around his toes. A hard shell of skin protected them like a first pare of shoes. The muscle near his arch on the side of his foot was blue with blood-filled veins. His thick, tough heal had a ridge of callous that grew yellow and wide. There were nicks and cuts and scratches everywhere, and black-laced scars where splinters had been healed over and accepted by his body like a fence post swallowed by a nearby tree.

What could Jenny have seen in his feet? One glance. What story had she already noticed? The young farm boy? The liar?

Bob slipped his feet back under the blanket. How could he have any life, but that of a liar's? Jenny, nor any woman, could know the truth. He remembered the betrayal he felt when the five roaming Negroes had lied to him.

His side ached. He had not even thought of his injuries until they throbbed or a pain struck through him like lightning. Now, his head hurt too, and his neck. He patted the book on the stand next to him, as if to say later. He stared out the window wondering how the day was proceeding for Jasper.

CHAPTER 24

Thanks to Hugh, Bob's ribs were not cracked or broken. Bruises dappled his arms and legs and side. As his muscle scraped and pulled against the tenderized skin and nerves, pain pulsed through him making his movements slow. But he could work. And he could get around just fine. No one had said so, but Bob knew that one of the men who attacked him was Jacob.

Another act was heading into town, five black women and an old black man, a baritone. Jimmy Finch needed the room for some of them. "An unusual bunch. And I don't know how the clientele's going to take to it, but I know several of the women. Grew up with 'em you might say, and they're good people."

Bob had dressed. Hugh had stopped by as an escort. Jenny stood behind and to the right of Jimmy, making occasional eye contact with Bob.

Bob, so hypnotized by her damp, sweet eyes, couldn't help looking over at her each time she caught his attention. At one point, Jimmy turned to look behind him, noticing Bob's attention shift elsewhere.

Jenny laughed and turned her face away.

After all the thank you's and small talk, Hugh led Bob outside and onto the sunny street. Mosquitoes and gnats were thick and annoying. Bob squinted.

"You all right?" Hugh asked.

"Fine. Why would you ask?"

"You're still walking pretty slow."

"More stiff than sore," Bob said. He picked up the pace.

Hugh stared ahead, "Mind if I ask you something?"

"Go right ahead."

"You're not thinking about Jimmy's sister are you?"

"She wouldn't want the likes of me."

"Shit. You are. God dammit. You can't go thinkin' about that."

"Why not?"

Hugh's voice quieted. He talked in a whisper out the corner of his mouth. "What the hell color you think your children would be?"

They kept walking. Bob didn't know how he felt about Jenny nor did he extend those feelings as far into the future as Hugh did. "Don't know," he said. "I didn't think about it."

"Well you'd better, my friend. Not just for your sake, but for hers."

"That family doesn't feel that way, though, you said so yourself. Look at all the Negroes moving through that house."

"That's different. I'll guarantee it."

"What the hell does that mean?"

"Those are acts. They're passing through. They're not family." Hugh squinted his eyes and swatted at a clutch of gnats, slapping violently at the air in front of him. "Not everyone in this town is so tolerant. And when they find out you lied, they're going to feel tricked and cheated. It won't be pretty."

"You're telling me I can't have a life?"

"No. I'm not sayin' that."

"You think I'm less than you."

Hugh grabbed Bob's arm. "God damn you. They'd lynch you sure as we're standin' here. Do you know that? Jesus Holy Christ you chose this life, now you God damned better live it like you told it."

Bob stared into Hugh's square face. The man's eyes penetrated with strength and logic. Bob wasn't interested in having either. "A baby could just as easily be white. Look at the two of us. Look at me. What do you see?" His teeth clenched. He knew what Hugh saw, but he also knew what Hugh knew, and the two didn't mix well, not even to Bob. But he wasn't about to let go, not then. He hadn't known a moment ago how he felt about Jenny. After Hugh stripped away layers of thought, Bob sensed his emotions more clearly. His interest in Jenny lay deeper than he'd understood at first. His interest penetrated more than mere curiosity.

Hugh walked Bob to the back entrance of Jasper's bakery. Another man, a one-armed man wearing a torn soldier's shirt, stood at the oven. "Hey, boss," the man said.

Jasper looked back over his shoulder, a big toothy smile across his face until he saw Bob and Hugh, then his lips tightened. "Ah, dammit," he said. "I'm sorry Bob. I had to find someone. I needed the help." He shook his head.

"Well, he's back," Hugh piped in.

Bob put his hand on Hugh's chest to stop him from advancing any closer to Jasper. Bob nodded to the soldier first, then to Jasper. He said, "I understand and it's all right."

"Bob?" Hugh said.

"No. I mean it."

"There're plenty of jobs you can do," Jasper said.

The soldier turned his head away.

"It's okay, Mr. Snipe, this man deserves to work too." Bob nodded again to the soldier, then he let a small grin slide over his face, a ripple of acceptance.

"I'm sorry," Jasper said as Bob left.

In the alley Hugh grabbed Bob by the elbow and spun him around. "What the hell did you just do? That was your job."

"Jobs don't belong to people."

"The hell they don't."

"The mill changed your job as soon as you got hurt. I can find something. I'm smart enough," Bob said.

"You're not acting smart," Hugh said.

"That man back there. When I saw him, I thought of you. He didn't choose the life he has. An accident and everything changes," Bob said.

Hugh held up his hand. "It's healing."

"You still have yours. Can you imagine how he feels after fighting for what he believed in? Jasper's a good man for hiring him, and a better man for keeping him."

"What happened to you to make you give a shit?"

Bob thought the question through. "I don't know. Another time it may have pissed me off. Things can go two ways. I can feel controlled or free. If I were passing for Negro and everywhere I turned someone was taking advantage or treating me poorly, I might be pretty mad. I learned, though, that I'm not a killer. Don't exactly know why. And now I know I don't take someone's job from them."

"I've seen beatings and lynchings and all sorts of other abuses. Inhumane behavior. Some men become more like beasts than men," Hugh said.

Bob remembered his beating as a child, how Mr. Carpenter had touched his mother's cheek, how he'd escaped being killed. "I've seen men act compassionately even when they didn't have to, when the pressure was against them." Bob pursed his lips and made a smacking sound with them. "I know I could be killed for what I'm doing. I know it. I don't think I realized it at first. There's no doubt now. I'm also living free right now and the feeling reminds me that not all people of one color are bad and not all are good. It's not easy, but you have to take each person and figure them out on their own."

"There's a lot of liars and cheats out there, too, don't fool yourself," Hugh said.

"Like me?"

"Ha. You don't even know."

"Know what?"

"How you feel. You're looking at your history, your ma and pa, not yourself. You look the next time you get a chance. Then we see how you feel. I'll tell you, if you're not standing next to your parents, everything about you says white. And I don't mean poor or ignorant white. I mean city white. Now, you can lie about your heritage, but you damned well can't lie about what's inside you screaming to come out."

"I never thought of it that way."

"Well, think of it. Stop pitchin' back and forth in the middle."

"Right now I've done enough thinking and too much talking. I've got to get work."

"Always work at the mill this time of year." Hugh slapped a mosquito that landed on his arm. A dot of blood appeared and he wiped it against his pants leg. Sweat dripped down the side of his head.

Bob's muscles loosened up. He walked straighter. "Not the mill," he said.

"You're right." Hugh patted Bob's shoulder. "You don't want to work at the mill. Look what it's done to me."

"I'll find something. But first I've got to get out of that boarding house and find something that's nicer."

"Tired of the piss smell or a few days in that bed at Jimmy Finch's spoil you?"

"I do like a bed with fewer bedbugs."

Hugh laughed. "You like a bed with a woman in the room. I don't blame you, but you better listen to me about that or your life might get a whole lot more complicated."

"I don't know. Look at me. The chances are—"

"Don't go back there again. I've seen Negroes, Indians, and white all mixed and you don't know what's coming out. You're brother might look opposite of you. And, Bob, you don't want to take that chance. You don't want to put Jenny or any other woman through that. I'm telling you," Hugh said. "You'd better listen."

Bob got the feeling something in Hugh's past must have given him special knowledge of the situation, but he didn't express his thoughts about it.

Hugh pealed off to work the rest of the day, while Bob headed for the boarding house. It might be more difficult to find a place to stay than to find a job, but he was willing to try.

The moment he entered the room, he knew he couldn't live with the stench any longer. His first thought was to leave his bedroll and books as well. Instead, he held his breath momentarily, walked to his cot, collected his things, and left for good. He had paid through the week. There was no reason to talk with anyone.

Bob wandered up and down Third and Fourth Streets while weaving in and out of the side streets too. Trying not to favor the pain in his ribs, Bob strolled from Arch Street to Market Street, stopping anywhere he thought might be able to put him up even if he didn't see a sign. When he found nothing, he traveled up Market Street and weaved up and down side streets between Park Avenue and High Street. Between those roads, he found a place on Green Street a block from Campbell Street, which conveniently led to the river. He wouldn't be in the thick of things, but he'd be close enough. A young family was renting a room in their house that had been cleared of personal items. Two young boys now slept in their parents' room.

Carl, the husband, introduced himself and showed Bob into the house. "I don't recognize you Bob," he said. "Then there's hundreds who work at the mill."

"I don't work there," Bob said.

"No?"

"I'm looking for a job now. I did work at Jasper Snipe's Bakery."

Carl's face lightened up. "Oh, I do know you." Then he stepped back. "Wait a minute. Used to?"

"I got jumped and he hired a soldier."

"Look mister I need this rent."

"I've got plenty. It's in the bank. I save everything."

"A week up front. I can't wait for payday."

"I understand." Bob pulled the money from his pocket. "Three dollars?" he said, quoting the sign he'd seen. He handed it over. "Here, let's do two weeks."

Bob looked at Carl's bandaged right hand. Fingers were missing. Probably all of them but the thumb. *The mill took lives a little at a time,* he thought. Carl took the money with his good hand, his left, and stuffed it into his pocket.

Carl led Bob down a short hall. The kitchen was to their right. Bob peered in as they passed.

"Look mister, I live here with my wife and boy. The kitchen's private. A few blocks down Campbell and you can get meals."

"I understand," Bob said. "I'll be as scarce as I can."

Carl nodded. "I heal fast. I'll be workin' again soon."

Bob looked at him. Regardless of his outward stance, Carl appeared pitiful, unsure of himself. His assurances were all too aggressive. He was scared. "As soon as you're on your feet, I'll find somewhere else," Bob said.

"A man's house is private. I'm only doing this 'cause I have to."

"I can see that, sir."

"Here's the room," Carl let Bob look in.

Two wood plank beds filled much of the space. A dresser stood against one wall between them. There was a mattress on one bed. The other must have been moved into the master bedroom. The room didn't smell of piss, but of sweaty little boys. Bob could deal with that. He'd lived with the smell of bodies his whole life.

"You can go in," Carl said with some apparent reluctance.

Bob placed his bedroll and sack on the floor. "Thank you," he said.

"It's done then." Carl walked away and Bob heard him in another room telling his wife and sons to stay away from the stranger in the house until, ". . . we get to know 'im."

Bob sat on the bed with the mattress for a few minutes. An unusual feeling came over him. He was alone. For years there were other people around him. Not always kind, but there was talking and rustling about. There was noise. He listened. He couldn't hear the river, either.

In a few minutes, he decided to buy some candles and to get another book from the library. He'd make sure he accomplished those two tasks while he looked for work. Walking toward the river from Carl's house, at Fourth Street, Bob turned left, the river to his right, and headed toward town past mansions belonging to the mill owners. Howard Mill, Kemp Mill, Paulhamous Mill, and farther upriver, Ritter Mill. He had delivered bread to these houses. He knew the staffs, black and white, men and women, working for the men of money and power.

He stopped in front of Henry Kemp's house and turned toward the door. He knocked. Liza answered. She was a smiling and delightful black woman of age, chubby in the cheeks and in the arms, but with an average body on the rest of her.

"Why Bob, where you bread? An' ain't it early?"

"I got hurt and Jasper hired another helper. I'm all healed now and was wondering if Mr. and Mrs. Kemp needed any help. A stableman? A fetcher?"

"I done know fer sure. I get 'im to tell me when he git home. Where you stayin'."

"A house up on Green Street. Six-one-two."

"Six-one-two Green. I think I can fine that. You know I lives right pass dare in wit a shack row." She laughed. "I ain't surprised if'n you all can hear us chantin' and singin' on Sunday."

"I just moved in."

"Due tell. Well, I done think there nothin', but I be sure to let you know."

"Thank you Liza," Bob nodded his head and walked down to Jed Howard's mansion.

Surprisingly, Jed's wife, Elizabeth, opened the door. Bob had talked with her only once before. She was a skinny slip of a woman with a sharp jaw line and boney elbows. Her voice often sounded as if it slid along her teeth and leaped out of her mouth with the force of her breath behind it, often cutting off the first letter of the first word she said. "'Es, 'An I help you?" Once she got started, she didn't force the words out so hard and they came easier and without as much snipping.

Bob stepped back, having expected May-Lou to answer the door.

Elizabeth appeared to recognize the surprise in his face because she then said, "'ay-Lou an' her family's all sick. I tell 'er and Emmil to stay home till they fine."

Bob stood there to register what she'd said and to contemplate what he wished to do about it.

"You da bread man."

"I am."

"'Ere's your bread?"

"I'm not the bread man any longer. Now, I'm looking for work."

Elizabeth looked into the sky as though Bob wasn't even standing there. "Oh, thank you Lord," she said. She sounded as though she meant it. Her voice so soft and so sincere that Bob wanted to reach out and hold her.

"'Ere's a lot a work." She stepped from the door allowing space for Bob to walk in. She moved quickly, closing the door behind him, then slipping past him on the side closest to the wall, where there was hardly enough room for a broom handle. Before he knew it she charged in front of him leading him deeper into the house. He hadn't even felt a breeze as she stepped by him.

He didn't have time to think. He never heard what his wages would be. Elizabeth hadn't even said yes to him about the work, nor did she say what he'd be doing. He just followed behind her, through the foyer, past a large reading room on the left, past what appeared to be a living room on the right, then the kitchen on the right, and a closed door on the left. She headed straight out to the back of the house, turned left and there, in front of her, was a carriage bent down as if on one knee. The wheel lay in the grass. The axle pushed into the dirt. And the diagonal wheel lifted into the air, held up by the weight of the shift and tilt of the carriage itself.

"I can fix that," Bob said.

"You got a woman?"

"No, ma'am."

"'An you find one?"

"Maybe."

"'E needs a cook, now, too."

"I'll check and see who might be interested."

Elizabeth pursed her lips and stared into Bob's face. She made a smacking sound and walked off without a word.

CHAPTER 25

B ob inspected the carriage. There was no telling how long it had been sitting in the same, unused position. The axle looked fine. He pulled down on the opposite wheel from the missing one and the carriage weight shifted. He easily got the wheel to touch the ground, but the end of the axle just slid back a few inches. It didn't lift. The carriage weight would be off the axle though. When he let go of the wheel, the carriage shifted back, but not completely. Both the back wheel and the axle touched ground now.

He stepped to the wheel lying in the grass, reached down and lifted it, pulling grass along too. It had been there long enough for the grass to have grown around it. He had to force the wheel against the long, slow grasping and tearing of the lawn.

On one knee, next to the wheel, Bob noticed that it had a split hub. No one had greased the wheel for a long time, which had been much of the problem, he surmised. Bob rolled the wheel next to the carriage and leaned it against the boot-board.

He glanced around the property and found plenty of rocks and wood, and dragged them into place so that he could prop the front axle up and off the ground.

Next, he inspected the other wheels. Two could be salvaged with a little sanding and some grease. One other wheel wouldn't make it to the edge of town and back. Bob knocked at the back door of the house.

Mrs. Howard answered. She looked calmer than when he'd arrived. A white fringed apron hung from her waist and she had taken the time to pin her hair up. "'Es?"

"The carriage will need a little work. One hub's broken and another can't be repaired." Bob looked around inside the house more as an indication that he'd been searching and not as though he were nosey. "Can't find any grease anywhere either."

Mrs. Howard opened the door a bit farther so that Bob could peer inside. "Anything here?"

"Don't see any." He stopped for a moment thinking that she might instruct him. "I'm not sure what it will cost," he said.

"Don't care."

"Would you like me to go ahead and fix it?"

"'E got a tab wit the stable. Tell 'em it's for the Howard's."

"Could you write a short note?"

She stood and stared at him.

Eventually Bob nodded. "I could write it for you."

She stepped away, went into the kitchen, and came back with paper and a stubby pencil. Handing it to Bob, she said, "Thank you," in such a whisper he hardly heard her.

"What would you like me to write?"

She looked to the ground.

"I'll just put down that you'd like two wheels and a bucket of grease put on your tab. I'll let you know how much that costs when I get back."

"No need," she said. "I truss ya."

Bob smiled as broadly as he could. He didn't know whether to feel good about himself or pity Elizabeth Howard. A trapped child stared out of her face. He hadn't realized it ever before, but that must be what it felt like to be a slave – as an adult. It didn't look good.

Before he could turn to go, she put her hand out and touched his arm. "'F you can write, why you wanna work like this?"

That was a good question. He pursed his lips, nodded politely, and stepped away letting her hand drop.

On his walk to the stable, he let her question roll around in his head. His bruises hurt more as he stood upright to walk than when he rolled and lifted the rocks and logs into place. Walking made his side muscles ripple with every step, shooting occasional pain clear through to his flesh. So he slowed, he sauntered down toward the stable as though he were on a Sunday stroll.

The street wasn't very busy and he hummed, not loudly, but the sound did resonate more than a whisper, right at that break between breath force and lung force.

By the time he made it to the stable, he wondered why he labored all morning too. And over a carriage that the Howard's obviously didn't care for properly. That's probably why they didn't want the stable to send someone to fix it, to escape the embarrassment of neglect. Indeed, why had he continually labored when he had also been able to out-think many of the men and women he'd met or worked with?

The blacksmith at the stable questioned his note. The man must have known the Howard's well because he instantly read the note and asked, "Did Mrs. Howard write this down for you."

"No sir," Bob said. "She can't write."

He put down his hammer and dropped a piece of metal into a water bucket. A fizz and sizzle rose with steam. He placed the tongs across his anvil next to the hammer. He stretched to his full height. A long torso, short stocky legs, and barrel chest gave him the stature of a rock. He shook hands with Bob. "Name's Willy, but everybody calls me Fist."

"Fist?"

"Been known to box." He laughed with a boom that caught Bob off guard.

Fist grabbed Bob's shoulder when he saw that he'd surprised him. The grip hurt, but Bob didn't cringe. Fist said, "That's when I was a kid. Now I beat the hell out of horse shoes and carriage iron. Made cannon parts in Philadelphia. Kept me busy during the war." He held up his hands. "That's why I'm all here," he said. "What about you?"

"I was farming."

"You was lucky."

"I'm starting to feel lucky," Bob said.

"So, two wheels and grease, is it?"

"Yes, sir."

"Only niggers call me sir," Fist said.

Bob quieted, answering questions but not participating in the conversation, which he knew Fist wanted him to do. The little pleasure he got from Fist's frustration with the conversation ebbed when Fist slapped a black man who worked for him. "Dumb son-of-a-bitch," he said when the man delivered the wrong wheel.

Bob thanked Fist anyway, biting his lip before doing so. Then he rolled the wheels out of the stable and down the street. The grease bucket handle slipped over his arm rested in the crook of his elbow and swung as he maneuvered the wheels down the street.

Bob had never seen Fist at Jimmy Finch's and figured it was because of how the man obviously felt about Negroes. As Hugh had said, some in town avoided the bar.

The going was slow. If Bob moved too quickly, the grease bucket slammed into his hip. He had enough bruises. He moved slowly as he returned to the Howard's.

Once again he sang while rolling those wheels. "Don't know why I'm walking/ down this lonesome road,/ just sure I can't stop talking,/ nor let go this heavy load./ People say I'm crazy/ for working like I do,/ but I say I'm not lazy/ missing life like some men do."

"Ex-cuse ma sir. Ex-cuse."

Bob heard a woman's voice from behind him and then heard feet shuffling his way. With some effort, he stopped the steady roll of the wheels. One almost fell over and, when he reached for it, the grease bucket slapped the other wheel almost knocking it out of his hand and into the dirt. By the time he felt balanced enough to turn around, the woman stepped beside him, then in front of him while two other women stepped to either side. The woman to his left reminded him of Martha and although he didn't wish it, his mind freed the woman's breasts and let them hang in the hot summer air, the nipples smooth against the flesh. He shook his head and looked at the others one at a time. "What can I do for you ladies?"

"Ladies? Well, my goodness," the one in front of him said. "We the Sistas of Rythmn."

"Except you aren't sisters," Bob said. Their noses, although wide, were not the same. And the way their eyes opened a space in their skulls were hollowed out on two of the women, but ran shallow on the other. Even the cheeks and ears weren't enough alike.

Not that they had to look the same, but typically there were similarities. These women had none.

She turned her head to the side, looking at him through a tighter lense. "An' you ain't you normal white man. Most cain't tell one Negro from another. We got to wear shirts so's they can tell men from women." She laughed.

A shot of blood ran through Bob. "I was raised by Negroes most of my life. Doesn't Jimmy Finch recognize you?"

The woman kept her head cocked. "I reckon on one level. You part of da railroad?"

"No."

"Come on Mary," the woman with Martha's build said.

"We heard ya," Mary said.

"Heard what?"

"Singin'. You make up them song words?"

Bob lowered his head. "Yes, but they come and go, just like everything."

"I'm Mary. This here is Joesy. An' here is Bet. How would you like it if we sang you song? We cain't pay nothin' an' we got little to trade."

"Sing what?"

"You song 'bout walkin' down dis lonesome road."

"You heard me?"

"Hell," Joesy said, "she hear what people sayin' clear 'cross town. You grow up in da South you hear a mob coming before they thinkin' about it."

"An' she remember the words, too," Bet added.

Bob smiled broad and toothy. "Yes, ma'am. You can if you can remember what I said."

"Johny write most a the new songs we got. We sing two or three a night juss to surprise the audience so's they wake up. Then we do gospels – ."

"Mostly in church on Sunday," Joesy said.

"An' war songs."

"Yankie only," Joesy said.

"An' even some Negro work songs."

"Johny gettin' tired is all. We like more if'n you can writ 'em down."

Bob looked from one woman to the next. His heart raced. The sun sparkled off the treetops. "I might be able to do that."

The women looked at one another and laughed like they'd been tickled. Then they hiked their skirts off the road. Mary said, "Come by tonight?" And before Bob could acknowledge her, they all nodded and scurried off behind him.

He sang louder as he headed to the Howard's. He tried to remember what words he had made up, but suddenly wondered whether the job might be more difficult than he thought originally. After singing the same words a few times, the songs sounded a little less interesting to him.

The rest of the afternoon, as the day's heat peaked and then began to wane, Bob worked with less concentration. He still packed grease and mounted the new wheels. He still managed to get the rocks and logs back where he'd found them. And he even thought to feed the carriage horses in the back of the horse shed.

By the time he finished, the sun had dropped into the treetops and the Lord's sweet song into night carried his words with it. The beauty inspired Bob to make up a song about a woman's beauty being like the sunset and fading from a man's life at the end of his days. Perhaps the lonely feel to the song reflected how Bob felt about his new room in Carl's house. Perhaps it was his pining about his mixed concerns over Jenny Finch. As Hugh had brought up, he might feel one way, but what might be practical – in the longer time period – stood opposite those feelings.

The longer and more deeply Bob sang, the more beautiful the evening crept into the Howard's back yard, and the stronger Bob felt about Jenny. He imagined she had no suitors because her beauty intimidated everyone. He recalled how his body had reacted to her glare alone. As he cleaned up after his repair work, Bob's song, the color of sunset, and his loneliness merged inside the remembered smoothness of Jenny Finch's face, the flow of her body in motion.

Bob wiped his hands on a rag he found near the disorganized tools in the carriage house. Stepping from behind the carriage after a final admiration of his work, Bob was surprised by Jed Howard bursting from the back door. Jed stood nearly six and a half feet tall, had bushy white hair and deep creases in his face and neck. Three duplicates of Jed followed him. The boys' hair weren't white, but brown and the creases were not so deep on any of them. But these three were Jed's boys, long and lanky, stringy muscles in their arms and big feet stretching out to hold them upright.

"Fine job. Fine job, Mr.—"

"White," Bob said. Holding out his hand, he said, "Bob White."

"Like the birdy?" the oldest boy said. The other two laughed.

Bob nodded. "A cruel joke, but a true one," he said.

Jed barely shook Bob's hand before he began his inspection of the carriage. "Didn't clean up very well, Mr. Bird Man."

The younger boy laughed nervously and repeated his father's words quietly. "Bird man," became a refrain.

Bob followed Jed and bent to see where the man pointed. Dirt was caked on the boot-board and a smudge ran across the carriage side.

"These scratches need paint." Jed forged ahead.

"Scratches here, too, Pa," the oldest said.

Bob tried to note each scratch, but couldn't be on all sides of the carriage at once. He resolved to look it over the next day. "You have paint?" he asked.

Jed shot up straight and peered at Bob as though he had spoken out of turn. "You should-a looked and picked it up all at once. Now you'll waste time going' to get it. Well, I won't pay for wasted time, Bird Man. No sir. You pick the paint up on your way here tomorrow."

The sun pitched into the sea of green setting a glow along the ridge of the mountains. The sky darkened. The back area where the newly repaired carriage sat shrouded in shadow was reduced to near darkness.

"I want this properly cleaned and properly repaired, every scratch, then polished by tomorrow eve." His chin jutted toward Bob, an unloosed arrow. "I'll inspect it then."

"I think I can do that," Bob said.

"Think? You don't Mister and I'll strap you like a nigger."

Bob looked into the sky for a moment. The first stars pushed through. The anger he felt rise in his chest and throat at the moment clashed against the serenity he was experiencing just before Jed split the clean air with his unclean words. Bob's teeth clenched and his ears rang. "Don't think you'll have the chance to strap me," Bob said, still looking into the night sky.

"I better not."

"'Cause I won't be here tomorrow," Bob said.

"You young, cocky son-of-a-bitch. You're too damned much a pussy or you'd be workin' at the mill like the other men. All except for war gimps and I'll have none of them at my mill." Jed slapped Bob across the head. "You take the work you can do, or I'll make sure nobody give you work."

Bob turned suddenly. His eyes bulged.

Maybe Jed thought he'd gone crazy. Maybe he thought Bob had just had enough. Either way, he stepped back and back, and his boys followed him.

Bob felt anger as he had never felt it before, head-splitting, jaw-clenching anger. Before speaking, he spit at Jed's feet. "You don't slap a man unless you're ready to kill him, Mister. You don't ridicule a job until you're man enough to do it yourself." Bob took a step and Jed leaned backward. For a big, rich mill owner, Bob thought, Jed's power was only in his mouth. "And, when you address me, you'll learn to use my name." He would not get paid for his day's work. He would not go back to that house. But he felt justified and relieved.

Jed nodded. Bob turned to leave around the side of the house. To his surprise, the youngest boy ran up as if to jump him. Bob heard the approach and whipped around and hit the boy in the ear. His heart fell. He had hit a white man. He could be killed on the spot if they knew his secret. The boy staggered backwards.

Before going to Carl's, he decided to have a drink at the saloon. He hoped he'd see Hugh there and be able to tell his story and ask for advice. He wondered whether Jed Howard really had the power to keep him from getting work in town. Hugh might know. This was no time to visit with the Sisters of Rhythm. Perhaps another evening, or early tomorrow, he would go there.

The dense and muggy air pulled on his lungs. His bruises made walking uncomfortable, but only occasionally painful. It was a good thing Jed hadn't hit him. Jed must be a sad and lonely man to feel that striking out at others would get them to work. Bob knew from childhood how a man could find ways to be lazy if he chose to. How planning made doing take longer. How one's pace could slow, making a day's work take two days to finish. How hiding often made work stop altogether. Bob was not proud of what' he'd said to Jed, but he did hum a happy tune on his way to Jimmy Finch's.

Hugh was at the bar and his mug stood brimming with foam.

"Just get here?" Bob said.

"Have one with me."

"All right."

Hugh motioned to the bartender and a beer mug slammed down in front of Bob. Foam spilled over the edge onto the smooth mahogany surface of the bar.

Bob paid, placing his money in front of the mug, near the bartender, who scooped it up almost like magic.

"Had an interesting day," Bob said.

"Tell me." Hugh turned to listen.

Eventually, Hugh laughed both when Bob told him about Fist and when he told him about Jed. Hugh then said, "They don't know who they fuckin' with."

Bob liked the sound of that: as though he were a man of some means. "And what do you think about the songs?"

"Ain't no money in it. So, why do it?" Hugh said.

"But people would be listening to my words. They'd hear what I had to say."

Hugh smiled at his beer. He shook his head. "You know, maybe you're right. For someone who seldom had a voice, even when I met you just months ago, you're finding it. Others should hear it to."

Bob laughed. "Yeah." He drank down his beer and ordered two more. Sisters of Rhythm were just stepping onto the stage.

CHAPTER 26

The room did not smell of piss. The bed felt comfortable to lie in. Carl's family remained quiet much of the time. And the house felt safe and secure, unlike many of the inns and boarding Houses and barracks Bob had slept in. Still, he slept fitfully.

He didn't belong there. The family didn't want him. He had displaced the sons. And, it was temporary. Carl would heal enough to start work again, this time in a different job, but he'd do it. And the mill owner wouldn't care as long as the work got done. Carl might even be better off in the long run. Regardless what happened next for Carl, Bob would not be wanted there.

By morning, Bob hadn't slept more than a few intermittent hours. He rolled out of bed, placing his feet on the bare planks, already warm. The day would be hot. Sweat slipped down from his armpit and beaded along his hairline and above his lip.

He had to go to the bathroom and get something to eat. The beer had made his mouth dry.

He shuffled around the room in the half-light. He had read the night before. The candle scent still hung in the room. The tart scent of Carl's sons had been replaced in one night.

Money was stashed inside his book. He kept the rest in his pockets. Thanks to his discriminate spending habits, he didn't need to worry about getting work for a few weeks, especially if he emptied his bank account.

He slipped on his pants and shirt and stood to go. He opened the door slowly and noticed that it didn't creek. After closing the door behind him, Bob walked down the hall and went out the front. He felt freed. He ran his fingers through his short hair. He took in the humid morning air. Mosquitoes already pestered him. He itched an old bite and slapped at a mosquito that landed on his arm. Blood dot. He wiped it on his pant leg.

The smell of bacon and eggs rested on the dead air, slight, but noticeable. He wondered whether the odor came from Carl's kitchen at the end of the hall, wafting outside through an open window instead of traveling through the blocked hallway. As he ambled down Campbell Street, the scent got stronger. Carl and his family were still asleep.

Bob ran into people heading toward town or one of the mills. Many said 'morning', others didn't. One man asked whether he'd quit working for Jasper and Bob ran through a quick explanation, while the two of them continued to walk.

Bob stopped in at the Park Avenue Eatery and took a seat. A middle-aged woman yelled from the door to the kitchen asking what he wanted. Several men turned to look at Bob as he answered, "Eggs, bacon, coffee." The rest of the clientele didn't look up, stop talking, or acknowledge the woman hollering from the back of the place.

Seven tables sat inside the small space. Bob could hear every conversation in there had he wished to listen. Instead he thought to himself, wandering through every possibility for his day. When he decided, he ate quickly, drank down his coffee, and stepped back out into the street, leaving his money on the table.

His heart pounded. His ears rang. Like when he talked back to Jed Howard and then punched his son, Bob's adrenaline took over.

By the time he reached the saloon, sweat dripped down his face and arms. He didn't know what he'd say, but stepped up to the door in the back and hit it hard with his fist. The wait was endless.

Jenny answered. "Oh my."

Bob knew why she said that. Her face blushed and she placed her hand over her mouth.

"Sweet Jenny," Mary said from behind her. "Why I would never a guessed it."

Jenny turned toward Mary who looked at Bob and said, "Why, you got the same look on you."

Mary put her arm around Jenny lovingly. Bob had never seen one woman do to another, let alone a Negro woman and a white woman. "Now I got no idea why you come," she said. "You wishin' to see me an' my sisters or just Jenny here?"

Bob stuttered and couldn't seem to get the words out. The room lighted up behind Jenny. The sun touched her hair gently.

"I get 'im first," Mary said.

Bob could tell that Jenny had no idea what was going on.

Mary hugged Jenny close to her, a little squeeze, and explained. "We meets this man on the street and he be singing what we never heard a-fore." She lowered her voice. "He gonna write us a song or two."

Jenny backed out of the doorway. "Well he'd better come in then."

Bob brushed past them and stopped. He suddenly didn't know where to go.

"We have a parlor," Jenny said.

"A parlor? Well, we usually use the gamblin' table in the back a the bar, but if'n you want us in the parlor dat's fine too," Mary said before leaving to round up the other women and John.

Jenny sat opposite Bob. She stared at her own feet. Her hands were folded in her lap.

Bob's hands shook, and he thought he felt his lip twitch. He knew the dangers of what he was about to do, but couldn't stop himself. "Can I come back later? Or can we meet somewhere?"

Jenny raised her face and looked into his eyes.

Bob's whole body tensed. His memories of women were not pleasant, but this woman, this feeling, pulled at him differently. In a strained voice, he said, "I'd come to tell you one of those stories my feet knows." He looked down at his stretched out legs and wiggled his feet.

Jenny laughed in a nervous way. "You most certainly can come by."

Bob's entire being took in her reply.

When the Sisters of Rhythm came into the room, Jenny stayed seated. No one seemed to care. Bob didn't know what to expect or what to do, so he sat and waited for someone else to begin.

Mary set paper and pencil on Bob's lap. Then she introduced the others one after another, and nodded to John when she was finished.

Bob picked up the pencil.

A moment later, John began to run a baseline rhythm singing, "Bum, bum, bum, do-dip, bum. Bum, bum, bum, do-dip, bum," repeatedly.

Bob listened. No one looked at him except Jenny who only glanced occasionally in his direction. He closed his eyes for a moment just to escape the room and its occupants. His nervousness rose to a pitch of its own. What if he couldn't do it? What if nothing came to mind?

Soon Mary, or Joesy, began to hum. It soothed him. Martha came to mind, humming in the corner of the white-washed shack. He was a little boy again. Another voice placed a twinkling, tighter rhythm over the other two. It was as if the entire room had been filled with music.

Bob followed the sound to the fields where he grew up. He opened his eyes, thin slits, only enough for him to see the paper where he wrote: "The yellow-tipped fields of grain/ where I grew to be a man/ are long behind/ here I sit blind/ at the end of life I stand."

The words continued – his life but not his life. An old man remembering youth, a youth that Bob never got to experience or live out. But in the sound, somewhere, there rode the possibility for him to live out a different life, one where he didn't have to work a day of double-chores, stealing time alone when he could. He wrote on and finished the song. The old man dying with a hint of a smile for the strength it took to travel through life.

When he put his pencil down, a tear braced itself at the corner of his eye. He brushed it away. He had fallen into a dream. The room and the voices had disappeared for a time. They could have eaten lunch and he would not have known it. The beautiful and empty feeling he experienced while riding the lyrics swelled inside his chest. He sighed out of relief and exhaustion.

Somehow Mary and John and the other Sisters understood the calm, the sacredness of what he'd just done. They stopped humming and singing, but did not say a word. No one reached for the paper.

Jenny sat still.

Bob didn't understand what he had just done. He didn't know how much effort writing lyrics was supposed to take. He wasn't aware of how it was supposed to feel. He just allowed it to happen its own way, just as he had done his entire life.

He stirred. Then he bent to look over what he'd written. He wasn't sure about the way the words flowed. What would the accompanying music sound like? Who would sing the words he had written down? "I don't know," he said, breaking the stillness, the silence.

The room came alive. Several Sisters stood up and left the room. John leaned back and placed a big hand on the top of his own head, then let his shoulders relax. Mary said, "I could juss feel it. Didn't I tell you, John?" She reached for the paper that Bob held onto.

He released it. "I don't think it's very interesting," he said.

John spoke for the first time. "You wouldn't know. Once it come out, it take somebody else to know. Mary tell you da truth. Yes, sir."

Bob looked over at Mary. She appeared to read the paper several times over, nodding at her own tunes. Each reading brought a different nod. "Well," she said.

Bob didn't feel good about how she said well.

"It's close." She slapped it in front of John, but she spoke to Bob. "John can fix it. We juss need our instruments." Just then the other Sisters came into the room carrying guitars and banjos and a fiddle. "Here they are," Mary said.

John read through the lyrics as everyone except Mary stood and took an instrument. Jenny and Bob stood too, but backed away and against the wall to give the group space.

Although Mary appeared to be in charge, she looked at John to lead them on. He had a deep voice that resonated like music even when he just talked.

"Gonna start happy," he said. "Da boy in his chile-hood play. When we gets to the part where he growed, life still good, but more routine." He looked at Joesy and Bet. "I'll signal the change. You all keep a repeat chord so's it sound like life be the same day after day." All the while he spoke, he picked at the guitar slung over his shoulder using a piece of frayed rope. His words and the notes he played mimicked each other. "The end. Da lass bar, that one he sad."

No sooner had he stopped speaking, he handed the paper back to Mary and began. The others came in a little clumsily at first, then smoothed out as they played. The transitions were rough and painful to the ear. Mary stumbled over words and would bend to her knee and mark the sheet. After one run through, John suggested a few more changes. Instead of 'yellow-tipped fields of grain', he changed it to read 'yellow-tipped plains', tightening the line to go at a faster pace. He made similar changes to each line for the first half of the song.

Bob sensed that he had failed to produce what they'd wanted because they didn't just accept the lyrics out of hand. Then, as the morning progressed and the music became more complex and smooth, he understood that their adjustments were necessary, and what he had given them was a solid foundation on which to build.

"We breakin'," Mary said late into the morning.

Instruments all went down near one wall and out of the way. "This song," John announced, "we picked up from an old black man, blind as can be, livin' out his final days in the sun next to the midwestern flat plains of his youth."

"I likes that," Mary said.

"Me too," Bet said.

And as they left the room, Bob realized it was no longer his song, no longer his childhood, but everyone's and no one's.

He turned to look at Jenny who had stood as silent and in awe as he had.

"I have never seen anything like that in my life?" She laughed as if in relief from the tension in the room.

"It was beautiful," Bob said.

"The song was beautiful. And sad," she said.

Those were the first words about the song that gave Bob the least bit of credit. He felt partly responsible for what had occurred, and that was enough.

"I have to find work," he said quickly.

Jenny touched his hand with her fingertips. "You said you'd come by. I'm looking forward to listening to those feet." Her smile appeared tight, her wet eyes sincere.

Bob's nervousness had his legs shaking, so he walked away. At the door he looked back. "I'll come by after dinner. We could walk somewhere?"

"I'll be ready."

Outside, Bob let out all the air that had been trapped in his lungs for what seemed like hours. He felt light-headed. He wandered a bit, stopped in for nut bread at Jasper's, who didn't charge him. They actually laughed together about nothing in particular, they were so happy to see each other.

"I pray you're doin' fine," Jasper said.

"Very fine," Bob told him.

"Well, you look it."

"And you too. Thank you for the nut bread."

"My pleasure."

With his lunch in hand, he walked to the swelled river, bleached with floating logs, dotted with river rafts. He sat on the bank and listened. A breeze kept the mosquitoes busy, and clutches of gnats hung over the water's edge as if they were held in place by a thin thread.

He noticed how his life had changed. He had run from harm, a black boy. He knew even growing up that he was treated differently than the other Negroes on the farm. And he had heard stories of even more horrible treatments than he witnessed. He had been different, and to a community of workers, like the clutch of gnats sticking together, different meant outside. And to people afraid of being outside, like Edna, that meant evil. Yet, Leon had been different only in his features and his skin color. But that had made all the difference in the world.

"Leon," he said aloud as though it were someone else's name.

In crossing the river, he had been baptized by dark and by water. He had walked through fear and survived. He had learned about his other heritage. His white heritage. But freedom, white freedom, had its complications, too. On either side of that color line, a trusting soul seemed difficult to find. Bob had been beaten worse as a white man than he had ever been as a Negro. He had been cheated, threatened, and emotionally assaulted because of his difference, whether for skin color or social aptitude.

The river carried the song of his life more than the fields he had written about. Perhaps a river song would come to him next? He had not gone far in his travels: a long walk, but a short distance. He was still perched along the West Branch of the Susquahanna River. He had crossed it a second time, returning, in a manner of speaking, as a white man. The river had truly cleansed him. He laughed at the thought. "Bob White," he said, and in a moment recalled his dead friend.

Bob looked at his own hands. How had he come out of Bess so white? Raised by the Negro farm-boss who should have been his father. A man and a family alienated by the color of a child born to them. He wasn't the only Fred Carpenter child born in that row of shacks. He bet that there were even more half-white children living there now that Hank and Earl had most likely taken on their adulthood.

Bob dipped his hands into the river. He washed the lard-induced stickiness off his fingers, and brushed them dry on his pants.

He thought of Jenny. Could he have a normal life with a woman, after what he'd been through? He tensed when around her, but the tension was not the same as he remembered. The tightness was in his heart not his skin and muscle.

Hugh had been wrong about him. There was no doubt that Bob was white now. He could only have white children. Perhaps one black skinned and one white skinned could bare either color, but two white skinned? It was common sense what would happen.

Bob strolled to the other side of town and beyond the streets, then stripped down and entered the river in a spot where an island had been created, where the current had slowed. He cleaned himself and his clothes, then sat under a tree until his clothes dried in the sun. He slept for an hour, which took the edge off his sleep-deprived night. His clothes were stiff as he put them back on.

The river sang. The wind had the trees and bushes chattering among themselves. Wrens flitted inside the bushes. He could hear them, but could only see the flurry of their movements inside the foliage, as if they were the live, internal organs of the trees and bushes themselves.

He wasn't hungry, but he decided to go back to town and eat anyway. It would kill time and the urge to eat later. He didn't need his stomach to churn while talking with Jenny.

Refreshed, relaxed, and satisfied by a small meal, Bob headed for Finch's. Before he could even knock on the door, Jenny opened it and stepped outside. Her hair was pinned back, one loose strand sticking to her neck, which glistened in the remainder of heat from the day.

The streets had filled, many of the men heading home, while others aimed themselves for Jimmy Finch's.

As Bob and Jenny walked east and out of town, heads turned to watch them. Bob couldn't decipher the glares they sometimes got. And other times people would smile and say, "Good evening," as if their walking together was a natural occurrence.

Jenny thanked him for coming by.

"I said I would," Bob said. He stared ahead, afraid to meet her eyes.

"I know. It's just that—"

"There are too many people who—," he started to say.

"Yes," she said. "Not everyone does what they say they'll do."

Unsure how to speak with her, he didn't add to the statement. He led her east, downriver.

She said, "At least when it comes to me they're not honest."

Bob spoke to the river. "Why would you say that?"

"It's the company I keep."

"Like me?" he said, turning to look at her.

Her laugh-giggle came out. "No, everyone else. Well, not everyone, but many of the others. It doesn't affect Jimmy and the boys like it does me. They can do that."

Bob stopped and looked at her. "What are you talking about? What's Jimmy doing?"

"Why, Bob White, you don't know?" She lowered her head. Her face flushed. "You might wish to take me home."

Bob scratched his head. "Do you want to go home? Did I do something wrong?"

Her head went back and forth slowly. "No. No. And, no again," she said. Then Jenny reached for Bob and rubbed his arms as if consoling him. "It's because of the acts. Because of what my ma and pa did. Running the railroad." She stamped her foot. "Goodness. I'm with Negroes most of my life. The white men don't appear to think that's okay."

Bob looked at her. She still held onto his forearms. Her comments continued to sink into his mind. Was that why he felt familiar around her? Did he notice how comfortable she was around Negroes?

She shook his arm. "Say something."

"I don't know what to say," he said.

Her hands dropped from his arm. "I understand," she said. "I'll go home."

He reached for her as she turned to go. When he pulled her back around by her elbow, she floated through the air toward him; so easily did she move that her body fell into his. Her arm slipped over his shoulder. He let go of her elbow and embraced her.

CHAPTER 27

Bob found that growing up on a farm where he did double chores, spent time with two lazy white boys, and learned to repair things using his own wits, now benefited him more than had he been a mere field hand. He learned quickly and the more odd jobs he performed around town, the more he could apply one set of concepts to the next problem. He, therefore, had a series of jobs from home repair, to general store cashier and operator, to part-time bartender. He also continued to write song lyrics even after the Sisters of Rhythm were on their way to the next town. At least once a month, he would send the Sisters of Rhythm, through the U.S. Mail service, several songs he'd written, knowing that had he heard them again they would most likely sound completely different than what he'd imagined.

His life appeared to have stabilized over time, except that he and Hugh were not in agreement about Bob's interest in Jenny Finch.

One night, Hugh threw up his hands and said, "Do what you like."

"You'll never understand," Bob said.

The two of them left Jimmy Finch's while in the middle of their discussion. The night sky turned black with clouds. The end of summer let go of the leaves and color had already broken out all over town and in the mountains where the trees had not been clear cut.

"I understand," Hugh said, "more than you could ever know. But Jenny doesn't."

Bob stopped in his tracks. He was sober and Hugh was drunk. He should have known not to get into a conversation with a drunk man, but it was too late. "That's not fair," Bob said.

Hugh swung around, stumbling to keep himself upright. "It doesn't have to be fair," he slurred. "It's true."

Bob said nothing. He knew it was time to leave. Hugh would be fine walking to the mill alone. But Bob didn't move. He hadn't felt punished enough.

Hugh stopped weaving. He glared at Bob. "You haven't listened to me at all. You're only comfortable with her because you both grew up around the same colored people. How do you think she'll react when she finds that out?"

"She won't."

"Then your life together will be a lie."

"I live a lie," he said.

Hugh's shoulders relaxed. He looked finished, but he got in the last word before Bob turned to go. "You don't live a lie with me."

Bob jogged back to his room in Carl's house. The exertion eased his anger. His mind cleared. There were many lies in his life and Hugh held only one of them.

Bob lighted two candles and pulled out "Leather Stocking Tales", another book by Cooper that he found in the library. Reading relaxed him further until he blew out the candles and fell off to sleep.

He awoke in the early morning, still thinking over what he and Hugh had argued over the night before. He had to offer more of his truth to Jenny. After all, she had never heard the true stories of his feet, only a few short tales of his life in a timber camp.

Bob left the room and wandered up the street, away from the river. He had taken to walking through the small Negro section on the Northwest side of town. Something about the sound of them talking, the clanking and banging of their doors and dishes, the sound of the children, brought back memories and feelings he'd thought he'd never want in his life again.

Hugh had told him once, that no matter how bad a childhood could be, there was always a yearning to return to it. Hugh had never told Bob what terrible things had happened in Hugh's childhood, but Bob knew that the big man talked as much about himself as anyone. And perhaps he was right. There was something about the idea of returning to the Carpenter Farm that appealed to Bob. Part of him wanted to touch the shack one last time, say goodbye to Martha, skip stones at the creek flat.

He would probably be killed on site.

Did anyone miss him? How did living in the shack change with him and Big Leon gone? Who took over as foreman?

He looped around a few blocks and headed back toward the Susquahanna. He slowed at the corner of the street. To cross it he would again be in the white neighborhood. Were the people all that much different? Years of resentment and fear had been handed down. For Bob, the memory of one way of life slammed into the uncertain and unfamiliar interactions of a new way of life. Were the differences between individuals more a matter of wealth than color? "I've seen Negro slave owners kill other Negroes for disobedience," Hugh had told him once. That act was surely a sign of the power of wealth over poverty. And there was Bob's own experience with Jed Howard, with getting beaten in the alley, and fights he had witnessed in the logging camps. There were many points of separation, color being the most easily noticed, but wealth and status gave men a reason to hate as well. Even education created a separation where one should not exist. He felt that separation at times himself. He even entertained the thought that it was his white half that allowed him the ability to educate himself. In discussing the subject of white versus black intelligence with Jenny later that day, she said, "I should think not."

"I knew it didn't make sense," he said.

"I've met Negroes who were highly educated and intellectually astute when alone or in small groups of like-minded people. Then when they are around whites, they talk down so they don't insult anyone. Most whites don't like a Negro who can articulate his views."

"Some people act stand-offish to me, too, even after they've hired me for some odd job. Maybe that's why Carl doesn't want his family around me."

"Jealousy," Jenny said.

The summer months had brought the two of them closer together. Bob felt at ease around Jenny, even if he still tensed slightly at her intimate touches and caresses. He hated for his chest or stomach to be rubbed and couldn't understand why it made him so angry. Sometimes the closeness of her breath unnerved him as well.

The two of them sat together near the edge of the river. The evening cooled down. Other couples walked together up on the roadside. The streets emptied as evening wore on. Farmers were daily bringing grain and vegetables into town. Harvests had been good that year.

"Hugh's hand has healed pretty well," Bob said.

Jenny leaned into Bob and placed her hand on his knee. "You're sad about that. Why?"

"I tried to talk him into finding a different job and to stay in town. He insists on cutting timber this winter. He knows a lot of the farmers who are staying here. They'll work together until spring planting and then the shift will happen again. If he lives through the winter, he'll be back in spring."

"He'll live," she said. Jenny kissed Bob's cheek.

"He could stay," Bob said.

"You'll miss him."

The sun reflected off the river. Bob took a deep breath. He had thought a lot about his predicament. He wanted to tell Jenny the truth, but didn't. Instead, he turned to her and said, "We could marry."

Jenny pushed away from him as if to take him in more completely. "Marry?"

Bob hung his head.

"Do you mean it? Someone like me?"

"Yes." He flushed.

"You've never said you loved me."

"Well, I do."

She threw her arms around his neck and kissed him.

His tense fear lightened as Jenny leaned back, shook her head, and smiled. What had he done? How would he tell Hugh?

They laughed together. Finally, she said yes.

Bob heard Hugh's concerns in the back of his mind, but he so wanted a normal life and Jenny seemed the right choice. He half listened to her as she rambled about a small wedding, a simple house, and – his heart jumped – children.

Jenny couldn't have known what he was feeling. She asked why he fell silent, but all Bob could say was that it was a big step and he was considering the details, worried over their living conditions and if he'd be able to support a wife and family.

"We'll be fine," Jenny said. She placed her hands on his cheeks and looked into his eyes.

Bob wasn't so sure, but Jenny's smile was contagious. He found that in a few minutes his delight in the idea grew to match hers. His concerns fell away.

"I know we can live in the big house with Jimmy until we find our own place. But we may not have to," she shrilled. "Homes are being finished up all over town." Her faced lighted up and her eyes grew big. "Or we could build our own at the edge of town."

"There is hardly an edge to town," Bob said. "Williamsport is growing so fast. It's like everyone is looking for a piece of the lumber business."

"Except you," she said.

"I like working odd jobs, and as a replacement for when someone gets sick or injured." He looked at his hands in the fading light. "It's easier on my hands, too. Lumber tortures the hands."

Jenny placed her hands into his, "I love your hands." She became giddy. "And I love your smile. I love your shoulders and neck and lips."

Her excitement worried Bob. Could he live up to her expectations? He had a lot of money in the bank. He needed very little to live, but what about Jenny? He didn't want to get a real, day-long job. He worried that he'd run out of things to say if they were together more than a few nights a week. And then there was the possibility of children. His thoughts wavered between the logic he had created and the unknown reality that Hugh had posed. What would he do if they had a Negro child? What would Jenny do?

Bob's stomach churned with acid put there by his own body. Worry and uncertainty attacked him. After dropping Jenny off, he took his time walking home.

Lately Bob worked at the feed mill. Wagon loads of grain and corn and hay needed to be unloaded, counted, and logged. He had tried to get Hugh to quit the mill and help at the feed storage, but Hugh stuck with what was familiar.

There seemed to be a different warehouse foreman every few weeks at the feed mill. Now it was a man named Josh, who had a similar build and skin color as Bob. Josh appeared to think they were the same nationality and often slapped Bob on the shoulder and said, "We got to stick together."

Bob just smiled and got back to unloading a wagon or filling grain bins.

Putting up hay was a big part of the feed mill's year long income. The larger the town got, the more horses and carriages there were. And the number of residents had practically doubled in size over the last year.

The stable had expanded into its own hay bins. Horses had taken over the entire lower barn space there. A third stable was already half built. Bob had helped to frame it in late summer.

Bob knew hay. He could tell whether it had been harvested a day too early or left on the ground too many nights. Horses needed clean hay, none that was too dusty or they'd get the heaves. Josh took Bob with him to look over about every third load that came in.

Bob did not recognize the wagon itself, but once he glimpsed the driver, he turned away. There were three loads. Hank Carpenter drove the first one. He had grown, in a few years, to look just like his father with thick red hair and a weeklong beard.

Josh seemed to know Hank. "Hey there."

"Hey," Hank said.

"Back again. It's a long haul down here for you, isn't it?" Josh yelled up to Hank.

"Long as yer prices is still better, we make the trip."

"How's your pa?" Josh asked.

Bob stood behind the wagon and waited, peaking around from time to time. He feared that any moment Earl or one of the hands would sneak up on him. It would be all over.

"See fer yourself. Pa's in the wagon coming along there." Hank pointed to one of the other wagons still making its way down the road.

"Bob?" Josh yelled. "Hey, Bob, where are you?"

Bob froze. His whole time in town had come to an end. He could run, but where to? And why? He could deny being Leon, but who would care once Hank and Earl recognized him? There was nothing he could do. He stepped around the wagon. Would Hank just shoot him down right there?

"Look this load over. Should be pretty good," Josh said to Bob. Then he turned to Hank. "You boys stayin' long enough to get a drink tonight?"

"As soon as we put Pa up someplace. This trip was hard on 'im."

Bob looked over the load of alfalfa. It did look good.

Hank had hopped down from the buckboard and came up on Bob. "This here's the best you'll find. Bob, was it?" He held out his hand.

Bob turned and stared at Hank. Right in the eyes. They shook hands. "It looks good to me," Bob said.

Hank cocked his head and leaned back slightly.

"Everything okay?" Bob said, trying to keep the quiver out of his voice. His heart raced and his knees weakened.

"Yeah. Yeah, it's okay."

"Check 'em all," Josh yelled.

Bob found it difficult to walk. He didn't know whether to feel relieved or insulted when he realized that Hank had never really looked at him. He had been a Negro farmhand, a slave really. He had never been seen. All those years he had been invisible.

Hank met with Earl, "Let's get a quick drink while they take care of this."

Josh put his arm around Bob's shoulder – way too familiar for Bob, but he tolerated it. "Now there's a sad story," Josh whispered. "Their pa was shot stupid by a runaway nigger that raped his daughter. You believe it? Later, she gave birth to a monster child.

Hank had to smash its head in and bury it. His sister ran away the next week. Never seen again."

Bob shivered. Blood rushed to his throat and pounded in his temples. They were coming around the wagon. He didn't want to see Fred Carpenter, but it was too late. A slumped, heavy-set figure, his hair cut to a stubble, his neck fat and humped, sat motionless.

"The boys," Josh was still telling his story, "went back and killed the runaway's whole family and anyone else who got in the way. Bloodiest night in history, at least on that farm."

Bob resisted Josh's pull on his shoulders, but the hunched figure on the buckboard must have heard them coming. He turned his head and shoulders together and in slow motion.

Fred's eyes, at first, were black, dead to the world and empty to life. But once he saw Bob, they opened wide. Bob expected his name to be called. Recognition burst along Fred's face. "Aaahhh." Drool slipped from his mouth. "Aaahhh."

Bob broke loose from Josh's weak grip. "Oh, God," he said. He ran to the side of the building and vomited.

Josh ran after him. "What the hell's wrong?"

Bob vomited again.

"Shit," Josh said. "Are you all right?"

Bob shook his head.

"You've got one weak stomach, my friend."

Bob spit onto the ground. "I'm sorry."

"No need. I understand. It's a pretty frightening sight."

Bob held back tears. "I need to leave."

"Go on. The loads look good. We can handle it from here."

Bob jogged as best he could back to his room where he buried his face in his hands and cried silently. He couldn't even howl like he wanted. He had thought that some day he'd return to see Martha, but now he knew he could never do that. The evil that he brought into the family burned them all.

His whole family was gone. Martha had done nothing but witness the horrible lives as they played out inside the shack. She was innocent.

He imagined the scene. The fury in Hank's and Earl's eyes would have been easy to decipher. Hate, their eyes would say.

Anger, their bodies would announce. The household, what was left of it, would be stunned by the attack. Bess and Martha – awake and waiting for Big Leon who would never return, being already dead. Hank and Earl and the men must have burst into the shack and shot holes into anything that moved. With Bess and Martha waiting for Big Leon, candles would have been lighted. The wind through the open door would have caused shadows, the breath of life forced into them suddenly, to scurry around the shack like so many rats.

Horrible and wild gunshots ricocheted inside Bob's mind. He held his hands to his ears. His eyes squeezed tight bringing only a clearer picture, Bess falling backward and Martha surprised to find she had been shot several times in the chest and shoulders. Understanding fell over her face and her humming ceased. And then a smile appeared. Satisfied that life was finally over for her, Martha nodded to her assailants – and to Bob. Blood bubbled from her lips and she mouthed, "Leon."

CHAPTER 28

Bob woke that morning in a thick sweat. His blanket lay on the floor. His head and neck burned. The area around his eyes felt caked with dried tears, although he was positive he ran out of tears long before morning. He reached up to rub his head and neck and pain shot through his shoulder. His fingers ached, too, as though he had held his fists clenched for hours. Then he noticed his legs and back. The progression of pain enlarged with his evolving consciousness.

When he opened his eyes, light already filled the room. He had run six, eight scenarios through is head, one more gruesome than the last. Several of his – were they dreams? –happened in slow motion. Several played out with him, as Leon, watching through a window from outside, one occurred with Leon participating in the killing. That was the worst of them.

He rolled onto the floor and his back snapped. He stretched in every direction possible and in complex ways, like a cat getting comfortable.

He could hardly think straight. He closed his eyes briefly and recalled Fred Carpenter's surprise. Ironically, his blood father remembered what he looked like. He had been seen as a child by someone he thought had ignored his very existence.

Bob stood to go. He didn't want to run into the Carpenters again, ever. How could he prevent that from happening?

The events of his life churned inside him. He had accidently shot his own father, who had shot Leon's acting father. And his half brothers killed his mother and aunt. His half sister had had his monster child. Bile crept into his throat again. He swallowed the bitter flavor and shook the facts from his head.

How long did it take to run the evil out of him? He thought he was through after crossing the river that night long, long ago.

He stopped in at Jasper's and bought a loaf of bread. Jasper took the money this time. Bob tore the crust open and reached into the loaf and removed the warm, soft center one mouthful at a time. The bread soaked up the acid building inside him. As he ate, Bob headed north. When he found himself in the thick of the Negro section of town, he sat at the edge of the street and watched the pickaninnies playing.

Autumn rode the underbelly of summer air. A shiver went down Bob's back. He wished he had been able to play like the children he watched now. The other mulattos from the farm, as long as they had Negro features, were accepted as Negroes, and he knew it. He wondered, once the thought came, if that were always true? Was that the only reason he was left out? Or was his ostracism partly because of his family's special treatment? Big Leon being foreman? Bess being Fred Carpenter's favorite? Had he been too ignorant as a child to see the real reasons behind the hate? It couldn't have been that personal, could it?

Bob noticed the children glancing at him as they played and handed one of them the leftover bread. "Share this with your playmates," he said. Even before he turned away the bread was being segmented into nearly equal portions.

Hugh would be working, but Jenny might be available. Bob rose to go. He took the long route around Jenny's house in order to avoid the downtown area. Most likely the Carpenter crew would be gone, but why take a chance?

He didn't know what he was about to say to Jenny. She'd surely want to know why he came by. She'd most likely see that he'd been up all night. Every time he tried to plan his visit, his headache drew his thoughts away. Perhaps that was a blessing. When he got there he knocked and waited.

Jimmy answered the door. He wore glasses and carried a feather pen in his hand. "Bob, what brings you around in the middle of the day?" He reached up and removed his glasses. Showing Bob his pen, he said, "Bookkeeping."

"Is Jenny around?"

"At the market. I could tell her where you'll be when she gets back." He cocked his head. "You all right?"

"Tired," Bob said. "Tell her I'll be down by the river." He motioned toward the end of town. "She knows where. I really need to see her."

Jimmy got a serious look on his face. "You won't be hurting her." It was a statement, not a question, an order from a concerned brother.

Not knowing what else to do, Bob just shook his head. "I hope not," he said.

Jimmy said nothing more.

Bob walked east, and the sun burned a little cooler. At the river's edge, Bob pulled at the late blossoms of wild tiger lilies, their orange heads trailing behind him where he dropped them. He sat near the river's edge and watched as the sun sparked and spit light from the surface. On occasion a ger-plunk sound indicated a fish surfacing to gulp down a fallen insect.

Bob threw a twig into the river and the current dragged it out of sight in a matter of moments. He lay back and stared at the sky, the river swishing and gurgling in the background, combing the tall grass at the water's edge. The image of the clear sky broke along the edges of his vision into yellow and red tinted leaves of choke cherry branches. He heard the twitter of wrens, the caw of crows, and the occasional squeal of hawk. Bob's shoulders relaxed into the ground, no longer tensed and rounded forward. With his hands clasped behind his head, he could use his thumbs to gently rub his neck.

He could be anywhere in the world, he thought, at any time, past or future. Nature, in that spot, felt timeless. The sounds, even if they changed from bird and fish to human, could not affect the color of the clear sky.

He allowed himself to go back, once again, to his childhood, what there was to it. He had been ridiculed as far back as he could remember. But that wasn't what mattered. He wanted to feel out being Leon. If he could recall how it felt to be Leon, he could project those feelings into the adult who had removed himself from time and location to lie on the riverbank. He could re-experience who he had been and place it alongside who he had turned into.

Bob struggled with becoming Leon. He didn't expect that to happen. The boy wasn't black, although he lived with blacks; he wasn't white, yet he worked side-by-side with his white half-brothers. And they never even saw him. They never looked at him.

The child Leon hurt inside.

Bob White sighed with regret.

Both wished that he could hate the people involved. The entire family eventually killed one another either emotionally or physically, and neither Bob nor Leon could figure out which death had been the worst. No doubt Fred Carpenter had suffered at his own son's hand for the sins he had placed on the Negro family. And the sins of the father *were* handed down to the sons. Hank, at least, since Bob had avoided Earl, looked plagued. His wrinkled-before-age face, the sound of his tortured voice, the blankness behind his eyes, all stood to declare the pain of living out such an awful and ruthless life.

Bob began to feel lucky and special that he had lived through what he had. He had not come through purely innocent by any means, but he had made it this far thanks to both his fathers, one whom he shot and the other who was shot while helping him to escape.

He could not repay either of them except to live out his life. The only question being, as whom?

Bob heard footsteps and sat upright. Jenny stood surrounded by tall grass, tiger lilies to her right, the sun behind and slightly over her left shoulder. His eyes adjusted to the slight change in light. Jenny had been crying. He stood and went to her, his hands out, taking hers. They faced each other. "What is it?" Bob said.

"Jimmy said I should be prepared." She sniffed. "But I didn't know for what, so I conjured the worst."

"Oh," Bob hugged her.

"Please," she said, "don't make it last. If you no longer wish to marry me, just say it."

"That's not what it is."

"Then what could be so serious and urgent?"

"You may not wish to marry me," he said.

Jenny pushed from him, a curious look crossed her face. "But why?"

"I've been lying here trying to figure out who I am and what I'm going to be. How am I going to live out the rest of my life? There is something I need to tell you, but I don't know how or where to begin?" Bob's eyes narrowed. He held back his own tears.

Jenny reached and touched his face. "Nothing can stop me from loving you," she said.

"Perhaps," Bob said.

She appeared calmer. Yet, her calm had been replaced, Bob thought, by other concerns he couldn't interpret. She waited to see what he had to say to her now and looked guarded.

"Let's sit together," she said, leading him back to where he had risen from a moment before. She held his hand. Their knees touched when they sat on the ground. She faced him. "Now, I'm ready."

"I am not who you think I am," Bob began.

"And who do I think you are, but a man I met and fell in love with?"

"My name's not Bob White."

Her eyes strained to continue to maintain eye contact. He noticed her flinch.

She swallowed. "Are you a criminal?"

"I never thought about it in that way."

"Thought about what? You are going too slowly. What is it?"

Before he spoke, he double-checked his feelings. His shoulders slumped. His face relaxed. "My name is Leon. My mother was black, my father a white farm-owner." There, he'd said it straight out. He turned away and looked into the river.

Jenny let go of his hands and let hers fall to her side. "Well," she said.

"There's an entire story."

"I suppose there is," she said.

"But I'd like to forget much of it. Even at that, it could take years for me to feel comfortable telling you everything."

"I've seen a lot of horrible things myself."

"I wouldn't blame you—"

"I know a thousand Negroes who would love to live like whites, but won't lie about who and what they are," she said.

He nodded.

"I have to think," Jenny said. "You have to think too."

He looked into her eyes.

She leaned forward. "Who are you and in which world are you going to live?"

She looked sad. Hurt that he had kept a secret from her. Or perhaps she worried for herself. Was she misinformed by his color as much as others might be? She might wonder whether she cared for him because he was black and that is what she had become used to? Why was she used to it? Did she curse her parents, then, for their participation in the underground railroad? For exposing her to more Negroes than whites? Was she questioning her own beliefs?

She sat so still and so silent that he had to wonder. Before she said a word more, Jenny fidgeted. Her fingers moved first, wiggling. Then her mouth set itself in a straight line. Her eyes narrowed. The birdsongs didn't affect her. A breeze pulled on her pinned-back hair, removing a few strands from the pin, letting those strands struggle in the breeze as if they were trying to get loose of her head as well. The freed strands panicked. Bob could see the deep sound of words growing inside her long before she spoke. "I have to go," she said.

He followed her until she began to run. He stopped. The sun lay warmly across his shoulders. A breeze from the river blew into his face. The corners of his eyes became cool where his tears had accumulated in sad pools. Regardless of the hurried conversation about his past, Bob felt relieved. He felt lucky for being alive, even at the cost of being submissive, at keeping quiet, at holding the truth close to his chest and hidden inside his mind. Lucky and unlucky. Black and white. His world consisted of opposites.

Jenny had stopped running, but she had never looked back. Bob continued to stand there, and as he did the realization of what he had done overtook him. His release, like sexual release, had been short lived. Fear reentered his life. Jenny would no doubt tell her brothers. Jimmy had already warned him not to hurt her. Bob suddenly felt vulnerable. Was this going to be a repeated situation, like the one with Hillary? He looked around to see whether anyone could have heard them. Chills ran down his back. The breeze appeared to be picking up. The trees leaned away from the river. Bob peered across the Susquahanna. His gut wrenched. Winter was coming. Logging camps would form soon. He fell to his knees and shook his head. He couldn't stay there. Surely someone would come for him. Once word got out, not even the logging camps would be safe for him. In fact, that would be worse. They would kill him. Just as he had walked for days over the mountains to get here, he would have to go even farther to escape Williamsport. He wished he could end it. Let them do what they will. Yet, something inside him would not let that happen. No matter what he suffered, he would go on. He should have never stopped at this town. He should go to another state where the chances of being found out would be near impossible. Like the Negro roamers he had been with, he needed to create a story that fit his life, a story that explained who he was and how he wished to be. The story the Lord had given him no longer worked.

His life could be recreated. But not here. Not in this town. He knew he wasn't invincible, yet, his life had been spared great pain at least twice before; perhaps this time it would be spared as well. He couldn't expect that to go on forever.

There was little time. Jenny had run off upset. Even if she wished to remain silent until she thought the situation through, her brothers might take it upon themselves to come for him.

Taking the long way home would be safest. On his way, he offered a young Negro of about twelve, twenty cents to go to the mill and let Hugh know to meet him at Carl's. Bob hoped he had a few hours, but didn't know for sure. He could always run.

He packed quickly, even though he thought he had plenty of time. He stood next to the window and peered out, watching the street, ready to rush down the hall he was told not to use, and out the back door. He also had the gun even though he didn't think he could force himself to use it. Just touching the cold metal to pack it brought back the image of Fred Carpenter.

It was funny to Bob how many Negro children had been separated from their families so that they had no connections in the world but their owner-employers. Fred Carpenter had, in many ways, created the same effect between him and young Leon by ignoring the boy all his life. Even Hillary must have felt that Leon was not part of her family.

And so, as horrible an image as Fred Carpenter had been, it was of little or no difference – a misfortune of a mere acquaintance. It is when Bob added his own hand and gun to the formula that he felt the connection. That frightening connection also meant that he could easily be hanged for a crime accidentally committed. A crime as much of self-defense and fear as of attempted harm to another soul. A crime of black against white.

CHAPTER 29

B ob lost all sensation in reference to heat and cold. He sweated as though the bedroom burned. His predicament, still rolling around in his head, was reminiscent of how he felt as he and Big Leon ran toward freedom. Yet, Leon had become a different man, a new person, and Bob had as much reason to stay as to run.

Standing as quietly and as alert as possible next to the window in his rented room, Bob alternately shivered and sweated, cried in defeat and bucked-up with a firm demeanor and clenched teeth. His knees wobbled and his mind became too self-absorbed, too preoccupied. If he had held back his own truth, this is what his life with Jenny would be like until the truth came out. And his secret would come out, somewhere, sometime, even if it happened one, two, three children down the road. He could see himself standing at another window, of some future house, while Jenny screamed from another room, giving birth to a Negro child.

When Hugh came down the street, Bob almost collapsed in relief. He thanked the sweet, sweet Lord that Jenny or her brothers hadn't appeared first. He had already accepted the fact that he would not touch the pistol in his sack, that he would step out and let them take him, shoot him, or whatever they chose to do. But it was Hugh who rushed down the street toward him. It was Hugh who showed up first.

Either Jenny had kept silent or her brothers had assumed that he would be long gone. And perhaps he should have been. As Hugh approached, Bob grabbed his things and left the room and the house. The cool outside air stung his fevered brow and neck. The pain lasted a moment, then faded into his skin like snow on a hot rock. "Follow me," Bob said.

Hugh caught up to his side and kept pace. "What the hell's wrong?"

"I'm in trouble," Bob said.

Hugh turned one corner after the next with Bob in the lead.

"Where are you dragging me?" Hugh asked.

"A little farther." Bob led the way past the shacks and into the hills above Williamsport. They puffed and gasped for breath as they climbed. Bob gleaned the area for a familiar place to hide. In a low thicket of pine scrub, Bob bent down and climbed along the ground until he felt they were hidden. They sat together for a few minutes to catch their breath.

After a long sigh – Hugh was in better shape than Bob – Hugh asked again why they were hiding.

"I told Jenny," Bob said between breaths. "I don't know what might happen."

"Whoa there for a minute. What righteous moment did you have that thought blurting out the truth would go smoothly? Jesus Christ, I told you to stay away from her in the first place. You know if you'd just get your pluggings from a Negro, it wouldn't matter what happened. But shit almighty you go and fall flat for some well-placed white woman." Hugh rampaged on, shaking his head and spitting out words like a preacher talking about damnation.

When Bob was able, he said, "I know."

Hugh's shoulders dropped. "What happened? Why'd you tell her? I should be asking why you didn't listen to me, but it's too late for that."

"The farm I worked for when I was a child. It's on the other side of Pine Creek."

"Holy shit. They came to town? Why would you stay so close? I'm sure you don't miss home. Christ."

"Hugh, please."

"All right. All right. No wonder you kept this secret. But it would of blown eventually anyway."

"I'm sorry. I thought I could get lost here. Never be found out."

"Did they tell the authorities?"

Bob looked at Hugh. "It's too complicated, too long a story, but my half-brother never even recognized me."

"Then what's the problem? Did someone else recognize you?"

Bob sat still and quiet. He searched for words, but found only the most mundane. "My white father."

"Holy shit." Hugh shook his head back and forth.

"But he couldn't talk."

"I don't think I'm following this. Is there a problem or not? If not, why would you tell Miss Jenny?"

"Haven't you ever done something without thinking?"

Hugh said, "Yes, but nothing I could get lynched for."

"I was upset and confused. Seeing my white pa. I shot him. I didn't know it until now. I don't know how he lived through it, but now he's stupid. He can't even talk." Bob shivered. He took a breath. Hugh remained courteously silent until Bob regrouped. "He had been with the posse who were chasing me. He shot and killed my black pa. Then he told the posse to stop chasing me. He let me go. When I found the gun, I twisted around and fired several shots, then ran off. I never knew what happened. I just found out that my half-brothers carried their anger back with them and murdered my whole family, every one who was left." Bob fell back onto the ground. He stared into the brush. "I was confused. I got sick and vomited when I heard what had happened. I ran away. I don't know why I felt like I had to tell Jenny that I was black, but I did. She doesn't even know the rest of the story."

"Why were they chasing you?"

In Hugh's eyes, Bob saw a huge gap in understanding.

"Terrible things went on," Bob said, not wishing to go back to that place. "My mind was muddled and all I could think was to get rid of all the lies. I just needed to tell the truth." Bob closed his eyes for a moment. "I never told her the whole truth though. And now I don't know if I'll ever be able to."

"You should have told me," Hugh said.

"I know. I should have never come here, either. No one should have found out. I should have kept it inside."

"That's a hard life to live," Hugh said.

"You live it, don't you?"

"My past is locked away. I never go there. Never."

"Then I won't make you go there. Just tell me, am I right?"

"You're right." Hugh reached back and patted Bob on the shoulder, closing the deal on their pact never to go there.

"What if she never tells anyone?" Hugh said after a few minutes.

"I can't stay here."

"No. Perhaps not. A lot of people know you. You've helped out more than you might know."

"It won't matter. So many have had me in their homes, trusted me with their businesses, their children and wives. Once they know I've lied to them, there's no telling what they might do. And there is that tiny fact about my shooting Mr. Carpenter."

"If you'd only gone black," Hugh said.

"I can't." Bob rolled onto his stomach and propped himself up on his elbows. "There is no way I can let a black woman touch me."

"I won't even ask you why."

Bob fiddled with some fallen leaves and pine needles. "If she didn't tell, if she went back and thought about it and still loves me, do you think she'd go away with me?"

"You are one fucked up and confused man."

"I don't want to be alone."

"And who will you be, then? The black man with a white wife? How will that be for her? For you, too? Your whole life will change."

"What life?"

"Dammit, Bob, you have a life. People like you now. They'll like you in the next town, too. No one will ever know as long as you don't tell them." Hugh sighed. "Come-on, you know it's true."

"But I can't marry, have a family, live normally."

"You aren't living a normal life now. You said that."

"I want to."

"You get used to being alone. It's not so bad. There's always the crew you work with."

Bob rolled back over and sat up. "You should know."

Hugh stared out beyond the thicket, not turning to look at Bob once. "This ain't about me."

"We all choose differently."

"I know. I know." Hugh lowered his head. "And we should choose for ourselves. And those we love, well, they should have the chance to choose on their own, too." He began to get to his knees to crawl back into the open. "Your life just ain't going to be normal no matter what you choose."

"Where are you going?"

"To find Miss Jenny."

"Don't. She's upset. She doesn't need this kind of trouble."

Hugh peered through the brush at Bob. "We'll let her decide her life." Then Hugh was off and down the hill.

The hidden sun let twilight slip into the scrub. Bob wondered what animal he might surprise when it returned in the morning. He thought to leave. He even got part way to his knees, ready to crawl out after Hugh.

He stopped short. Hugh had been through something. Bob wanted to know what it was, to compare it with his own situation. Hugh had closed that part of his life away, though, and Bob didn't wish to cause Hugh any pain. All Hugh was really saying is that he had made a choice in life and had learned to live with it. He wanted Bob to do the same. On his own. But Bob wasn't so sure he wanted to decide.

His memories sickened him, but would not let him sob. He knew that whatever happened to him was through ignorance, uncontrollable sexual urges, and, when it came to Fred Carpenter, by accident. Age, intelligence, and experience discolored everything he knew from his past. He thought that he had left the evil of his life behind, but now he had stepped back into it. The more he knew, the more he remembered, and the more disgusting his whole life opened to him. Was it even possible to change a past like the one he lived through? Would he have to carry it with him forever? Of course he would.

Vomit crept into his throat. He scurried into the open. Throwing up near a tree – amidst the familiar odors of pine needles and loam – is where the hole in his memory tore wide open. His sickliness as a child had not been that of a weak body, but that of an innocent one torn by an evil he had been too young to understand.

He tensed. Memory exploded. He retched, coughed, and retched again. Bob fell to the ground, his elbows holding him up, his face close to his own vomit. Dry heaves leaped in and out of his throat. His lungs burned. Images of his mother fondling him burned like flames licking at his mind's eye. He had never understood why he hated the tickling, the touching. He never fully felt the pain and pleasure so keenly. His mother's hand squeezing his balls, rubbing his erection until his pain burst, his body jerking and squirting its fluid, the wrong in it, the evil in it, all coming down on him. Vomiting at the side of the shack or in a bucket became his way of erasing what had happened.

How Big Leon lived with him and Bess was a mystery. The mental torture that man must have gone through. Yes, Bess was Fred's favorite: they shared a tenderness that excluded Big Leon. The only way to keep Big Leon away was to disgust him. Was that it? Or was it that Bess struck out at both men? Was Martha sympathetic to Big Leon or did she love him? It was a fact that he could not have children. Were he and Martha lovers?

Bob rolled onto his back. The sky opened as the day closed. Twilight turned to starlight before his eyes.

He would never know the answers to all his questions. But he was alive. He was real.

Bob's skin cooled. Evening breezes turned to night winds. Mixed clouds shifted and moved, turning into new shapes. Between the clouds, stars flared up and came close enough for Bob to reach out and touch.

He shut his eyes and images of his past fell before him, the curtain drawn, the catastrophe of his life playing out. He'd watch awhile, detached by the feel of his own skin, the scent of the ground, and the hoot of an owl. When the play in his mind became too horrible, he'd open his eyes and breathe in his present life. When nearly elated with just being alive, Bob would close his eyes again.

That is how he spent the next few hours, turning his memory on and off, reminding himself of the difference between a life past and a life being lived. For years he wondered who he was, and how he should live his life. Would he ever know the answer?

As the night wore on, his tears dried. His shoulders relaxed. His jaw let loose its tension. Knowing what he had held all those years allowed him to release it. The memory might remain, but the emotion fell away. The emotion would return, but he'd be ready for it. He was no longer innocent. He was no longer that child that could be manipulated and abused. He no longer had to blame blacks or whites; he no longer had to choose black or white as his savior. They were merely people back then, individuals, most of whom were gone now. He alone had escaped.

Bob unrolled his blanket and moved back into the hollow of the pine grove and underbrush. He stretched out and put his hands under his head. He was not out of hot water yet. He knew that much. But he felt real, more real than he'd felt for years.

By the time he dozed off to sleep, it was only a few hours before morning. His dreams were sweet and free. His body fell into the earth and disappeared. He slept whole. He slept completely, but he woke with a start.

The voices took a long time to feed through his deep unconsciousness, but when they did, he recognized them. His heart raced. His blood built pressure as it rushed to his brain. His eyes opened. Jimmy and Jerry Finch kneeled next to Hugh. Their faces big as the opening Bob had crawled into. His first thought was that Hugh had betrayed him.

CHAPTER 30

G et the hell out-a there," Jimmy said.

Bob rolled to his side. Sleep held to him like dew held to the morning grass. He felt the gun under him and his hand closed around it.

"Come on," Jimmy said.

Bob stretched his legs and slipped the gun under his blanket, then began to roll them up together. He wanted the pistol near, but not seen, not threatening.

The three men backed up and let Bob slide out from the brush. Once Bob was on his feet, Jimmy Finch cold-cocked him and he fell back down. The bedroll dropped from his hands. He saw Hugh scoop it up. As he got to his knees, Jimmy hit him again.

"You said he'd be safe," Hugh yelled out.

"That's for hurting my sister's feelings." Jimmy rubbed his fist with his other hand. He glanced at Hugh. "Had to do it." Hugh's interruption had changed the tone of attack. Jimmy looked as though he was getting ready to hit Bob again. Instead, he turned to Jerry, who looked equally surprised at the attack. Rather than swing at Bob, Jimmy pulled a gun.

Bob's eyes opened wide. He looked at Hugh holding his bedroll. "I just told her the truth," Bob said.

"I don't care what you did. She cried half the night."

Bob lowered his hands and stared into Jimmy's eyes. Jimmy wasn't going to shoot him. Bob could tell. Drooping eyes and a slack mouth indicated that the man burned with sorrow, not with anger, for what his sister had been through.

Jimmy waved the pistol for Bob to get up and move in front of the three of them.

"I didn't know," Hugh said to Bob.

Bob nodded. What had Hugh told them? How much more did Jenny know now? How much did Jimmy and Jerry know? He questioned himself, but knew that he wouldn't get an answer until Jenny appeared. The thought hurt his chest. How would she look at him? What would she see?

As the four of them walked down through the north end of town, children came out to watch. Jimmy held the gun on Bob like a false security against him running off.

Mathis Williams, one of the more outspoken Negroes who had run abolition meetings long before the war, stepped out into the street. Bob recognized him and knew that Jimmy's parents had helped him get from Virginia to Pennsylvania and into Williamsport a long time ago. "What's goin' on here," Mathis asked Jimmy.

"Private matter," Jimmy said.

"When there's a gun in the street, the matter ceases to be private, my friend."

Jimmy swung around to Mathis.

Bob stopped walking and watched out the corner of his eye.

"This is a *private* matter," Jimmy said. "We'll be off the street soon enough."

"Son," Mathis said.

"No, Mathis. It has to do with family. You understand."

"Be careful, son. Holding a white man at gunpoint when you're already a Negro sympathizer might not sit well in this town. You got enough trouble."

Jimmy thanked Mathis, who stepped back inside his house.

Bob didn't want to bring pain to yet another family. Everyone he touched got caught in the storm of his evil.

Whether Mathis got through to Jimmy or his sadness for his sister eased, he slipped the gun into his shirt and patted it with his hand.

Bob had no intention on running.

When they reached the house, Jimmy shoved Bob inside. Bob tripped over the door jam and landed on all fours.

"Shit, Jimmy, take it easy." Jerry said.

Bob could see into the parlor down the short hall. Jenny sat with a handkerchief to her nose.

"In there," Jimmy said.

Bob glanced back. Jimmy had put his hand over where the pistol was tucked into his shirt. Jimmy should have finished him off in the underbrush. That certainly would have been better than facing Jenny like this.

"Get!" Jimmy said.

Bob jumped up and went into the parlor. He braced himself against another shove, which didn't come.

Jenny looked up. "Oh, your face." She stood up.

"Sit down," Jimmy said to her. He handed Bob a bar towel. "He'll be fine."

"I didn't mean for this to happen," Jenny said to both men.

Bob touched his burning cheek with the cloth. There was little blood. At least he hadn't been hit with the pistol. He felt lucky in that.

"Leave us alone." Jenny sat back down.

Bob remained standing.

When the others were gone, Bob said, "I only wanted you to know the truth." The words were harder to say than he had imagined. His lips quivered. He could, rightfully, be hanged for what he'd done. That wasn't what appeared to matter though. It was Jenny that mattered. He had not wanted to hurt her. "I thought," he whispered, "that getting the truth out now would let me love you better."

"You've carried your secrets long enough," she said. "I can see that."

Bob thought back. He didn't even know whether he kept secrets or merely kept silent. That, too, has its own link to deceit, but it's not the same. It never felt quite the same.

"If anyone finds out—"

"It could be bad." She rubbed her eyes. "I sometimes wonder what it would be like to be totally accepted for who you are and not who your family is, or what your family had done. I wonder what would have happened in my life." She laughed pitifully, disingenuous. "But that is not what happened. That is not what led me to this moment. I know you could die at the hands of others for your truth – even what little I know of it. Passing as white should not be a crime, but it appears to be. Being black shouldn't be a crime either. That's what this town was built on. But you can't change those who move in." She put her hands into her lap and jutted her chin forward. "Is it worse to be lynched quickly or to be avoided and ridiculed much of your life? I only played with Negro children when I was small. There were plenty of other families who believed like my parents, don't get me wrong. The boys? Well, no one cared what they did. Most of the girls grew up and left town for a new life. I swear what my parents did was the right thing for them and the Negroes they helped, but not the right thing for a little girl too innocent to know what she did."

"I'm sorry," Bob said.

"I grew up in a white family, but for years learned nothing but black ways. My parents were curious people, willing to learn anything new and to try it out on their own. When I started school, I didn't even act like the other children. I didn't talk like them or think like them. My brothers went to fight for what they believed in, and God went with them and brought them back alive, but sadder.

"I stayed home and helped Ma and Pa raise twelve Negro children whose daddies and older brothers went to fight. Just like my own brothers, the ones who came back were sad, different. They took their children, sisters, and wives, and left town like it was a bad memory. If you looked into their eyes, you'd see that their whole lives had become a bad memory." Jenny lowered her head.

Bob waited. He didn't know what to say. He slid down to the floor, his back against the door jam. He hugged his knees.

"I felt like I'd been left behind. Ma and Pa died. Jimmy lets me live here. You'd think with all the drink and laughter at night that this would be a happier place."

Bob let his legs stretch along the floor.

"Then you come along," she said. "Even with your own sad story, you brought something good. I thought that a white man would never love me. Until you. You didn't care about all the

Negroes coming and going around here." She looked up and tried to produce a smile. "Now I know why," she squeaked.

"I'm as much white as black." Bob tried to make her see that it wasn't all a lie, that it wasn't so bad.

"You're sweet to say that."

"It's true. I have few happy memories with my black parents." He thought about what more he could say, but came up empty.

"You must tell me everything. Your name. Where you're from. How you lived."

Bob froze. He'd have to run if he told her. He'd have to go far away if anyone knew the truth about him. He breathed deeply, opening his mouth to pull in gobs of air and letting the air out through his nose. He looked around the room. He could lie. He had become good at making up stories that sounded real. And what of his latest memory? What about the information he had just learned himself? How could he tell her something, out loud, that he literally couldn't stomach even as memory? His lips pursed. His eyes filled with water. His nose ran. He sniffed. He knew he was going to tell her now. He waited for the courage to well up, to take over his body. He always knew long before his mouth could open that truth was about to be spilled, like the blood that had spilled over and over again in his life. His body began to sweat. His breath became hesitant. He drew his legs close and hugged them.

Jenny stared at him, with patient eyes, waiting for him to be ready.

"My name is Leon. I lived on the Fred Carpenter farm from birth. He was a kind man," Leon hesitated, "and a cruel man. He loved my mother. He trusted my father with the farm. My father," he raised his head. Tears slid down his face. "My black father tried to kill me when I was born and when he couldn't, he killed himself, little by little, until he was shot, dead, by my, my—"

Jenny lowered herself to the floor and went over to Leon and sat with him just as they had near the river the evening before. She took his limp hands into hers. "You've got to go on."

"I was born, so I was told by my Aunt Martha, during the Lord's sweet song into night. When my black pa came home from the fields he tried to rip me out of my mama's arms and she never forgave him that." Bob swallowed, then went on. He spoke of all the meaningful details including how he began to escape mentally by making up songs in his head. He walked Jenny through many of the stories of his life clear up to when the Carpenters came into town to sell hay. He explained how he recalled the awful truth of his mother's molestation. To Leon, it brought all things to a point of clarity. He left out details only to hold back his own nausea.

Jenny collapsed onto him. "It's not your fault," she said. "How could you know?"

Her understanding, her forgiveness, broke the logjam inside him. Finally, it truly wasn't his fault.

He held onto Jenny, his arms across her back. He felt her shiver and cry. She cried for him. She wasn't going to expose him, or kill him, or run from him. There was a release that happened inside Leon that pulled him together, drew all the pieces that had been taken from him, little by little, and drew them back to him. His own tears dried.

There were still questions inside him. "What, now, shall we do?"

Jenny looked into his face and asked the one question he couldn't answer himself, the one question he'd asked over and over again his entire life: "Who do you want to be?"

In that moment, he knew that he needed to honor his past, yet move into his own private future. "Leon. . . Leon White."

She then let him pull her onto his lap, and they stayed together for a long while.

ALSO BY TERRY PERSUN:

Novels

Giver of Gifts

Wolf's Rite

The Resurrection of Billy Maynard

The Witness Tree

Poetry

Every Leaf
Barn Tarot

CPSIA information can be obtained
at www.ICGtesting.com
Printed in the USA
FSOW03n1214110717
36280FS

9 781537 513492